ABOUT THIS BOOK

Secrets can be good (a surprise party) or bad (an affair). Secrets can be big (international spycraft) or small (I saw Mommy kissing Santa Claus). Secrets can be shared between two people or spiral out of control with a whisper campaign.

But no matter what, secrets forever alter the people involved.

Writer and editor Dayle A. Dermatis assembles a compelling mix of stories that run the gamut from crime to fantasy to romance, from happy to sad to thrilling. They all share one thing: incredible voices of some of today's top fiction writers.

NO SECRETS
BETTER KEPT
AN ANTHOLOGY OF HIDDEN TRUTHS

EDITED BY
DAYLE A. DERMATIS

SOUL'S
ROAD
PRESS

No Secrets Better Kept
edited by Dayle A. Dermatis

Print edition published 2023 by Soul's Road Press

ISBN: 978-1-946462-23-7

Inquiries should be addressed to

Soul's Road Press
info@soulsroadpress.com
http://www.soulsroadpress.com

Cover image © anskuw | Depositphotos.com
Soul's Road Press logo: Designs by Trapdoor

CONTENTS

INTRODUCTION
I HAVE A SECRET...

When I came up with the idea for this anthology, I had a fear. Even though I was expecting stories from some of the top writers I know—some of the top writers in the business today—I knew that a theme like this could invite what some of us call "low-hanging fruit."

In other words, stories that don't go anywhere new. Such as, a spouse thinks the other is cheating when in reality they're planning a surprise.

I even said in the guidelines, "I want you to surprise me."

And to my great glee, they did. So much so that I could've filled two anthologies with stories. However, the contract I had with the publisher was firm on the word count, and there were wonderful stories I had to reluctantly let go. I'm sure they found good homes.

I also said, "Make me laugh, make me cry, make me turn the pages." And boy oh boy, did that ever happen, too.

Secrets can be good (a surprise party) or bad (an affair). Secrets can be big (international spy craft) or small (I saw Mommy kissing Santa Claus). Secrets can be shared between two people or spiral out of control with a whisper campaign.

But no matter what, secrets forever alter the people involved.

Herein you'll find a heart-wrenching story from Robert Jeschonek that involves secrets upon secrets upon secrets. A short, sharp, creepy-as-all-get-out story from Patrick Mammay.

Heartwarming stories from Lisa Silverthorne and Annie Reed, and thoughtful stories from Dory Crowe and C.J. Mattison.

No anthology about secrets would be complete without a spy story, and Juliet Nordeen gave me a nail-biter. Michele LaFramboise and C.H. Hung gave me completely different and completely wonderful historic fantasies, and Stephannie Tallent gave me a tense otherworld fantasy in a world I hope she'll revisit.

Phillip McCollum made me giggle-snort, and Leah R. Cutter made me (as she always does) stop and think about life choices. Rob Vagle presented me with another of his unclassifiable but always amazing looks at life.

We can't live our lives without secrets, no matter how open and honest we try to be. The best thing we can do is keep our secrets to ourselves, because, as Benjamin Franklin said, "Three can keep a secret, if two of them are dead."

But never mind that. Let me tell you a secret...

You're in for a great read.

—Dayle A. Dermatis
June 2022
West Linn, Oregon

CLIENT PRIVILEGES

DORY CROWE

T he autumn I turned ten, Dad's dad—The Old Man or Pop to Dad, Mypa to us kids—came to live with us in Manly Manor. He brought Theesta, his housekeeper, with him.

Our old Victorian house—built higgledy-piggledy from the inside out with cubbyholes and towers and not one iota of concern for any exterior design—hardly qualified as a modern home. If our name had started with a C, Mom would have called it Castle C—. It would still have been as rambling and drafty with plumbing as unreliable and heating out of the Dark Ages.

It faced the Park Avenue of our middle-class suburban New Jersey town. There was no park and not much of an avenue, but the house sat far enough back from the concrete-paved roadway, narrow grass median, and root-heaved slate sidewalk to accommodate neighborhood Wiffle ball tournaments on our front lawn. Every spring Dad reseeded the grass. Every summer we re-wore the base paths and pitcher's mound to bare dirt.

Dad's law office—two large rooms with a private

entrance off the side of our wraparound porch—filled what was once a library and music room. Sometimes he used the dining room for conferences.

With five bedrooms on the second floor, if my sister and I went back to sharing a room, there was plenty of space for two more, if Mypa had still been able to climb stairs without danger of falling. Theesta, every bit as old and creaky, moved into the servants' quarters on the third floor.

Mom moved the television out of, and Mypa into, the second-best parlor. He took over the downstairs office bathroom next to the butler's pantry. Miss Nancy, Dad's secretary, complained about the musty old man smell from the day Mypa arrived. I heard Miss Nancy's shrill voice loud and clear through the wrought iron heating grate. It created a speaking tube between my bedroom and Dad's inner office.

I could hear everything down there, if I slid the register open and lay with my ear next to the vent. At ten, I knew about breaching attorney-client privilege. It could get Dad in big trouble and not just because he'd kill me if he knew I was eavesdropping. I was too scared to breathe a word I overheard, but not scared enough to stop listening.

I'd learned the hard way to keep my mouth shut at school when kids repeated the lies their parents told them; lies like where Lucy Perkins' older sister really went to "lose weight" or how come Sammy Jones' father didn't live with them anymore.

When I was in second grade, Dad almost caught on to my secret.

I tried to set Joanie Wilkes straight about why, in the middle of the school year, Miss Cervelli replaced Mr. Grayson as the fifth-grade teacher.

The school said Mr. Grayson had to move away "for family reasons."

Everybody had a guess what that meant.

Tall, dark-haired, with a perfect white smile and wicked twinkle in eyes as blue as a summer sky, Mr. Grayson was young, friendly, and as handsome as Lt. Rip Masters on Rin Tin Tin. All of us girls had a crush on Mr. Grayson. He wasn't married, had no kids of his own. Family meant parents, brothers and sisters, grandparents. Joanie Wilkes' parents told her Mr. Grayson had to move back home because his father had died suddenly and his mother needed him.

I knew better.

Shouting through the heating grate told me what really happened.

That secret opened my private window on Dad's legal world.

I was quarantined at home until just before Christmas while I got over the chicken pox. Past the fever and the worst of the itch, I felt fine, but Miss Nancy had never had the chicken pox. Mom made me stay upstairs in my room during office hours.

That day an arctic wind howled so hard it rattled my windows. I had the heating register open wide. I was building Fort Apache on the bare oak floor with my nine-year-old brother, Kenny's, Lincoln Logs, when the shouting started.

Dad never raised his voice around us. A low, disapproving tone; a stern look over the tops of his tortoiseshell glasses and an "I'm disappointed in you" was more than enough. I barely recognized his voice; it was so loud and angry. I did recognize Mr. Grayson's voice. He shouted plenty during games at recess.

Their words made little sense to me then. Only after Miss Cervelli showed up in Mr. Grayson's classroom after Christmas vacation did I understand that keeping the boys after school for special education got Mr. Grayson fired. I didn't understand what "special education" meant until high school. Nobody talked to little kids about sexual predators back during the Eisenhower Administration, not in the safe suburbs. We knew not to take candy from strangers or get into their cars. Our parents thought that was enough.

Joanie Wilkes' dad told the school board chairman the rumor Joanie had heard about Mr. Grayson—the rumor she'd heard from me.

Dad almost lost the school board, his best client.

———

I was nibbling the crust off a Swiss cheese sandwich and slurping my way through a bowl of Campbell's cream of tomato soup when the pocket doors between Dad's office and the dining room slid open. His deep-set eyes behind his round, tortoiseshell glasses were slitted to half their normal size. His finger crooked in our direction.

Kenny, sitting across the dining room table from me, gulped and pointed to himself.

Dad shook his head.

"Suzie."

Dad's finger uncurled and crooked again.

I almost choked on a spoonful of soup going down the wrong way.

"Me?" I croaked.

Dad nodded and headed back into his office.

Kenny snickered.

"You're gonna get it."

I kicked him in the shin.

"Hey." He grabbed his leg and rubbed. "What was that for?"

As if he didn't know. Brothers!

I dragged the toes of my Keds on my way toward Dad's office, leaving brighter hued furrows in the cream-colored broadloom carpet. We kids never ventured into Dad's inner sanctum uninvited. Most invitations meant trouble. At seven, I'd already been inside more times than I cared to remember.

Miss Nancy sat in her corner, behind her square wooden desk with the central typewriter well open and her steno pad tented on one of the pull-out writing boards. She didn't look at me, much less say her usual "hi." Her eyes—behind rhinestone-studded, cat's-eye glasses—remained on the steno pad. Her fingers pushed the type-writer keys. They struck the platen in a rhythmic clackity-clack.

A skinny, bald-headed man I didn't know sat in one of two cushioned wooden arm chairs tucked inside the bay window in the opposite corner of the room, on either side of a small table piled high with magazines. His long legs, crossed at the knee, revealed, under the cuffs of his grey suit trousers, an ankle clad in yellow, black, and red Argyll socks. Their pattern matched his tie. A grey fedora rested on his knee.

He wasn't smiling.

A winter-cool noon-day sun shone through the windows. It glinted off the dark, polished wood-paneled walls and Dad's framed diplomas, making them impossible to read, even for someone who could read Latin.

Dad stood beside the pocket doors. As soon as I crossed the threshold onto the bare oak floor of this outer office, he slid the doors shut behind me.

"This is Mr. MacLeod, Chairman of the School Board," Dad said. "He's going to ask you some questions."

I swallowed hard against the tomato soup still stinging the back of my throat and resisted the overwhelming urge to cough.

Dad's palm in the center of my back urged me forward.

I took two small steps and stopped.

"Go ahead, Ian," Dad said.

Slowly, Mr. MacLeod picked up his fedora and placed it on top of the camel hair coat draped over the second armchair. He uncrossed his legs and unfolded himself from the chair.

He was taller than Dad, much taller. He was the tallest man I'd ever seen. He ducked his head around the brass chandelier hanging by a chain from a plaster rosette in the middle of the ceiling. He stopped in front of me with the toes of his polished black oxfords only inches from the toes of my much-scuffed Keds. His head tilted down like a buzzard surveying its prey.

"You're Suzie," he said.

I gulped and nodded.

He stuffed his long fingers inside the pockets of his suit jacket. His elbows bent out like wings.

"I understand you talked to Joanie Wilkes about Mr. Grayson."

I peered up over my shoulder at Dad.

He gave me the kind of half-hearted smile that made me wince.

"Go ahead, Suzie. Tell Mr. MacLeod the truth."

I nodded and shifted my gaze up into that hawk-nosed face.

"What did you tell Joanie?" Mr. MacLeod asked.

"The truth," I said.

Mr. MacLeod squinted down at me. "Which was...?"

"That Mr. Grayson got fired because of the special education."

Miss Nancy stopped typing.

Dad gasped.

Mr. MacLeod's lips squeezed tight together. He stared over my head at Dad. His eyes shifted back to me.

"Who told you that?"

"They were shouting," I whispered.

"Who?"

"Dad and Mr. Grayson."

Dad's hands clasped my shoulders. He turned me to face him.

"Where were you?"

I couldn't look at him. I hung my head.

"Home with the chicken pox. Upstairs." I fought back tears. "I didn't mean to hear."

I looked up.

Dad's face had gone red.

"You were shouting," I whispered again.

"It appears," Mr. MacLeod said behind me, "that we have an innocent misunderstanding here. The board will reassure the Wilkeses. I'm sure you will address this matter with your children, Ken, and we won't have any further problems."

"No. I mean, yes. I mean, I'll talk to the kids." He sighed. "Thank you, Ian."

Dad spun me back around and held me against his legs.

"You can tell the rest of the board this will never happen again."

Mr. MacLeod nodded at Dad. He smiled down at me.

"Pleasure to meet you, Suzie Manly."

He picked his hat off his coat, placed it on his head, and threw his coat over his arm. Without another word, he ducked out the door.

———

Dad called me and Kenny and my five-year-old sister, Tammy, into his bookcase-lined inner office. He placed all of us in a row in the middle of the room. Backed against the large wooden table he used as a desk, arms locked straight at the elbows, hands gripping the front edge, he read us the riot act.

"And you will not, I say again not, repeat one word of anything you might overhear in this house. Ever."

"But, Dad—" I blurted, already thinking of all the things we heard that had nothing to do with Dad or his clients or anything worth calling a secret. I was born parsing my parents' words.

"No buts about it. Not from you—" he pointed at Tammy "—or you—" he pointed at Kenny "—and especially not from you, Miss Nosy Parker."

He pointed at me and stared over his glasses.

I puffed out my cheeks and stared back.

Dad pulled his glasses down his nose until I could see the steel glinting in his eyes.

I blinked. My cheeks deflated like a punctured balloon.

Dad shifted his gaze to Kenny. "Understood, son?"

Kenny nodded.

"I can't hear you."

Kenny continued nodding and muttered, "Yes."

"Yes, what?"

Kenny's head stopped bobbing. He threw his shoulders back. Looking directly up at Dad, he answered like one of the soldiers who'd followed Captain Kenneth Manly, Jr., from the bloody beaches of Normandy to bombed-out Berlin. "Yes, sir."

Dad gave him a curt nod.

Before he could turn his attention to Tammy, she squeaked out, "Yes, sir, Daddy."

The corners of his mouth quirked upward. They turned down as soon as his gaze fell on me. "Suzie?"

I couldn't look at him, much less meet him eye-to-eye.

"Yes, sir," I muttered.

"Kenny, you can go. Take your sister with you."

Before I could move an inch, Dad's fingers dug into my shoulder. "Not so fast, young lady."

Tammy slipped her hand into Kenny's.

He turned to go, but not before he shot me a you're-in-big-trouble-now leer.

"And close the door behind you," Dad said.

Dad's finger lifted, pointing to one of the padded chairs usually reserved for clients.

"Sit down." The tone of his voice said, "or else."

I climbed onto the chair, inching rearward until my butt hit the slats on the back and my legs stretched out straight in front of me.

Dad hitched one knee onto the edge of his desk. His dangling foot remained motionless.

"I don't think you understand the gravity of this situation, Suzie-Q."

I opened my mouth to say I did.

"Don't even start with the back talk, missy."

My mouth clapped shut like a clam closing its shell.

"You know why I call you Suzie-Q?"

The long pause after his question demanded a serious answer.

"Because I ask so many questions. I'm Suzie Questions."

"Right. You know why I'm talking to you and not your brother and sister?"

"Because I have a big mouth?"

He almost smiled.

"That, too."

The almost-smile faded to a grimace.

"Mostly because they lack your curiosity. If I tell them to do something, they don't ask why. They just do it. You —" his finger raised in my direction "—on the other hand, never stop until you have an answer that satisfies you."

Once opened, my big mouth couldn't stay shut.

"Isn't that a good thing?"

"Not always. And not—" he leaned over me like a crow about to peck my eyes out "—when it comes to my clients."

"Was Mr. Grayson your client?"

Dad massaged his chin.

"Mr. MacLeod is my client. Mr. Grayson worked for Mr. MacLeod."

"And Mr. MacLeod fired him."

"He did. With cause. But that's not something I'm at liberty to explain, nor would you, hopefully, understand if I tried."

Dad stood. He circled the desk and sat in his chair. He rested his elbows on the desk and his chin atop tented fingers. His eyes, squinting behind his glasses, never left my face.

I squinted right back.

Dad let out a deep breath. He pulled his glasses down his nose and peered over them.

"Suzie, you know what I do for a living."

"You're a lawyer." I'd known that since before I could remember. I was born knowing my dad was a lawyer.

"Do you know what that means?"

I had no idea. I shook my head, as astonished as I was embarrassed.

Dad pushed his glasses up his nose and leaned back in his chair. "I didn't think so."

"Is that a bad thing?"

"I'm not sure I understand your question, Suzie. Being a lawyer is not a bad thing." The start of a tired smile crossed his lips and vanished almost before it began. "Some people would beg to differ on that, I'm sure. But a good lawyer— and I like to think I'm one of the good ones—helps people. When a person hires a lawyer, they become his client."

"Like Mr. MacLeod."

"Yes, like Mr. MacLeod. Clients can tell their lawyer anything—even a very bad thing they might have done or seen—because of something called attorney-client privilege."

I nodded as though I understood all those big words. I didn't.

"The client has to have full trust in his lawyer. Which means that no matter what, a client's lawyer has to keep everything the client tells him a secret."

Dad leaned forward. His glasses slid back down his nose. He peered over them. He jabbed his finger onto the table with each word.

"Do. You. Understand?"

"No matter what?" I asked.

Dad took a deep breath. He leaned back. His eyes scanned the volumes of law books filling the built-in bookcases. He raised his face toward the ceiling, as though looking for answers in the plaster rosette over our heads.

I knew better than to say another word.

Finally, he lowered his head and turned squinted eyes back on me.

"If you weren't a female, you'd make one fine lawyer someday. You ask all the hard questions." Again he leaned forward, palms flat on the desk. "There are exceptions, but only when the client's secret means he intends to commit a crime or harm someone in the future. Breaching attorney-client privilege is not something a lawyer does lightly and it is not up to an eavesdropping little girl to make that decision."

Again he jabbed the desktop.

"Do. I. Make. Myself. Clear?"

As mud. I shook my head.

An exasperated breath rattled his closed lips.

"I hesitate to ask what you don't understand." He rested his forehead in one hand. "What don't you understand?"

"When is it okay to tell?"

He sat up straight. His finger poked toward me.

"For you. Never."

"But you said—"

His hand slapped the desk.

"I SAID NEVER."

He shouted at me.

I tried hard not to cry, but the tears seeped out of my eyes.

"Oh, honey, don't cry." Dad opened his arms. "Come over here."

I climbed out of the chair and slow walked around his desk. He slapped his knee and I climbed onto his lap.

"Let's make a deal."

His arms circled around me.

"You don't tell anything you hear in this house unless I say it's okay. If you have any question, you come to me. I'll tell you if it's okay to repeat. Deal?"

I craned my neck until I could see the hairs inside his nose and the kind look in his eyes.

"And you won't be mad if I ask?"

"Promise." He crossed his finger over his heart. "Scout's honor. I won't get mad."

"Okay. Deal."

He squeezed me tight and kissed the top of my head.

No matter how much I wanted to tell something I heard through my heating grate, I kept my part of that deal. For three years I never had to ask a single question, until Mypa moved in.

That fall, while the weather remained warm, we played Wiffle ball after school and on weekends. The switch to football happened after the Yankees won the World Series again, withered oak leaves scudded across our bare dirt base paths, and thoughts turned to ghoulish Halloween costumes and spectacular hauls of candy. All the neighborhood kids old enough to hold the light plastic bat or catch a football played, all except Tommy Hatfield.

Mr. Hatfield—a hands-on developer who'd bought the empty lot two doors down and fought the town zoning board to allow him to squeeze a small ranch-style house into our Victorian neighborhood—had spent three years building a house and a feud worthy of his name.

Tommy and his mom moved into the half-finished house that fall. They hauled a few sticks of furniture over the ramp of loose planks that ran from their muddy front yard to the front door. We never saw Mrs. Hatfield after that. I saw Tommy at school. We were both in Miss Cervelli's fifth grade. We walked the same way to school, at the same time, but never together.

Tommy wasn't the most popular kid in school, but he did make friends, just not with me or my best friend, Patty Williams, who lived in an apartment on the other side of our school district.

Tommy's dad had something against mine.

Tommy had something against Patty.

I was rummaging through my closet on the Saturday before Halloween, trying to decide if I could still fit into the lion costume I'd worn the year before or should pull my head inside a sweatshirt and call myself the headless horsewoman, when the shouting started in Dad's office. I dropped down beside the heap of lion on the floor and opened the heating grate.

"You sorry syphilitic son of a bitch," Mr. Hatfield shouted in his Southern drawl. "You all called the building inspector, I know you did. Admit it!"

"I did no such thing."

Dad's voice was calm, almost too quiet to hear.

"You think I don't know what you and all your fancy-pants neighbors are up to? You think you're the only one with friends at town hall?"

"I didn't call anyone, Tom."

"Before I lose my house, I'll sell. You know who I'll sell to?"

There was a long pause before Mr. Hatfield shouted, "Negroes. The blackest sumbitch I can find."

Dad said nothing or I couldn't hear him.

"How's them apples, Mr. Butter-Wouldn't-Melt-In-My-Mouth? You can tell all your rich clients you blew it big time. You all don't like me and my white trash family, you can see how you like living next to jungle bunnies."

"Tom—" was all Dad got out before a door slammed and I watched Mr. Hatfield stalk across the Carter's manicured lawn, up the planks, and into his house. His work boots left clods of black mud behind on the raw wood.

I didn't know why Tommy didn't like me before, but that day I sure learned I didn't like Mr. Hatfield. Not one bit.

———

The Saturday before Thanksgiving was bridge night. Mom and Dad's duplicate bridge group—four neighbor couples—took turns hosting. They set up card tables in the dining room and living room at our house.

After stocking the drinks and bowls of peanuts and Chex Mix, Theesta went to the movies. Mypa went to bed in his room. We stayed upstairs out of the grownups' way.

Kenny wanted to watch Killer Kowalski and Haystacks Calhoun fake wrestle on the old black and white TV in the hallway at the top of the stairs. I wanted to watch anything else. Tammy sided with him.

I sat moping on the landing, where the staircase made a right turn out of the living room. I couldn't see the players, but I could hear them talking, the slap of cards on the table and the tinkle of ice in their drinks. The blue haze of smoke from their cigarettes wafted up the staircase.

Mom and Dad were partners against Mr. and Mrs. Carter. I wasn't paying much attention until the bids of "Two hearts" and "Six no trump" turned into a conversation about the Hatfield's house.

"I tell you, Ken, that man has a buyer," Mr. Carter said. "He went straight to one of those blockbusting organizations and offered it. They're so eager to put a negro family in a white neighborhood, they're willing to pay top dollar."

"You don't know that, George," Mom said.

"I do," Mr. Carter said. "They applied for a loan at my bank."

"Oh, dear," Mrs. Carter said. "Can't the bank do something?"

Someone cleared his or her throat.

I craned my neck to make sure I was hearing right.

"It's not so simple. There are too many bleeding hearts on the bank board. I'm afraid they may give them the loan."

Someone groaned.

"But, surely, if they can afford a house in this neighborhood, they can't be such bad people," Mom said.

"That's where it starts, Maureen. First one buys and the property values drop. Then somebody else gets out while the price is still half good. He sells to another one of them. Pretty soon your house isn't worth the powder to blow it to hell."

"Only if you sell," Dad said.

"You want your kids living next to the likes of them, Ken?"

"Our kids go to school with the negro kids from the apartments. I can't see that it's hurt them any," Dad said.

"Then you're blind," Mr. Carter said.

"But what can we do?" Mrs. Carter whined.

"I'll tell you what we do. We form a neighborhood corporation. We buy the damned house. Then, once this whole thing blows over, we sell it to the right kind of people."

"Is that legal, Ken?" Mom asked.

"It's not illegal," Mr. Carter said.

"But is it moral?" Dad said.

"Is losing the value in your house moral, Ken? Or don't you care? Maybe you're one of those bleeding hearts." Mr. Carter wasn't exactly shouting, but there was a meanness in his voice I didn't like.

"I'd have to think it over," Dad said.

A voice, shouted from the dining room, "Hey, we're done in here. How long are you going to be on that hand?"

"It's your play, Ken," Mr. Carter said.

"Right." Dad didn't sound too sure. "Right, my play."

———

At recess on the Monday after Thanksgiving, Patty Williams came back to school. She'd had the chicken pox. Her skin was clear and she sounded fine. She pulled me under the metal fire escape at the back of our brick school building, our special place to share secrets. She was all smiles.

"Guess what?" She gave me a hug. "We're going to be neighbors."

She released me and stood back.

"But you can't tell anybody, yet. My daddy says if the wrong people find out, they could keep us from buying the house."

"Your dad's buying a house near me?"

She nodded so hard her pigtails bounced up and down. I thought her head might fall off her neck.

"Isn't it great! Daddy says it needs a lot of work, but he's been saving forever and we have enough to buy and fix it up before we move in."

A lump formed in my guts. I'd been friends with Patty since kindergarten. We did everything together at school— and nothing outside.

I'd never been to her apartment. She'd never come to my house.

We shared so much, and so little.

We were the same age, same size, the smartest kids and best athletes in our class.

For the first time I saw my best friend through different eyes. I saw her black hair braided into tight pigtails, her dark brown eyes, the gleaming white teeth in her smile.

I saw the color of our skins.

"That is great," I said, trying to make it sound as though I meant it. Did I?

Of course I did. Theesta was even darker than Patty and she lived right in our house. Whatever Mr. Hatfield said couldn't change that. He couldn't change the way I felt about either of them.

I gave Patty an even bigger hug.

"I can't wait."

I followed Tommy Hatfield home from school that day, walking behind him and making sure I never caught up. He wore his usual worn jeans and a T-shirt under a bomber-style jacket that looked as scuffed and worn out as his shoes.

I wished I'd never met him or his father.

I wanted things to go back the way that they were before they moved in.

I didn't want to know that Patty Williams was a negro and I wasn't and that somehow that made a difference.

I wanted Patty to move next door.

I didn't want to lose our house.

I needed to ask Dad.

I didn't want him to know I'd been eavesdropping.

"Why the long face, Suzie-Q," Mypa said from the living room couch as I closed the front door.

He folded the New York Times and patted the cushion next to him. "Come tell the Old Man your troubles."

I took off my coat and hung it in the closet under the stairs, taking my time before sitting down next to Mypa. I picked up the paper to sit down and read the headline: Redlining and Blockbusting.

I pointed to the paper. "What's redlining?"

"It's when real estate agents refuse to sell houses to certain people in certain areas. They draw a red line around the area." He poked my shoulder. "But that's not what's eating you, I'd bet."

"How about blockbusting?"

"That's kind of the opposite. It's when people who have been excluded—"

"Like negroes," I asked, regretting the question as soon as it flew out of my big mouth.

Mypa cocked his head before answering. "Yes, like negroes are excluded from some areas. So they try to get their foot in the door. Once one gets in, others follow, until the whole neighborhood changes."

"And everybody loses their houses," I said.

Now one bushy eyebrow rose. "I think you know more

about this than you're letting on, missy."

He put a gnarled hand on my shoulder and had a twinkle in his eye. "I promise I won't let your parents know if you tell me a secret."

I swallowed. "What about Theesta? She's a negro, right? She lives with us."

Mypa shook his head. "Is that what's bothering you?"

"Yes. I mean no. I mean, I don't know."

"You sound confused to me. But I'll tell you there's a difference between a domestic living with the family she serves and a negro buying his own home in a white neighborhood."

"What's the difference?"

"Equality, or the perception of it."

"So if Patty Williams' dad buys Mr. Hatfield's house it's not the same as Theesta living on our third floor?"

"Who's this Patty Williams and what does she have to do with the Hatfield house?"

My secret was out. I only hoped that Mypa would keep his promise. I told him everything. He guessed about the heating vent.

Theesta served meatloaf and baked potatoes for dinner that night. I hardly swallowed a bite. As she finished serving coffee and slices of apple pie à la mode, Mypa touched her hand.

"Theesta, you need to hear this." He tapped the empty chair next to him. "Take a seat."

Theesta looked from Mypa to Dad and back to the Old Man before placing the coffeepot on the sideboard and perching on the front of the chair.

"Son," Mypa said, "I understand that you and some of the other neighbors are preparing to buy the Hatfield house out from under some potential blockbusters."

Mom gasped. She hid her lips behind her napkin.

"How...?"

Mypa glared at his son, my father.

Dad bowed his head. He barely whispered, "We've been considering it."

"I want you to take a good look at the woman sitting next to me."

Dad cast a sidelong glance at Theesta.

"A good look, not some slithering snake glimpse like you're ashamed. You've known Theesta for most of your life. Take a good look."

Dad looked Theesta in the eye.

She stared back.

"Now if Theesta wanted to live in a house of her own, how would that differ from living in your attic—as well furnished and comfortable as it is?"

Dad swallowed.

Mom dabbed at her lips with her napkin.

Kenny and Tammy stared wide-eyed from Dad to Theesta to Mypa and back again to Dad.

I wanted to sink through the floor.

"I said we were considering it."

"Well, consider no more. If a fine family of negroes wants to move into that hellhole Hatfield calls a house, then you'd better reconsider. I didn't sell my own perfectly comfortable home and move in here so I could help you with the mortgage and provide a little comfort for your family to have you deny it to others. Do I make myself clear?"

"But, Pop. Having a negro homeowner could drive down property values," Mom said.

"You think Hatfield hasn't already done that?" Mypa pointed at me. "Did you know that the buyer in question is the family of your daughter's best friend?"

Both Mom and Dad stared at me.

"Patty?" Mom whispered.

I nodded. "She told me not to tell."

"And right she was," Mypa said. "What were you fighting for in Europe, Ken? Land of the free, home of the brave. Be brave where it counts."

"I'll think about it," Dad said. But the warm look he gave Theesta and the stony resolve reflected in his father's eyes made me sure I'd have a new best friend for a neighbor.

Mr. and Mrs. Carter moved out the day Patty Williams' family moved in.

They'd seeded the Hatfield house lawn and built concrete steps to the front door. Theesta baked a welcome-to-the-neighborhood casserole—macaroni and cheese. Mom delivered it.

None of the other neighbors sold.

Mypa kept my secret, but made me promise to stop listening at heating grates.

Dad got it wrong about what was good for the neighborhood, but he got it right in the end.

He was wrong about female lawyers, too. Now that Patty's joined us, we're the biggest and best firm in town—Manly & Manly & Williams, Attorneys-at-Law.

DON'T GET CAUGHT

JULIET NORDEEN

T he cold morning breeze off the snow-covered lake had teeth, which surprised Jessica Fournier, because at 2700 meters the air was thin enough to induce a headache like a vise clamped over her ears. She and Kason D'Angello, her partner for the inspection, stood among hundreds of Chinese tourists and a handful of South Korean pilgrims at the edge of Heavenly Lake. The sky above was deep cerulean kissed with wisps of white and the mountainous bowl surrounding the caldera lake was alternately dirty white, where the bare rock was tufted with dead bunch grass, and coniferous green, where the hearty pines had sloughed off the scrim of snow from the night before. The lake itself, which nearly glowed aquamarine in warmer months, was flat, white, and homogeneous in the way that only a newly formed layer of lake ice could be.

"Who knows we are here?" Kason asked quietly, the only English voice among the susurrant sounds of Mandarin and the more intervolcaic Korean.

"Well, I know you're here, and the Director General knows I'm here." Jessica ticked off three ruddy red fingers.

"So unless you told someone, that makes three," she answered, equally quietly.

"Plus the fish truck man we are meeting?"

"Plus him. Four."

"Plus the father of that man?" There was a suspicious tone in Kason's voice that Jessica could forgive, and a condescending one that she chocked up to lack of experience and then ignored. He would learn, someday, that it was impossible to do their work without some measure of faith. For that to happen, one had to extend cautious trust.

"Okay, five," she said, knowing but unwilling to admit to him that having that many cooks in the kitchen might not turn out to be in their favor. "Again, unless you told someone."

Wanting to put some distance between them and the crowd, Jessica walked casually toward the left edge of the clearing where the tour bus had dumped them beside the lake.

"Who could I have told?" Kason argued as he followed her. "I did not even know we were flying into Beijing instead of Seoul until you dragged me across three concourses at Charles de Gaulle."

"I apologized for that." Jessica blew warm breath across her icy fingers as the wind kicked up again, blowing strands of her greying hair across her face. She wished she had packed a tuque into her backpack, not just a warm scarf. "It is critical that—"

"—that we preserve the secrecy of our presence until such time as you wish the regime to become aware of our location. Si, io capisco," he said, finishing her sentence. The droning tone of his slip into Italian gave Jessica hope that the young investigator was at least open to a new understanding of how hard the job at hand was going to be.

Jessica stopped at the edge of the clearing where the dead bunch grass smelled sour in its dormancy and surveyed the sweeping crown of mountain peaks that surrounded the lake. Starting on the western edge, which belonged to China, she circled counterclockwise toward the border with the People's Democratic Republic of Korea, North Korea, where she could just about make out soldiers in pea-green greatcoats shoveling snow off the long cement staircase that marked the border between the two frenemy nations. As she brought her attention back along the remaining circle of peaks she also scanned the crowd they had just stepped away from.

"I am curious, what made you ask?" she questioned.

"Because everyone is staring."

Relieved, Jessica permitted herself a smile. "Have you never been away from Italy before?" She knew that Kason had earned his nuclear education in the Italian Navy, but it would be unwise for her to assume that naval maneuvers somehow made him worldly.

"Of course I have."

She looked and saw his bashful shrug. "But only to the rest of the continent, and to the United States, eh?"

"And Canada. Eh?" he challenged, with a dig at her countrymen's verbal quirk.

"But not to Asia?" she countered.

"First time."

"And do you not, at some level, feel a little bit like Gulliver in the land of the Lilliputians?"

"Che cosa?" It was obvious that he didn't understand her literary reference.

Jessica wanted to smack him upside the back of his curly-black-haired head. "You are easily a head and a half taller than even the biggest of them. Or had you not noticed?"

Kason squinched up his mouth and murmured, "Hhmmmph."

"They are staring because you are so obviously—what is that American phrase?—not from around these parts. That's all."

"Okay. But that guy." Kason pointed with his right hand toward the crowd. "He's staring at you, not at me."

Jessica quickly reached out and covered Kason's pointing finger with her left hand. "That is rude here." She showed him how to point courteously, with the downward facing thumb of his left hand, with his other four fingers cradled beneath it. Then she turned to see who he had been pointing to.

A middle-aged Korean man had separated himself from the crowd and was moving their way. He was short, only a meter-fifty, and had large, round glasses with bulky frames that accentuated the roundness of his face. His hair was worn long in the front, bangs nearly covering his eyebrows. The energy in his step and the vitality in his skin did not match the impoverished, rough-spun trousers and coat he wore.

"That's because he is Bike. The man we are here to meet." Jessica took two welcoming steps in Bike's direction.

Kason moved up to stand beside her as Bike approached. She initiated a bow before Bike could, showing deference and gratitude. Bike bowed next and then Kason got the hint and bent shallowly at the waist, until Jessica reached over and tugged at his lapel, lowering his bow until it was a deep as theirs.

"He does not look like a fisherman," Kason said under his voice as the three of them straightened up.

Jessica smiled patronizingly at her young partner, making sure that Bike saw. "Because he is not a fisherman. He is a seafood supplier."

"And he speaks English," Bike said, with a slight trace of a British accent.

"Speaks it quite well, in fact," Jessica added, and was glad to see that Kason flushed slightly as he offered an apology.

"Quickly, please." Bike extended his hand, and then led them back toward the parking area where the bright green Chinese tour buses had been joined by a delivery truck that would kindly be called a shanty if it were a building instead of a vehicle. The faded Hangul symbols painted on the corrugated side of the van box looked like they had last been touched up shortly after the end of the Korean conflict. Bike hauled on a canvas strap that rolled up the cracked, black vinyl drape like a window shade rising above the rear bumper. Inside rested a half-dozen empty wood-slatted crates, cube shaped and a meter long on each side. They sat in two rows of three with a narrow aisle in between. The crates reeked of their previous cargo, ghosts of shellfish past. An unpadded bench awaited them against the back of the cab. A tiny window between the two spaces would pass through a little light and possibly some conversation, if you shouted loudly enough.

"We have many kilometers to travel," Bike said as he helped Jessica up into the truck and handed up her backpack.

Kason balked when Bike offered hand, much like a horse reacting to a snake, even tossing his head a little.

"We must cross the border on the day watch today or we will have to wait until Thursday," Bike explained, by way of prodding. Though Kason seemed unmoved, Jessica knew how aggressive it had been for Bike to prod at all. She raised an eyebrow at her young partner and was on the verge of using her "Mom voice" when he relented and allowed Bike to help him into the back of the truck.

"Thank you, Bike," Jessica said before he dropped the curtain and left them in near darkness. A moment later the truck rocked on squeaky springs and then the slamming door echoed in the enclosed space around them. The starter whined until the engine coughed itself to life, sending harmonic vibrations through the whole truck. Vibrations which grew to full-on rattles as the truck got underway, its manual transmission winding up gear after gear.

"This thing is a deathtrap," Kason yelled over the noise.

"Not here, it isn't," Jessica yelled in return. "Welcome to the Third World."

Economic sanctions placed on the misbehaving DPRK by the rest of the world had strangled legitimate trade and predictably set up black-market practices at most of its border cities, especially for food. Undertaking the illegal movement of goods through border checkpoints would be a tricky thing, and smuggling people would be even harder. On the Chinese side it was the expensive yet well-accepted practice of greasing the Maoists' palms. To the east, they'd be dangerously flouting the Juche-flavored Communism created by Kim Il Sung and carried on by his deified-yet-knuckle-headed grandson, Kim Jong Un. Bike had said he could get them safely across. He picked an identically named pair of towns, Hyesan and Hyesan, for the crossing. It was likely that facilitating friendly officials on both sides of the border had cost him nearly a year's wages.

As the truck reached road speed Jessica began to feel a hint of motion sickness. It could have been that they were riding backwards. Could have been that they couldn't see beyond the walls of the van. Could have been the awful stink of the crates.

A peek at young Kason showed him to be a little green around the gills as well. But there was more. He looked like he was choking on a question.

Jessica had to raise her voice to say, "Okay, kid, spit it out."

Kason turned toward her slightly on the bench, until his knees banged into the crates in front of him. "Why this guy? Why is he helping us? Why do you trust him?"

Since it was impossible to talk without yelling, and yelling would exhaust her voice, Jessica kept her explanation short. Mostly she gave him incomplete sentences and waited for him to nod, showing that he understood so she could jump to the next point.

It all boiled down to Bike's history with the Kim Regime. He, Song Beyok, had been the country's chief propaganda artist, first hired by Kim Jong Il, and so he had been allowed free access to news and media content from all over the world.

"He had to know what messages were potentially sneaking in so that he could counter them," Kason shouted, showing the kind of deductive reasoning Jessica was hoping for in an inspection partner.

As the technological revolution exploded and the information age came into its own, the DPRK fell further and further behind the rest of the world. Through his work Bike lost the naïveté that most North Korean's carried, their blind faith in the divine nature of the Kim family and the truth in their edicts. It became impossible to reconcile the knowledge he carried with the "goat shit coming out of their great leader's mouth." Three months into Kim Jong Un's dictatorship, Bike had had enough and he defected.

"He was shot as he sprinted across the DMZ to the South Korean border." Jessica needed Kason to know that the man driving their broken-down truck was as brave, as valiant, and as tough as any soldier or agent he had ever known.

As Bike recovered from his wounds he developed a fake identity as a somewhat legitimate seafood magnate, giving him reason to travel between coastal communities in the DPRK and eastern China. Reborn as Bike, he left behind the man who had spread lies and helped keep his countrymen ignorant and docile, swearing to aid anyone who wanted to curtail or disrupt the regime.

"Like you and me," Kason yelled.

Jessica nodded, her voice having grown hoarse, and trusted that Kason would put the pieces together from there. Jessica suspected that Bike had other reasons, personal reasons, to hate Kim Jong Un and all that he stood for, but she allowed the man his secrets. She didn't need to know all the painful details to be able to trust him. The enemy of my enemy is my friend, or some such thing.

Aside from a tense thirty minutes at the border, during which she and Kason had to stuff themselves under the bench so that the Chinese and then the Koreans could perform their less-than-successful inspections of Bike's "empty" fish truck, their travels were relatively uneventful. The ambient light outside flared brightest at midday and then slowly died away in the pinholes and cracked seams of the tired old truck's van body. The cold intensified after dark and they huddled together, glad for the warmth of friction as they bumped and rocked along the pothole-pocked roads.

"I haven't heard any other vehicles on the road," Kason yelled. Or at least that was what Jessica thought he yelled.

He was right, there had been no clamor of other engines or rushes of displaced air from oncoming trucks. It was one of those peculiarities of North Korea, and the biggest reason they were riding in the stinky ass-end of a dilapidated delivery truck. The country had about eleven vehicles for every thousand people, including military hardware, and so a personal vehicle traveling the winding Tonae Road between the border and the sea would have stood out like the Oscar Meyer Wienermobile.

Since it would take too much breath to explain all of that over the truck's calliope of rattles, Jessica reached into her backpack and pulled out her torch and her satellite map of mountainous Hangyong Province. She placed the pages on Kason's lap and traced her fingertip along the starkly empty road they were currently traveling and then handed him the flashlight so he could look at the image for himself.

It took Kason only a minute to realize what she was showing him. As members of the iPhone and GoogleMaps generation, when everyone carried access to satellite images in their pocket, it didn't take people his age very long to clue in to what was missing. Cars. No cars cruising the roads. No cars parked in the city squares. No traffic anywhere, unless you counted bicycles, and Jessica's satellite image was printed at a resolution too imprecise for that.

Just then the truck slowed, walking down its many gears, and slewed through a hairpin turn to the left. Jessica motioned to ask for the satellite images back and shuffled through the pages until she found one with a higher resolution capture of their pending disembarkation point. She showed Kason the corner they had just taken, the short distance of the road they would travel, and then held up four fingers to explain that their ride was four minutes from being over.

To his credit Kason understood that it was time to change out of their personal clothes and into the kind of rough-spun clothing that was the best a common Korean might be able to afford north of the thirty-eighth parallel. Up close the disguises would never hold—both Jessica and Kason were too tall and too well-fed to be any kind of Korean—but at a distance it might keep them from being ratted out by a casual observer looking to score points with the local party boss.

Also to Kason's credit, he didn't ogle Jessica as she stripped down to change her own clothes. This kid might grow up to be one of the good ones. One of the best.

They had their belongings repacked and were ready to depart the moment that the truck came to a stop.

"Hurry. He cannot idle here for long without risking attention," Jessica said. They quickly slipped out underneath the vinyl curtain and hustled up the driver's side of the truck where Bike had risked exiting the truck to say goodbye. Jessica bowed deeply and using both hands she offered him a rubber-banded stack of Euros. Small bills, two different sizes, colorful and plasticky. Spendable anyplace in the world with a black market.

Bike politely declined, a somewhat chagrined smile on his face, but Jessica knew what it had cost him to get them over the border. She worried more about what it might cost him if anyone ever found out about his role in their affairs, and knew that her financial offering was just a token of gratitude in return for his very real, very critical help.

"You must take it," she insisted as she pushed it into his hands. "Use it to help someone less fortunate."

After a moment's pause, Bike agreed and bowed deeply. "If you find trouble..."

"Yes, I know," Jessica said. She turned to make sure that

Kason would hear her say, "If we have trouble we should follow the stream that flows from the test site to the sea and then hike down the beach until we reach Kimchaek."

"Yes, and stay out of the stream as much as you can," Bike warned them unnecessarily. "Each morning at sunrise my father's boat will be waiting for you at the jetty across from the cannery. Look for the red tile roof."

Jessica nodded and remembered that Bike's father was infamous for feeding scraps of his catch to the local seabirds. "We will look for the skiff with all the cormorants."

"Hurry now!" Bike shooed them off and climbed back into the cab of his truck.

Hoping desperately that none of the folks from the little town up the road had chosen the frigid, starry night for a stroll among the rolling hills, Jessica and Kason dashed across the packed-dirt road, through a dry drainage ditch, and scrambled fifty meters up a loose gravel embankment into the tree line. There, under the cover of a stand of winter-stunted pines, they rested for a moment.

The engine noise from Bike's truck faded gently for a few minutes in the still and dark night until there was a sudden drop in decibels, probably after rounding one of the many sharp corners of the valley, and then its noise faded all together. If it had been spring or summer, the night around them would have been filled with the song of crickets or the conversation of the field hands who worked the cabbage patches along the valley road beneath them. But, being winter, the forest was quiet except when a gust of wind caused the bottle-brush-shaped evergreens to dance and sigh.

Jessica pulled her hair back into a tail and then dug her

compass, a red-filtered torch, and the satellite images out of her pack.

"It's so quiet, so dark." Kason said. "I could almost imagine that we are the last two people on the planet."

"Yeah, I know."

Having grown up in Toronto, Jessica had really never experienced the kind of emptiness-of-place that exists in underpopulated areas. Not until she joined the IAEA and devoted her life to enforcing the Test Ban Treaty. Since then she'd seen some of the most desolate places on Earth.

By God's grace, most nuclear powers had the decency to test their bombs in locations that didn't risk a high casualty count in the event of a catastrophe. But if North Korea's or Iran's little science experiments ever bore fruit, the whole world could wind up with a serious case of being under-populated. "That's exactly what we're trying to prevent."

"This is starting to get real."

Jessica responded by checking her watch. 2200 hours. They had approximately nine hours to get to the test site in the river valley, the infamous Pungge-ri.

She showed Kason the satellite image of the area they were in, one last run through on the plan now that they were on-site. It was procedure.

"Up that hill," she pointed behind them, "we will find a power line trail that runs due east about six klicks. We can stay on the pathway until we reach the scree field for the West Portal venting tunnel." She pointed to a light patch among the trees where boring action had created a patch of gravel that no one had bothered to disperse, even though it betrayed their actions preparing spaces below ground.

Kason nodded that he followed her. She was proud of him for dutifully listening even though this was their third time reviewing the plan together.

"From there we will have to move under cover of the trees until we reach this compound." She pointed to a small clearing about 500 meters west of the scree. Inside that clearing was a perimeter fence around two equal-sized buildings that might combine to make 300 square meters. An incongruous lattice-line of shadows in the image implied that an object seen only as a small bright dot by the satellite was very likely some kind of communication tower. "This is new since the last inspection, but our analysts are pretty sure it's a guard post and listening station."

Once past the guard post and its electronic surveillance, they needed to cross the bowl of a mountain valley that was nearly the same size and shape as the caldera that held Heavenly Lake. Only this bowl had lost the contents of its rain-fed reservoir thirteen years before, mysteriously drying up in October 2006 after Japanese seismographs detected an unnatural single jolt registering just over 3.5 on the Richter Scale.

"Perhaps the lake drained down into hell," Jessica muttered to herself.

The bowl was the most open stretch of their journey and crossing it before moonrise was their best bet.

"Then we better get moving," Kason said. "Andiamo!"

With only their red-tinted torches to light the way, they found the power line path relatively quickly. Following along the path went equally well, but Jessica admitted to Kason that her nerves were high after startling a second time at an imaginary noise as they approached the guard post. If she'd been working with a more experienced inspector, she might not have said anything at all. She wanted Kason to understand that being afraid was expected at times in their line of work, but that they also needed to keep going, walking through their fear. That's how they did their job.

"May I ask a question?" Kason asked when they finished taking low-light reconnaissance photos of the monitoring station for the analysts back in Vienna.

"Go ahead," Jessica said as she pulled the micro-SD card out of the camera and tucked it into her bra.

Kason checked his watch. "If we had taken our original flight from Paris to Seoul, used the UN Ambassador's team to transit to the DMZ, and then contacted Kim Jong Un's people to escort us to Pungge-ri, wouldn't we be done with our inspection by now? Be on our way home, instead of freezing our asses off out here in the radioactive darkness?"

She had been waiting for this question and was mildly disappointed that it had taken him so long to ask. "You'd think so, wouldn't you?"

Jessica put a new memory card into the camera.

"But you don't?" he asked.

"Nope." She took a drink from her water bottle, stored it, and then hoisted her pack and started hiking again, carefully placing her feet on the downslope of the bowl. Kason followed.

"In 2008, I did my first solo job. A surprise inspection of Lashkar Abad, north-central Iran." The story was one she had told dozens of times, censored one way or another for the audience. She was grateful to have a chance to pass the whole experience on to someone who could use it one day, and telling it helped her ignore the screaming ache in her quads from the extended downhill trek. "I figured, no big deal, the site is literally only eighty-five kilometers from the Tehran airport."

"But something happened."

"They knew I was coming, that's what happened. Even

though the IAEA didn't officially announce the inspection beforehand, all they needed was to see my name on the airline's manifest. Surprise inspection blown."

"I'm guessing it took a few hours to get to the site?" Kason asked.

Jessica stepped on a loose rock in the dark and her feet skidded out from under her. She slid twenty meters down the slope on her backside, raising a cloud of dust. Agile as an Alpine goat, Kason picked his way down and helped her up.

"It took me two days just to get out of the airport."

"Two days?" Kason asked. "How is that possible? You carry United Nations' credentials."

"And the flunkies employed by dictators are often phenomenal idiots. Or very capable of faking it. It took the Director General threatening a personal visit to get me out."

"Did you ever get to Lashkar Abad?"

"I got there, eventually. First they took me to a very lovely medieval mosque in Arak. Then we saw a breath-taking mountain peak outside Kermanshah."

"That's halfway to Baghdad."

"I know, right?" Jessica said, a phrase heard often among the fresh grads in the office. It earned her a laugh in the darkness.

"Three days later, five full days after my feet touched Iranian soil, I was finally allowed access to the plant and found nothing more dangerous that some technetium-99m headed for Shahid Fahmideh Children's Hospital."

"So the moral of the story is that you can move a lot of hardware in five days?"

"Especially if you build it that way from the ground up," Jessica agreed.

They reached the bottom of the empty lake bed and the

going got easier. By Jessica's watch, they still had an hour until moonrise and four hours until first light, plenty of time to cross, climb out, and find the rectangular clearing that marked the best place to negotiate the ridge between the bowl and the river valley. From the ridge it would take them less than two hours to hike down the valley that held the tunnel entrances, the Portals of the Pungge-ri underground nuclear test site.

"Do you really think the Koreans are prepping Pungge-ri for more tests?"

Jessica had been rolling that exact question around in her mind for a month. A recent defector, a man much like Bike but from the scientific wing of the government rather than propaganda, had negotiated asylum in America. He had traded details about the DPRK's plans to build and test low-yield nuclear devices for a cattle ranch in the high desert of New Mexico state. The IAEA was unsure whether he was playing into their worst fears, the DPRK with an arsenal of nuclear-tipped long-range missiles capable of EMP attacks, or if he was telling the truth.

"We always wondered why Kim's regime left the South Portal untouched when they imploded the North and West tunnel systems for all the world to see back in May."

"Their test destroyed those tunnels; they just wanted to make a show of buttoning it up for the international press," Kason said, repeating words that Jessica had heard often since the sixth North Korean nuclear test in September 2017.

"Either way, we have to know what's going on inside that South Portal. What they might be able to do there, and what they're actually planning."

"And you think this the only way to find out?"

Jessica stopped, turned, and shined her light in his face.

She couldn't tell if it was just the red filter that gave him such a devilish look, or if he was flush with irritation and anger. Though he was a few inches taller, she did her best to give him a level stare.

"Me, and the Director General, and about two dozen heads of state who are not only smarter than you, but have gone round and round with this damn regime more times that you've spanked your willy."

She saw the embarrassment and humiliation cross his face, but it quickly turned to anger and he clenched his jaw. She had intended to provoke those emotions because she needed him to get past them, quickly, before they moved on toward the test site. He was no good to her until he faced what he feared. Straddling the ridge above a dry lake whose contents had been flushed toward hell by an underground nuclear blast seemed as good a place as any to confront it all.

"But what if we get caught?"

And there it was.

That was the other question she'd been waiting for. Back in the offices in Vienna, during their training, the possibility of capture had been more of a theoretical question. Here, deep inside a dictatorial state, with enveloping darkness all around them, it was a different matter.

"We're doing everything possible to keep that from happening. And, God forbid, if it does, we will have to rely on some help to get us out."

"But only three people in the whole world know where we are. A bird-brained fisherman, his ex-artist son who thinks he's some kind of spy, and the Director General, who is a world away from here."

"And that's a big risk. But it's also the best chance we have to avoid trouble in the first place."

Kason turned away and scuffed his boot on the rock of the ridge. The next step was for him to bitch about not having his mobile phone.

He turned back toward her and shined his red torch in her face. "I'd feel better about all of this if you'd just give me my damned phone back."

"Can't." Jessica shrugged and started down into the river valley where the fog had come up from the coast in the night and left behind a sparkling layer of frost. "It was in that bundle of money I gave to Bike."

She didn't look back. Either Kason would jump her from behind and smash her head in with a rock, or he would follow her. It took a good twenty seconds, but then she heard his footsteps fall in behind hers.

"When we get out of here you're going to buy me a new phone."

"Fair enough," she said. And they walked.

The gentle downhill slope of the valley gave them speed as they weaved their way through the dead pine trees, and the carpet of frosty needles quieted their passing. As the brown trees thinned, a pathway developed and then widened as it led toward a large clearing ahead, proof that theirs were not the first or only feet to travel the valley. Unwilling to encounter any of those folks, because they would likely be better armed, highly surprised, and entitled to shoot, Jessica and Kason edged away from the easy vector down the valley and found the first rocky signs of the dry tributary that would reach the sea about forty kilometers to the southeast. The satellite images showed that the Portals to the three underground test sites, a handful of buildings, and the roadway through the site all straddled the meandering stream, so their next goal was to find the fence line and follow it clockwise around the compound.

True to their satellite's surveillance, the fence was nearby. Though the images did not show it, the rusty chain-link was three meters tall and capped by razor wire. A strip of weed-free but frost-laden ground a meter inside the fence showed signs of roving security, but not too recently. Jessica lead Kason around until the fencing dropped two meters into a gully. She was tempted to hunker down there and wait for daylight, but the faint smell of urine and a wide field of castoff cigarette butts told her this was one of the guards' usual stops. They followed the fence line another hundred paces and then squatted among a stand of white-barked birch trunks for a rest.

"I think those cigarettes were Russian," Kason commented.

"No doubt," Jessica answered, fishing out her water bottle.

"So much for the sanctions."

A glowing orange dawn crept over the ridgeline to the east, giving them their first real look at the valley. The native trees were a mixture of birch, elm, and pine. Most of them dormant or dead, it was hard to tell.

Researchers studying the data from the worldwide radionuclide sensor network after the last test detonation had hypothesized that a majority of the radioactive parti-cles, anything heavier than Xenon gas, had been trapped in the cavities of the mountain. Looking at the signs of death around her made Jessica worry that either the IAEA's scien-tists had been wrong or the local groundwater had been horribly contaminated over the years. She remembered Bike's earlier warning to stay out of the stream; he had been kind to remind them.

"Too bad there's never a Geiger counter around when you need one," she joked. Kason didn't find it funny and she had to fight with herself about whether or not to apologize for her gallows humor. When she realized that he was as afraid as she was, it seemed callous to make a joke like that.

"I'm sorry," she offered.

After a long moment he said, "Me too."

"Okay then," Jessica said, and pushed her hands against her knees to stand up on chilled and weary legs. Neither of them had slept since deboarding the Air China 787 in Beijing more than twenty-four hours before. It was time to muscle through. "I think you Italians say andiamo?"

Kason agreed. She retrieved her compact SLR camera from her pack, they both reshouldered their bags, and they quietly made their way along the fence.

"That looks pretty permanently destroyed," Kason said as they stopped at a scree pile that spilled across their path to study the compound. The tumble of rocks and stones and dirt initiated above them at a pile of haphazardly stacked railroad ties half-buried in the hillside. From there it passed through the fence and ended in the dry stream bed where the smaller bits had been carried away, leaving fist-sized grey-blue rocks behind. It was all that remained of the North Portal. The entrance to a series of deeply questing mineshafts that had almost withstood a blast three times as big as the bomb that wiped out Hiroshima. Almost.

Jessica pointed across an open area inside the fence. Four rectangular irregularities in the dun-colored dirt were all that was left of the buildings that had once stood guard over the entrances. One had housed an industrial compressor for forcing breathable air into the shafts. Another had been a machine shop. The third had either been a barracks or storage; the analysts could never agree. The fourth was where the trigger buttons had been pushed.

Across the clearing from the North Portal were signs of the location of the West Portal. Online videos of its destruction had shown a series of four explosions that closed its black maw and then collapsed its throat with a triple whammy.

"No telling how long it would take to dig that open," Kason commented.

"Not with a thousand golden shovels, my boy," Jessica answered. She was satisfied that the North Portal was done. As with the West Portal, she hoped it never breathed another breath of the outside world. "Not for a million pounds of diamonds."

They declared themselves satisfied and moved along. The brightening morning induced them to be more and more cautious. Jessica thought of area of the test site that served the North and West Portals as the "head" of the valley, and so their destination at the South Portal could be called its "heart." It took ten minutes to reach it.

There, through the fence, beyond a group of seven plywood-sided buildings that had been built in a figure eight pattern around two courtyards, the road crossed the stream and passed through a hockey rink–sized clearing at the base of a tree-covered hillside. Here the pines grew lush and green, as healthy as their cousins upstream were distressed.

Oddly, the hillside beneath the trees had been cut away and supported on thick, horizontal steel beams, leaving just enough earth to anchor the weight of the trees and preserve their roots. A row of great concrete pillars, spaced just two meters apart, supported the beams. Beyond the pillars there was an open-air space, like a covered patio, but huge.

"Well I'll be damned. They dug back into the mountainside, made a portico over the portal."

"I bet it would never show up on the overhead images because of the overhanging foliage," Kason said.

"No, it wouldn't," Jessica agreed, feeling both angry and vindicated at finding that the Koreans were working the South Portal, despite all of their claims to the contrary. "We didn't even see evidence of its construction."

"And the guy the Americans brought over, the defector, did he tell them about this?"

"It wasn't in any of the written reports they shared with us." Jessica started taking photos. She steadied the camera against the fence, zoomed tight, and used long shutter times to get as much detail as she could about the site and its construction.

"So either he's a liar, or this is very recent."

"Or both," Jessica answered as she widened her focus to record the whole compound.

Even if the American's man had lied, it didn't matter anymore. What he'd said had gotten the Director General's attention. What he'd said had gotten them on a plane. Now they knew what was real and what was a lie, and her photos would provide incontrovertible evidence.

"Don't you think it's a bit too quiet in there?" Kason asked as they picked their way along.

Jessica checked her watch, nearly eight o'clock. "Probably staying warm in the barracks, enjoying a second cup of tea. We should have about thirty minutes before their day starts. Did you bring anything with better optics than this?" she asked, pointing to the lens of her camera.

Kason dug into his pack and came out with a scope, monocular vision like a sniper rifle's. He traded it for her camera, and she poked the business end through the chain-link to get a better view while he took over documenting the scene.

"They've got power, lots of lights along the tunnel walls," she reported, keeping one eye closed and the other focusing hard as she swept the scope across the new, wider portal opening. "And I see concrete foundations deep beyond the pillars. Might have caught them getting ready to build."

"Do you see any rail tracks?" Kason asked. Her camera gave a staccato of shutter clicks as he kept taking photos.

Nuclear devices might ultimately be optimized for missile delivery, but they were bulky and heavy during their development stages. Not the kind of thing that gets carried into the bowels of a mine by a cadre of shuffling scientists. Rails were a smoother and less risky way to transport a bomb to the test site. It wasn't the only reason that mines had rails, but it was a sign of planned testing when there were no obvious signs of commercial digging going on.

Jessica searched the areas of the cement floor that she could see from their vantage point and quickly found a pair of bright lines converging together as they disappeared into the darkness.

She was about to confirm the presence of rails when a subtle rock-on-rock scraping noise behind them froze her in place. The noise repeated a second and third time, and then it was outdone by a deep, throaty growl.

"Kason," she whispered as the growl continued. "Turn around slowly. Very slowly."

Jessica also turned around and found the largest and hairiest mastiff she had ever seen. It had to weigh at least seventy-five kilos, it was almost as big as a yearling calf, and its lips were peeled back to show sharp, white canines. If its coloring had been blond instead of black and brown, she might have mistaken it for a young lion.

They backed against the fence as much as they could,

but the dog kept coming. Its paws looked as big as salad plates and its growl kept intensifying.

"It's going to bark soon," Jessica warned. "Then they'll know we're here."

"Should we try to run?" Kason asked.

Jessica wondered if one of them might have a chance if they dashed in opposite directions, but it seemed a poor gamble. If the dog was well trained it would know to run down whichever one of them ran away from its handlers, and the other would be spared a dog bite only to run right into armed guards.

"No. There might be a chance for running later, but not with that dog in the mix. Right now, we have to think about the job."

The dog advanced another step.

"Okay," Kason's voice shook.

"On the count of three, I am going to keep the dog focused on me, and you need to get the memory card out of the camera and stash it where they won't find it unless they strip search you."

Kason groaned. He knew exactly what she was talking about. "Won't they know to search us carefully when there's no card in the camera?"

"We have to try to decoy them," Jessica said, keeping her voice calm for the dog's sake. "I have another card in my bra. As soon as you see one of the guards, smash the camera on the rocks. I'll drop the extra card and we'll have to hope they think it popped out."

The dog advanced. When it was only a half meter away, Jessica started her count. After two she took a deep breath and summoned every drop of courage she could, and right after saying three she dropped to one knee and tried to baby-talk to the huge, ferocious dog as if it were her neighbor's beloved golden retriever. Her movement provoked the dog's first bark, but they got lucky and were able to execute her plan before a pair of guards in standard-issue pea-green woolen overcoats and fur-covered hats arrived to find them cowering against the fence, the camera and the scope smashed to pieces on the ground around them.

To say the guards were surprised was an understatement. The older one looked to be about twenty, and the younger-but-larger one reminded Jessica of Baby Huey. They shouted orders in Korean that neither of the inspectors understood, but the anger in the guards' faces and the aim of their machine guns said plenty. Jessica encouraged Kason not to resist as they were yanked from the fence and shoved down.

"Be ready," she whispered as the larger soldier pinned her to the ground with one giant boot and the older one restrained Kason. "As soon as I say go, you run."

Kason was thrown over onto his belly and patted down by the guard. "What about you?" he grunted as a knee in his spine knocked the wind out of him.

Baby Huey looked like he didn't know whether or not it would be okay to frisk Jessica. Maybe he had never dealt with a woman in his job. "Don't worry about me," she said as she smiled at Huey, trying to confuse him further. "If they put that dog back on its lead, you have to try to escape."

Only they didn't leash up the dog, though its demeanor changed from ferocious lion to cuddly teddy bear once she and Kason had their hands bound behind their backs. Apparently Huey didn't feel like executing a pat-down, so the older guard made Huey pick up the pieces of the broken camera while he checked Jessica for weapons himself.

They were force-marched farther along the valley,

through a rusty gate in the towering chainlink fence, and farther along the road. Jessica knew that the command offices and barracks were about two kilometers further along toward the main road. They didn't get that far. Instead they were shoved into a bare cinder-block building with a tile roof that sat just north of the main road, about halfway between the barracks and the Portals. The analysts had always called it Mystery Building One, guessing that it was about twenty square meters inside, and now Jessica knew that it was a cold storage building for food. A spring bubbled in an open-topped cement basin at the back of the room, surrounded by the hanging carcasses of hogs and stacks of crates filled with cabbage, onions, and squash. Stacked bags of rice flanked both sides of the door.

When the guards untied their hands and locked the door behind them the room was dark except for a narrow rectangle of indirect light that came in through a high window in the door, like a badly installed mail slot. Jessica rushed to look out the window and saw the two guards arguing on the road.

"Please, please, please," she whispered to herself, and was rewarded when her fondest wish came true. The older guard leashed up the dog and began walking in the direction of the barracks, leaving Baby Huey standing guard over them.

She turned to Kason. "Are you ready? We're only going to get one shot at this."

Kason shook his head. "We should stay together."

"No," she said sternly, trying to keep the fear out of her voice. "No, this is the job."

"But, but, but…" Kason stammered.

Jessica knew that he was afraid for her; she was afraid for both of them. "One of us has to get out." She grabbed him by both biceps and shook him, trying to keep him from looking away. "One of us has to get out, or we'll both die for nothing."

"But why?"

"Because there have to be rules," she said, and uttering those words brought on an almost magical sense of calm. "There have to be rules," she repeated.

In a very motherly fashion, she started buttoning up Kason's rough wool jacket to protect him from the cold as he made his escape. She brushed dust and bits of pine needle from his sleeves. Then, grabbing both of his icy hands, she looked deep into his eyes and tried to help him find the steel in his spine. "We caught them. Caught them with their pants down. They were breaking the rules and you have to make sure they don't get away with it."

Unwanted memories pushed their way into her thoughts. She had been so much younger then, even younger than Kason was standing in front of her, submitting to her fussing and demands. She had still been in college, medical school. It was a hard time. She wasn't sure what specialty to follow, wasn't sure she really wanted to be a doctor at all. But her husband, Louis, insisted. Truth be told, all she wanted in her life was a baby.

They tried. For months. For years. All through her graduate program. When he wasn't on tour with the band, wasn't detoxing, wasn't relapsing, they tried. They tried, they lost, they tried again. She refused to give up until her gynecologist, a longtime family friend, diagnosed her fertility issues. Untreatable. Louis took the news in stride, but she insisted that their life would not be complete without a baby.

After tearful fights and sleepless nights, Louis relented. If she finished her program, stayed on track, then he would agree to start the adoption process as soon as she began her residency. So she studied and she worked and she waited. The day she clocked in at the ER for her first shift they signed the application and e-mailed it.

The provincial screening process to adopt was gruesome. Jessica insisted that they be brutally honest with the children's services staff, except for one thing, Louis's history with drugs. It was all in the past. Done. Over with. No one needed to know. It was a lie of omission she was happy to tell. And it worked. They were approved. Placed on the list. First available baby, it didn't matter what gender, what race, what reason.

Fifty-eight days later the best news came. An expectant teenaged mother was making the right decision. Adopting out. It would be a girl. Jessica painted the nursery shell pink and decorated it with hippos and giraffes.

A week before the mother's due date, children's services arrived at their apartment for a surprise inspection. Jessica was at the hospital, the second half of a twenty-four hour shift in the ER.

Louis was home.

Passed out on the couch.

An antique silver spoon, a bottle of de-ionized water, a strip of rubber tubing, a butane lighter, a bag of cotton balls, a syringe, and half of an eight-ball of Mexican heroin on the coffee table next to him.

Jessica never got her baby girl.

There were rules, they had said to her when she begged for another chance.

"There have to be rules," she whispered aloud, only half aware of where she was and what she was saying.

She followed the rules when she got a divorce. Because of who Louis was it was public, and it was ugly. The humiliation of it all drove her out of her residency. She worked hard and rebuilt her life on a foundation of honesty, integrity, and bravery.

A tear slipped down her cheek. Its cold track pulled her out of her memories. "Okay then," she said as she wiped it all away as simply as brushing the tear away with the rough-spun sleeve of her jacket.

"You really mean it, don't you?" Kason asked.

Jessica nodded, squeezed his hands, and then let them go. "In another minute I am going to cause a fuss. Screaming. Pounding on the door. Whatever it takes to get that door unlocked. Thankfully the dumb one is out there on guard. By the time he decides to open the door his buddy with the dog ought to be a kilometer down the road."

Kason bounced on his toes and breathed heavily, like football player psyching himself up before taking the pitch for a championship game. "Do you need me to help you take him down?"

"It's probably our only chance."

They talked about the best way to take the guard down and decided that Jessica would go high and Kason would go low.

"Once we get him on the floor, I want you to run. Just run. Get to cover first. Then get over the fence and do whatever it takes to get down to the sea."

"I can't believe I'm going to do this."

"You can!" Jessica said. She squeezed his shoulders and gave him a brave smile before she turned and began pounding both fists on the inside of the door.

It took minutes of screaming to draw the guard, but once Jessica felt the knob turn in her hand, she leaned back and got ready to yank the door wide open.

They caught Baby Huey off guard. He failed to let go of

the knob on his side of the door and Jessica was able to pull him forward into the building. Kason tangled the guard's giant feet by shoving a sack of rice into the door opening and then ensured that the big Korean would fall by pinning his knees together. Baby Huey landed on his face with a wet thud. His uniform fur hat tumbled across the concrete floor, rolling to a stop against the spring's basin at the back of the storeroom.

Jessica pounced on the guard's back. Her arms circled his neck; her interlocked wrists squeezing hard against the soft flesh at his throat. As he tried to rise to his hands and knees, she wrapped her legs around his torso so that he could not shake her loose. Her arms burned and it was all she could do to keep her ankles locked together around his bulky, pea-green coat.

She spared a moment's focus to look through the open doorway for Kason and was rewarded with a brief peek of his curly dark hair as he dashed across the road, racing for the fence.

"Andiamo!" she yelled after him, knowing that he was one of the good ones. One of the best.

STATUESQUE
LISA SILVERTHORNE

Harper Bolton bought the San Juan Island cottage because she felt as haunted and abandoned as the hundred-and-ten-year-old beachfront property. Along the secluded rocky coast, mystic wooded landscapes, and lush inland pastures, a strange magic resonated as tourist season waned and autumn's serenity approached the Washington State island.

Dispelling secrets. Drawing like souls together.

Despite the stories of magic and connection, no one ever stayed in the isolated, single-story cottage for long. Complaints of strange sounds in the overgrown English garden, presences in the house and along the private beach —even piano music in the house. No one used the word ghost outright, but that's how Harper got the house so cheap. Her divorce settlement barely covered the asking price and essential renovations. San Juan Island, Washington, was the farthest place she could run from her cheating ex—and his rich new wife.

At twenty-three, the last thing Harper Bolton wanted

was another man to break her heart. Especially one hiding secrets.

The English garden was an overgrown, stone-walled square of unruly green grass overlooking the rocky beach below. She'd weeded and trimmed, coaxing the unkempt perennials back into beds around the garden's perimeter and cleaned the mold from the two gold gazing balls nestled among the lavender and roses. She followed the waves of rich purple lavender that flowed along the flag-stone path, its clean, crisp scent carrying her past tall spires of white and pink foxglove, violet allium balls as big as grapefruits, and stands of sweet, spicy stargazer lilies.

Toward the huge, mature Madrone tree—and the statue.

She'd pruned the skeins of delicate, ballet-pink English roses that climbed the beige-plastered stone walls (matching the cottage's smooth beige plaster now) in tight, double-bloomed spirals. Their soft floral scent floated through the garden, mixing with cool, salt-tanged air and crisp lavender, calming her anxiousness.

She was alone now. Something she faced for the first time in her life. And the secret that Rick hid for more than two years—along with the lies. She hadn't suspected a thing until Maryland's Somerset County sheriff was on her doorstep back east, serving her with divorce papers.

Harper brushed her dark, shoulder-length hair back into a hair tie, the deep teal waters of the Salish Sea a soft whisper against the island's western shore as she stood under the Madrone tree, taking photos and making notes on her phone. The garden (and the house) needed a lifetime of work, but for now, it was essentials only. Taming the garden hadn't been essential, but it was great therapy.

She turned back to the cottage, admiring its restored

plaster walls, freshly painted trim, adorned gables, and newly repaired slate roof. She'd painted the roof's buttressed eaves a deep teal to match the original trim and replaced all the broken windows and doors.

Shivering, she zipped her pink fleece jacket up to her chin, keeping the cool sea air at bay. August's warm, seventy-degree days cooled into the forties at night. Even during the day, the raw channel winds bit through her jeans and grey canvas Vans. Shaking, she steadied her phone and snapped images of the garden and huge Madrone tree at its center. It spread thick, bony red limbs and curling orange leaves toward the crisp cerulean sky and warm gold sunlight, its smooth red trunk peeling in rust-colored strips like old paint.

Beneath the sheltering limbs stood the haunting marble statue of a tall, lean young man with sleek, chiseled features. The statue's fine facial features and detailed clothing were still sharp and defined after all this time. A tailcoat, double-breasted vest, and trousers from the early 1900s had been masterfully carved down to the perfectly spaced pinstripes and two-toned boots.

With a forlorn expression, the statue stretched one arm toward the Salish Sea, other arm at its side as it stood like a guardian over the garden and house.

No one remembered the man's name or who'd sculpted the statue, just that he'd built this house for his new bride. But someone must have taken care of the pristine statue all these years because damp sea air destroyed marble.

Harper didn't understand why most buyers found the statue and cottage unsettling. She found the statue comforting, protective like the Madrone tree, both softening the pain of loss and the heartache of betrayal. She winced, still in shock that Rick had taken everything from her. Love. Security. Her self-worth.

Like that young bride, she'd lost everything.

She reached up and touched the statue's cold cheek, intrigued by the strong chin and jaw line. And the story the locals told. Short hair framed the gentle oval face, patrician nose, full bottom lip, and large, wide-set eyes. Eyes that looked so honest. So innocent. She moved closer. Innocent but wounded.

What color were his deep, soulful eyes? His hair? Did he love his wife?

The hundred-and-ten-year-old statue was an attractive likeness of (and touching tribute to) the wealthy young man who'd built this cottage and garden for his new bride back in 1910. A month after moving in, he disappeared off the beach during a storm. His widowed bride erected this statue of her beloved, but soon after, she left the island, leaving the cottage dormant for two decades. After that, it changed hands like the flu virus, no one ever staying long. Or so the story went, according to locals.

Harper felt a kinship to the widowed bride, under-standing some of the pain and loss she must have endured, losing her husband so soon after marrying. All alone on this isolated coast. It must have been terrifying. She'd loved Rick with all her heart until his betrayal broke it into a million pieces.

But this statue's handsome face was captivating. Enchanting. Depicting such a kind face and honest eyes that might have darkened with disapproval at Rick's secrets and deceptions. Throughout their two-year marriage, she never suspected dishonesty in Rick's soft, puppy-brown eyes whenever he said he loved her.

She clenched her hands into fists, feeling ashamed at

being so trusting—so gullible—never suspecting a thing. Blindsided by the truth. She felt sick that he'd kept his infidelity a secret for almost three years—from the beginning. She never truly knew the man she'd loved. The man she married. Even when they moved in together after a year of dating, he was sleeping with Tori Winstead—and her father's fortune, his secret intact.

No, Harper never suspected a thing. It was way more than an affair. Had he ever loved her? No, he'd catfished her into a sham marriage. And it hurt like a razorblade to her soul. She was just Rick's backup transaction. In case his plan to marry into the billionaire Winstead family fell apart, Rick still had the daughter of the well-off Bolton Industries founder on the hook. Money had been the only quality he'd sought in a wife.

She winced, fighting back tears, every thought of Rick's secret relationship making her sick. And furious. At first, she'd wanted revenge, but in the end, she just wanted out. Freedom and the fastest escape possible. Far away from Rick's new beachfront Maryland mansion, a wedding gift from the Winsteads. Where no one knew her.

Right now, she needed a place to heal, a place to find true north again. Magical or haunted. Abandoned or not. Harper wanted only to be alone and tame this overgrown, frowsy garden.

She'd been in the house two weeks when music began in the attic. Around three a.m., it reverberated through the house, waking her out of a sound sleep. Her first since leaving Maryland. And Rick.

The haunting, tinny echo of a music box filled the silence.

Harper froze, afraid to move beneath her red and white quilt as the chilling, high-pitched chords plinked out a frantic, chime-like melody. Her hands went cold, heart racing as the unfamiliar song ached through the darkness, each metallic note vibrating against her eardrums until they hurt. But the realization took her breath, the cold fear immobilizing.

The attic was empty. And she didn't own a music box.

She couldn't stop shaking, teeth chattering as the strange melody reverberated through the deathly quiet hallway and rattled every west-facing window and door as the song repeated twice.

On its third playthrough, the frantic lament slowed, knife-point sharp notes softening until the song dissipated like fog in sunlight, echoes fading beneath the soft surge of waves against the rocky shoreline. A hint of brine hung above the soft scent of roses she'd put in a cobalt blue vase on her dresser, the mirror above it trembling.

Pale pink petals fell onto the varnished alder dresser as wind howled around the cottage eaves with horrific moans. Windows rattled and surf churned. Waves crashed against the garden's stone walls, growing taller as the music box heralded a windstorm along the craggy, evergreen coast and rock-strewn beach.

She gripped the creaking, white iron bed frame with both hands as it trembled against the queen-size mattress.

The islanders all told her that surviving her first storm season on the island was her first test. If she got through it (and the ghosts) and stayed in the cottage, she'd officially be a local. Being accepted as a local was a different story though.

Harper hated storms. She was seven when the old oak came down in a shower of lightning and fire, smashing through her bedroom window. When she was with Rick, she always snuggled close to him and he held her until her shaking stopped and the storm had passed. This was the first storm she'd faced alone. There'd always been someone else in the house. Not some ghost playing a possessed music box until the plaster walls cracked and the paint peeled. How long before she ran screaming for the next ferry to the mainland? She clenched her jaw closed until it ached. No, she wasn't scared.

She was terrified!

Sixty-mile-an-hour winds and twenty-foot surfs crashed along the beach, waves swelling around the garden wall. She winced. Probably obliterating flowers, hedges, and all her hard work. At least she had pictures on her phone if she had to start over again.

It wouldn't be the first time.

Waves pounded the beach, the sound thundering through the cottage like the approach of a nor'easter, the half-empty house magnifying the cacophony of wind, rain, and waves.

Terrified the waves might wash away the whole house, Harper climbed out of bed and pulled on black yoga pants and a grey hoodie over her red nightshirt. Grabbing her flashlight and phone off the marble-top nightstand (left behind), she slid into her Vans and crept into the dark hallway toward the living room.

The spacious, east-west living room, smelling like orangewood oil, held all the furniture from the house in Maryland. The furnishings dampened the echo of storm winds, making her feel safer. Down the hall, the empty parlor/library with only some of her books just magnified the sounds. So did the small, sea-facing music room, empty except for an old upright player piano. And lots of dust.

Wind moaned like harpies around the eaves of the house, shaking the walls. Light fixtures swayed. Dusty maple hardwoods creaked. Wall sconces flickered.

A loud clap erupted like a gunshot, the report reverberating through the entire cottage, as if the walls were coming apart. Then the house went eerily silent as lights went out and the furnace stopped. Still, the storm resonated through the dark house, moments of eerie silence heavy between gusts of wind and wild surf hitting the shore.

Harper turned toward the double doors that led outside to the patio and dark garden, flashlight in hand, but the frosted glass panes kept her from seeing outside. She unlocked the doors and struggled to open one just a crack.

A large tree limb from the Madrone tree lay dark and in pieces in the center of the garden. Her heart leaped into her throat.

No! The statue!

She ran out into the storm toward the Madrone tree, wind almost blowing her back against the house. Her heart sank when she reached the fallen limb.

A pile of rubble gathered where that statue had stood pristine and unharmed for more than a hundred years.

She bent down, fumbling through the hunks of white stone. Could someone put it back together?

"Help!"

The shout startled her. She jerked her head up, dark hair whipping into her face as she glanced around the dark landscape. The closest house was a quarter mile up the beach.

Her flashlight caught a glimpse of a dark figure

sprawled below on the sand amid tangles of seaweed and driftwood.

"Help me!"

A man's voice, sounding thin and ragged. Injured.

Harper hesitated.

"Someone—please!" he shouted again.

Harper hurried out of the garden and down the rocky footpath to the beach below.

She knelt in the wet sand beside a sandy-haired man, barefoot, wearing a soaked white dress shirt and drenched dark pants. When her flashlight beam lit his face, she gasped.

His big eyes were the palest blue pools of light she'd ever seen, outside corners gently angling downward into an almost hurt expression. His chin was strong, nose chiseled and aristocratic. He was beautiful.

He took her breath away.

She struggled for a breath when he grabbed her arm, his hold weak, eyes intense.

"I wished on a falling star and they sent me an angel," he said in a raspy whisper, eyes bright, British accent warm like hot tea with milk. No, hotter. Like buttery, melting caramel. "Are you granting my last wish or hers?"

Harper shrugged, shaking her head. "Don't know anything about falling stars or wishes, but the halo was too small and I pawned the wings."

She smiled at him. Had he mistaken the Perseids meteor shower for falling stars?

The corners of his mouth tried to lift into a smile, but he was shivering too hard.

"I know it's August and still summer, but a three a.m. swim during a storm might just kill you," said Harper, sliding her arm underneath his shoulders. "I need to get you off this beach before you die of hypothermia."

He nodded, still staring at her, looking confused as she got him on his feet. He glanced up and down the beach, his gaze frantic in the stormy darkness.

"She's here, isn't she?" he cried, fear shining in his eyes as he struggled to hold on to Harper.

Had he lost someone out there in the storm? A wife? Girlfriend?

"Was someone else with you out there?" Harper asked, gently shaking him until she had his attention again.

She turned him toward the footpath

"No, I was alone," he said, his shivering beginning to fade, eyelids drooping. "They warned me about wishing aloud near the sea," he said, shaking his head as his teeth stopped chattering.

He looked groggy now, almost sedated.

She had to get him out of the storm. Now.

"Why can't you make a wish by the ocean?" Harper asked, distracting him as she steered him onto the footpath

"Because," he said in a weary voice. "Something swimming past might just grant it."

Well, that was sufficiently terrifying.

She didn't believe in magic (or magical creatures), but she didn't want to tempt the unknown either.

He leaned against her, his bare feet dragging as the footpath curved up toward the garden. She pushed ahead, struggling to keep his tall, lean body moving along the sandy path. He was at least six-one to her five-seven height.

"Where am I?" he mumbled, sounding confused as he brushed wet, sandy bangs out of his eyes.

"San Juan Island, Washington," Harper said as they reached the garden.

She cut across the grass, struggling to reach the patio. His arm around her waist slipped. He was getting weaker.

"Hang on," Harper urged. "We're almost there."

He nodded, looking at her through hooded eyelids.

She tightened her grip around his waist, half-pulling, half-pushing him onto the flagstone patio. His eyes brightened as they approached the back door and she wanted to swim in his limpid blue eyes. She looked away, focusing on the door, reminding herself that she'd come here to get away from dating and relationships. From men.

Besides, eyes like that probably hid more secrets than Rick's accountant.

Three steps from the back door, he slumped against her shoulder, a dead weight now. She had to get him inside and out of those wet clothes.

Harper summoned all her strength and dragged him to the threshold. She threw open the door with her right hand. One last time, she pulled with all her might until both of them fell through the open doorway into the cottage. She shoved the door closed with her foot and sank back against it, chest heaving from the exertion.

The man lay unmoving on the dusty hardwood, skin pale and clammy. He looked like a drowned sailor. She leaned over him, making sure he was still breathing.

Had he been swept off a boat in the storm and washed up on the beach? At three a.m., who else would be out in this weather?

She sighed, shaking her head as she began unbuttoning his soaked dress shirt. She'd run more than three thousand miles away from the divorce and Rick's secret life to forget that he (and all other men) existed. Not even a month later, someone drops this stray guy on her doorstep. It was the last thing she wanted to deal with right now.

Where was he from? What was his name? She sighed again. Did he even need one with eyes like that? What secrets hid behind his chiseled features and wounded blue eyes?

Risking her heart one more time to discover them all might just destroy her.

The next morning, Harper's stray opened his eyes.

She'd put freshly laundered, yellow cotton sheets smelling like soap and sunlight on the brass bed in the spare bedroom. It was just across the hall from the master, a stained glass window facing south. She draped a thick turquoise quilt across him that smelled like rosewater.

The south-facing room had pale aqua plaster walls and white baseboards, empty except for the brass bed, white nightstand with a brass lamp, beige wingback chair beside the bed, and a walnut chest of drawers against the west wall. Sunlight pooled across the maple hardwood floors, dust motes settling as morning became afternoon.

"How do you feel?" Harper asked. She wore black yoga pants and a grey hoodie again.

He was even more handsome in daylight, those light blue eyes intense, watching her every move. His hair was lighter than she'd expected and he looked younger, too. About her age.

"Alive," he said with a faint smile. "You saved my life last night and I don't even know your name."

His voice resonated in smoky summer tones, smooth British accent warm and buttery. He seemed to study her movements, the clothes she wore, the way she wore her hair. Not in a leering or condescending way. He just seemed genuinely curious. Anxious.

Harper kept her distance.

She extended her hand. "Harper Bolton."

He stared at her hand a moment, as if he didn't know what to do, and then gently held her fingers between his thumb and forefinger in an old-fashioned manner. As if he planned to kiss her hand. He tried to act strong and able, but the weakness in his clear blue eyes betrayed him.

"Noah Lancaster," he said, watching her intently. "Thank you for the attentive care you've shown me."

Harper sat down in the chair beside his bed. "You're lucky to be alive, Noah," she said.

He nodded. "That I am."

She motioned toward the window. "That storm beat this place up quite a bit, but everything's fixable." She sighed. "Except for the statue."

It survived more than a hundred years without a scratch. Until she moved in and it got destroyed. It was as much a part of this cottage as the garden and now, it was gone. Reproducing it wasn't an option.

"The statue?" he asked, staring at her with a confused, almost intrigued expression.

Harper nodded. "There was a statue in the garden of the man who built this house for his new bride. According to the locals, the groom died in a storm a month later, so his distraught widow commissioned a statue of her husband."

Noah's eyes darkened. "His distraught widow?"

That was a strange reaction. She studied his face, jaw clenched, muscles taut as he chewed his bottom lip.

"You sound skeptical," she replied. "Why do you say that, Noah?"

A deep sigh shuddered through him and she couldn't

read the emotions warring in those clear blue eyes. He gripped his hands together, twisting his fingers against his palms. He seemed anxious. Worried. Frustrated.

Something felt off-kilter. She'd felt it from the moment she met him on the stormy beach that morning.

She glanced over at the chest of drawers. Where she'd lain out the clothes he'd been wearing when she found him. She'd washed and dried them. The white dress shirt had a stiff, removable collar and the pants had pinstripes, both with labels she'd never see before. They seemed more like part of a costume than anything current.

She wanted to recoil from the whole situation. More secrets. And if she confronted them, she already knew what would follow. Lies and justifications. Deceptions explained away until time revealed them for what they were—half-truths. Outright lies.

And then she'd lose herself all over again.

But something about Noah felt so genuine that he quieted that tiny little voice inside her head telling her to give up and run before she got hurt again. Part of it was just admitting that she was incredibly attracted to him. And part of it was letting go of Rick and his devastating secret.

Noah sat up in the bed, his fingers worrying at the edge of the quilt as he fixed Harper with his lucent blue eyes.

"Harper, there's something I need to say. It's probably going to be the most outlandish thing you've ever heard, but please, hear me out first. There's not much time, but the first thing you need to know is that you're in danger."

"What?" Harper cried. "What do you mean in danger?"

Noah sighed again, a deep, heavy sound that was almost a lament as fear crept into his wounded blue eyes. Dread. She felt it tremble through her hands, her fingertips turning cold.

She sat down beside him on the bed, wanting to comfort him, reassure him that whatever he was facing, she wouldn't let him face it all alone. She winced.

There goes my heart again.

"First, total truth," he said, staring at her, unblinking. "No secrets."

Harper nodded for him to continue, holding her breath, not wanting to break whatever delicate magic fueled his directness and stark honesty.

"When you found me on the beach, you knew nothing about the secret I've carried for over a hundred years."

Pain ached in his face, mirrored across his eyes as he watched her every reaction.

"A hundred years? What are you talking about?" She shook her head, the words a jumble and she couldn't string them together into a reasonable statement because of him tossing out the word secret.

She gritted her teeth, wanting to rage at that word and all the destruction it had already caused in her life. And what did he mean, a hundred years? How did he know how much time had supposedly passed?

He was shaking now, the words trembling as he forced them out.

"The statue, Harper. This house! And the abject lie about a bereaved widow honoring her dead husband."

He ground his teeth together, hands balling into fists.

Harper reached out and laid her hand on his, squeezing, feeling the outrage quake through him.

"There was no statue!" he shouted. "No bereaved widow. She was a monster. A gorgon eager to refuel her immortality by preying on a gullible, lovestruck fool. She took everything from me and then like a spider encasing insects in its silk to devour later, she used her magic to turn me to stone for a hundred years. And when it wore off, she would devour my soul, adding another two hundred years to her immortality."

"My God, Noah," Harper cried, cradling his hand in hers. "Is that true? How do you know it was a hundred years?"

He nodded and his eyes glistened with moisture, his bottom lip quivering.

"I stood in that garden for a hundred and ten years and nine days, unable to move or speak or dream while the years rolled past. While everyone I ever loved or cared for passed on, one by one. And every single day, I scratched a line on the inside of my stone prison, counting the days and the nights until my fingers bled."

He brushed back a tear that slid down his cheek. "I was born in 1886, Harper. 1886! I never got to see my parents or siblings again. They all lived their lives, thinking I was dead while I stood frozen in time, watching everything change." He slammed his fist against the mattress. "Watching my estate broken up into pieces around me, unable to stop it being sold off and destroyed bit by bit as my entire family disappeared one by one. Watching strangers move in and take a little bit more until the estate was abandoned and in ruin."

She was stunned into silence. Noah's pain and loss was unimaginable. He'd truly lost everything except his soul, but apparently, that was his last asset this monster would cruelly snatch from his defeated hands.

When she looked up, he was smiling, that beautiful light an afterglow in his pale blue eyes.

"And then you stepped into my garden and touched my cheek," he said in a solemn tone, his hand against his face. He wiped away another tear. "You were the first person in over a hundred years to see me. To acknowledge my existence, that I'd lived and breathed and inhabited a time and place once. Even if it was such a short moment in the long stretch of emptiness."

Noah reached out and took both of Harper's hands in his, kissing her fingers.

"You rebuilt my garden. You brought my cottage back from extinction, caring for it like a cherished heirloom." He winced, pain shuddering across every feature and every muscle. "But I need to ask you to leave, Harper."

"What? Leave? Why, Noah?"

He gripped her hands tighter, cradling them against his chest. "The gorgon knows I've awoken from my stone prison. She set the music box in the attic to play when I awoke. Now, she's coming back to take my soul and if you're here, she take yours, too. I'm too weak to protect you. I feel her out there. She'll be here by morning...and there's nothing I can do to stop her arrival. Or her taking my soul."

Harper felt the fury rise at her temples, the hot flush burning across her cheeks and down her neck. First, her garden statue became human. Now, gorgons were about to invade her garden and turn her to stone with a look. The statue had been a stretch, the gorgons over the top. But it didn't matter whether or not she believed in the magic because Noah believed in it. And right now, Noah needed someone at his side.

She gripped Noah by the shoulders, forcing him to look at her.

"Noah! Don't you dare just give up. Fight her. Fight back!"

She felt the hopelessness of defeat weighing him down. He'd lost everything, immobilized for so long. He had nothing left to give. But she did. She had her outrage and she had Noah. If he couldn't fight, then she'd fight for both of them. If this snake-haired bitch really existed, she'd make her pay for everything.

He shook his head. "Even if I could fight her, one solid stare would turn me back to stone. For good. Then she'd take my soul like a stolen wallet."

Harper slid her arms around him, holding him close until her mouth found his, kissing him with all the fire and determination she possessed. In order to fight the gorgon, Noah Lancaster needed to feel loved. When he was confident enough to stand up to her, he wouldn't stand alone.

And together, they'd take this immortal werebitch down. Where it all began, because she had a plan.

Noah miscalculated the gorgon's arrival. She slithered out of the sea and onto the rain-slicked patio just as the setting sun burned across the horizon in flaming orange and pink fingers. As the golden hour settled across the estate like Maxwell Parrish's Daybreak, lavender and lilies perfumed the air, the island's magic awakening.

As Harper Bolton prepared for a fight.

She stood at the door, dressed in black yoga pants and pink fleece jacket. Noah Lancaster stood beside her, dressed in unfamiliar clothes that she'd found throughout the house. A pair of faded jeans that were too big and a navy blue hoodie. And a pair of slip-on tennis shoes covered in paint.

"Noah, darling, it's time to end this," the gorgon called from the patio, her alto voice gravelly and condescending. "Come out and face me. Your soul already belongs to me."

Guess this thing was real after all. Her thoughts surged

back to college and the Greek myths she'd studied for a final paper. Just needed one little detail—how to kill it.

Arm and arm, Harper and Noah stepped onto the patio. They both stared at the ground, relying on peripheral vision to watch the horrid grey thing slither like a serpent onto the flagstone patio. Snakes writhed like dreadlocks across its scalp, Harper only able to capture its movements at the edge of her vision. In the puddles of rain water, turning rose-gold with the setting sun.

Looking this creature in the face meant an eternity of stone. She remembered that much from the English Lit and mythology classes she took in college.

"You own nothing," Harper shouted, tugging Noah toward the garden. "If you want his soul so badly, then come take it. Bitch."

The gorgon shrieked like a harpy, its body twitching as it oozed across the flagstone path toward her.

"Don't stop moving until you reach the Madrone tree," said Harper against Noah's ear as the tree's protective red boughs burned in the darkening sky. "Grab hold and close your eyes."

"Harper, please," he pleaded. "Don't do anything stupid!"

She shook her head, feeling the horrid creature approaching. "Nothing stupid, I promise."

When Noah grabbed hold of the tree trunk and closed his eyes, facing west, Harper bolted across the garden as the gorgon's writhing shadow stretched across flagstones and flowers.

"I'll gorge myself on both your souls!" the gorgon shouted, surging toward Harper.

Harper launched herself past the thick stands of lavender and into the dense skeins of English roses.

"Ladies first," the gorgon hissed.

The slithering creature was so close that Harper heard the snakes in its hair rattling. She felt the bursts of breath as their forked tongues tasted the air. Seeking a target.

"Turn and face me, mortal!" the gorgon ordered, rising up to its full six-foot height.

"Harper, no! Don't!" Noah shouted from the Madrone tree behind her.

Hunched over, Harper turned. "It'll be my pleasure. Bitch!"

She whirled around, gold gazing ball clutched in her arms. She turned her head to the side, lifting the mirrored ball up to the gorgon's face as the snakes lunged forward.

The gorgon screamed, the sound cut short as her oozing, slithering body turned to granite. Right where Noah had stood silent and immobile for more than a hundred years.

Grinning, Harper rushed toward Noah, who was smiling now. She set the gazing ball in the grass and threw her arms around him. He lifted her chin and kissed her hard on the lips, his arms tightening around her. He was shaking, looking relieved for the first time as he spun her around and kissed her again.

For the first time in a long while, she looked forward to the future. Noah had trusted her with an incredible secret. Now, it was her turn to trust him with some of her own. Starting with the life she left in Maryland. She and Noah would each work to reclaim what they'd lost and rebuild something new together. Starting here with his lost estate.

Harper smiled. But first, they had a statue to destroy. It was blocking the sunset.

THE FREEDOM OF METAL

STEPHANNIE TALLENT

J ess Miraca was as invisible as she could make herself.

Shoulder-length, slightly wavy, sort of curly, grey-streaked light brown hair. Brownish-green eyes, muddy against her dark skin. Even features: nothing ugly, but nothing striking, bare of makeup. Plump figure, clothed in baggy khaki trousers, a faded plum-colored blouse, and a dull maroon quilted jacket.

It might be the only thing that would keep her alive for her mission.

So many had died. So many enslaved in the thirty years of Lenarian occupation of her country. A generation. Longer. A second generation of children living under tyranny.

She entered the Az Contrada city train station, a white-washed brick and plaster behemoth of a building, with sky-reaching ceilings supported by slender, gleaming, pale blue columns and beams of azural steel and a pitted grey-and-white marble terrazzo floor.

Originally a prized example of the New Zorrah style of

the last century, any decorative flourishes had long been destroyed by the Lenarian occupation.

The lack of basic maintenance beat the once-glorious station down as well. No one mopped the coal grime from the floor before it accreted into sticky plaques. No one repaired the plaster cracks in the walls from the shiftings of hundreds of minute earth tremors over the past thirty years; those cracks had widened into crevices, big enough to be murine palaces (she actually saw mousy whiskers poking from one). No one patched the tiled roof before polluted, chemical-filled rain etched and pitted the azural beams and the marble floor.

It wasn't a slap in the face; more of the constant pressure of a jackboot between your shoulder blades, pushing you into the mud until you suffocated.

Yet the azural still gleamed rebelliously in the weak, late afternoon sun.

Azural, the prized metal compound created by Azcorra's engineering guild, both strong and flexible, and a natural reservoir of magical potential. Even non-mage-talented people could use azural-based spells.

Azural. The main reason Lenaria had turned its attention to Azcorra. Her small country, tucked up to the Az Wend mountain range to the south, southwest, and southeast, wasn't situated opportunely for trade, or expansion. But it had a resource the Lenarians decided they needed. So Azcorra fell, like most of the other surrounding countries.

Several extra inspection stations, shoddily constructed plywood stands built just for this week, were shoved in between the blocky, brick, permanent booths built thirty years ago by the Lenarians. Manned by inspectors assisted by extra, shark-eyed armed guards, the stations fully blocked free access to the actual concourse and platforms.

The Lenarian Emperor's first son, a reprehensible, arrogant piece of work just like his father, was concluding his tour of Azcorra with his visit to Az Contrada earlier this morning. Jess suspected the extra booths and extra guards would be gone by tomorrow morning.

The Lenarians were, if nothing else, efficient, with matters they cared about.

She chose what looked to be the booth with the shortest line, and settled into outwardly patient waiting, occasionally shifting her weight, trying to ease the soreness of her feet encased in stout leather-laced flats. The reek of the rancid oil of the fry fish vendors who set up on the periphery of the lobby, hoping to make a little cash off ill-prepared hungry travelers, turned her stomach as she waited. She'd eaten a hearty lunch, potato and onion stew, flavored with a few lumps of lamb in honor of her mission. Now wishing she'd skipped lunch, she breathed shallowly through her mouth.

But she retained a placid appearance, even when she heard a voice rising in panic two lines over.

She was too short. She couldn't see past her nearby, line-waiting neighbors. She didn't try.

A gunshot echoed off the coal-stained ceiling. The azural beams hummed softly in response, the frequency of the shot resonating.

An anguished scream, cut off by another gunshot.

The wet, heavy sound of guards dragging someone away along the floor.

Thirty minutes later, she finally reached the front of the line.

She fished her papers out of her worn leather satchel and handed them to the train travel inspector, a tall, bulky, cold-eyed man with a vicious scar bisecting his upper lip and coursing up his cheek, ending just under his right eye.

Insignia upon his uniform, golden eagles clutching arrows, indicated prior elite guard service. No azural. Just pure Lenarian gold and brass.

She wondered who he'd pissed off. How he failed. Maybe when he got that nasty scar?

"My daughter-in-law just had her first baby," she told him, meekly looking down, not meeting his eyes. "That's why I'm travelling, to see my grandbaby—"

"I didn't ask," he snapped, activating an azural ring charm and scanning her papers, running his finger along each line of raised silver dot codes, each one with a minute amount of azural in the pigment, then her photo.

She cowered. He would expect it.

He handed her papers back to her, saying nothing until she looked back up at him.

"There is an irregularity," he finally said as she shifted back and forth anxiously, clutching her jacket tightly around herself. The guard standing behind him loosened the holster for his weapon, a blackened ceramic firearm. Standard issue, probably loaded with magicked steel and azural ammo designed to cause as much damage as possible. A perversion of the azural. That agonized scream. The guards usually aimed for a gut shot first. Or a knee.

Of course there wasn't any irregularity with her papers. Those were the best forgeries Rudy, the team's document man, could provide. They were perfect.

Jess's chin trembled, and she willed a couple tears to leak down her cheeks. "I—I—" she stammered, then gulped. "They are from last year, but they haven't expired, they—"

He stared at her, split lip twitching cruelly. "Papers of

natives are required to be renewed sixty days before they expire."

What was the point of the expiration date, then, you lying piece of shit? But she didn't say that. She started to hiccup in misery. She could be an ugly crier. Especially if it got her past this brute.

"You can pay me the fee to renew them."

Of course.

She meekly extracted her wallet and pulled out a twenty mark bill. Then a second.

And finally a third. Maybe there really was an irregularity with her papers.

He nodded, took the bills, then motioned her along, allowing himself a satisfied smile. It made his face even uglier.

Stupid as well as ugly. If one of *her* people, in the same situation, didn't question why a middle-aged, native Azcorran, obviously lower-middle-class woman had that sort of cash...well, they wouldn't be one of hers anymore.

They wouldn't be anybody's.

She slid past him and the still-silent, lurking guard. The guard didn't even bother to search her. She could see most of the other guards searching the other travelers.

The power of a middle-aged woman: invisibility.

She was the only one of her team that had *that* power, sheer invisibility. Rudy, ten years younger than Jess, originally trained as an artist, had his talents as a mage-gifted forger; Sara, sweet-faced and curvy, young enough to be Jess's daughter, had her skills with explosives; Race, her second, a few years older than Jess and a former accountant, his prowess as a spy.

Which was why she assigned herself this mission.

She entered the concourse. Platforms and rails

stretched to either side, some rails empty, others occupied by the coal-belching, squat, ugly trains the Lenarians ran in all their occupied countries. Regardless, travelers filled the platforms, jostling to board their trains or just be in position to board. The Emperor's son had likely boarded his train hours before.

She found the departure board, and identified the platform for the train to Az Placeria. Platform 40, last one of twenty to the right, and the train was due to leave in just a couple minutes. She didn't like cutting it this close. She'd underestimated the time she'd had to wait in line. Sloppy.

She shoved her way lithely through the crowd of fellow travelers, sleek movement belying her clothes, figure, and age, finally slipping through the heavy steel platform gateway (another Lenarian addition to the station, another way to control her people) just before it slammed shut.

She boarded the second class car, found her seat near the back of the car, and settled in.

Second class meant three assigned seats in each row, two on the right, one on the left, of the central corridor for the conductors and ticket checkers, and an enclosed latrine at one end of the car, maybe, just maybe stocked with toilet paper and soap.

At least she had a single seat, threadbare as the horse-hair-stuffed cushion was, and had an illusion of personal privacy.

There weren't many other people in the car. A young man and woman sat up front near the latrine, dressed in post-wedding finery, her with small white flowers nestled in her hair, him sporting a faded but clean embroidered vest. They both clutched oil-stained paper bags of fish. Sigh. She could smell the fish from her seat.

A scattering of a half dozen passengers, mostly older

men in worn business suits, sat either singly or in pairs throughout the rest of the car. The closest, two rows up, was a middle-aged man in a worn brown suit, hat pulled over his eyes as he slouched against the window.

Enough seats were empty that most passengers could stretch out on the double seats overnight to sleep: except if they'd not paid for those seats, they would be fined and jailed at the next stop.

Before, she'd have warned the young couple not to try it. Everyone was young and stupid once upon a time. She knew the ticket checkers would come through at least twice after midnight.

One was her contact, after all.

She ate her supper, a pungent, sharp sheep cheese sandwich and one precious citrus fruit, a blood orange, her favorite, tart and juicy, a couple of hours later. Lenarians always got the best produce. They stole the best of everything. Rudy had filched it for her from a shipment from his family's farm to the mayor's compound. She wiped the back of her hand against her chin, and licked off one sweet drop. She sipped watered wine from her flask, so dilute it was more like wine-flavored water.

She wanted her mind clear tonight.

The brilliant scarlet of the setting sun cast a muddy red glow across the faces of the train travelers as it streamed through the coal-grimed windows of the car.

It was beautiful. So beautiful.

The conductor had come through once, about an hour before, verifying everyone's papers with an azural ring charm much like that of the inspector.

He didn't say anything about any irregularity.

Rudy's work *was* good.

The air was cooling in the cabin. Second class didn't have heat. She was glad of her quilted coat. It had been her mother's, worn the day the Lenarians gunned her down in the street in front of eighteen-year-old Jess. Jess had washed off her mother's heart's blood, sewed up the bullet holes, and dyed the whole thing the color of dried blood, a deep maroon shade.

A secret was sewn into the lining, a secret worth her life, the lives of everyone on the train. But, it was nice for everything to have more than one purpose.

First class, and only first class, had heat. Not second class, just physically one car away from first, but really, ever so far away otherwise, or third class, with the Azcorrans packed in like cattle, and never mind the last two cars carrying slaves, Azcorrans, children and adults, grandparents and teens, fathers and mothers, bound for Lenaria.

Didn't pay your taxes? Didn't properly address a Lenarian? Didn't bow low enough, didn't scrape your head in the muck as a Lenarian walked by? They didn't mess with jails. Just years of "service," depending on the transgression.

No heat. No matter how cold it got.

Heaters, powered by gas and magic, warmed the Lenarians, Lenarians only, in first class.

The Emperor's son was in first class.

Six hours later, she awakened to a firm grip on her right shoulder. Her contact. She straightened, fully alert. Everyone else was sleeping. The businessman two rows in front of her leaned against the window, hat still pulled over his eyes, snoring so loudly she was surprised even she had slept through it.

And sure enough, the young newlywed up front lay stretched out on the pair of double seats behind his wife.

"It's two a.m.," whispered the ticket checker. His half-Lenarian, half-Azcorran features, proof of his mother's violation forever on his face, highlighted by the burnished silver moonlight streaming through the window, were tight with fear. He handed her his insignia, a brass pin with an azural sparrow in front of a setting sun. It would allow her to access first class. "We can time this, right? I can uncouple the cars behind this one—"

She stared at him with pity. "Of course," she lied. "Of course we can." Was he kidding? Anything, anything could set off suspicion, and ruin her mission.

"And why would the cars need to be uncoupled?" The man two rows ahead was upright and fully awake, hat pushed back so his cold grey eyes glared at them, pointing a black ceramic gun, identical to those of the train guards, at the ticket checker.

At the ticket checker.

Jess didn't take the time to sigh. She reached into her coat, into a clever interior pocket no guard had ever found, even if one even had been conscientious enough to not to underestimate her, and in one effortless motion, pulled out a ceramic throwing knife and flung it at the man's throat.

He barely gurgled as he slumped back against the window again, blood coating his shirt front and suit jacket, pulsing from the neat puncture in his neck.

Maybe it was the *lack* of his fake snoring, that sudden absence of sound, but the newlywed boy was now sitting up, staring at them, trembling.

Gods above. She stood, shoving past the frozen ticket

checker, hissed, "Uncouple it. Uncouple it as soon as I leave this car," and ran lightly, softly, down the center aisle to the boy.

"You must be quiet," she said. "Can you be quiet? Can your wife be quiet?"

His blue eyes, flecked with amber, Azcorran eyes, bright against his dark face, widened, then he nodded mutely.

"Take her, and go into the next car. Don't leave it, until after. You will know. Then run, both of you, run away from the tracks. We're about fifty miles south of Az Placeria." At least, if the train was running on time. And the Lenarians, damn them to all the Twelve Hells, were efficient. Their trains ran on time.

"Remember this address: 212 Fontana. Tell the woman there that Jess loves her. Loves her so much. Give her this ring." She tugged off her azural-inset wedding ring and handed it to the young man. "She'll keep you safe. The Lenarians will have your information, you understand? From when you boarded. They'll know you were on this car. You can never go home."

Tears streaming down his face, he nodded. "Thank you," he said.

She nodded brusquely, then walked past the latrine, to the door that led to the coupler joining the second class car to first. Holding her breath, she clutched the ticket checker's insignia so tightly she could feel the sun's rays pierce her palm.

The door opened. She exhaled and tucked the bloody insignia deep into her front pocket.

She stepped onto the small platform, leapt across the coupler, and nearly lost her footing as the first class platform shuddered.

The other cars behind second were uncoupled.

Reaching into her jacket, she ripped the lining next to her knife pocket. A thin chain, links of azural, finely made and etched with spells, slipped out and snaked over her hand.

Now or never.

She entered first class. Heat engulfed her. The gas and the magic heat.

The car had been modified for the Emperor's son. Brass light fixtures emitted a golden glow throughout. Close to her was a carved wooden table, the luster of it reflecting the glow of the gas lamps, with a bowl of blood oranges and a carafe of ruby-red wine artfully placed in the center. She could smell the sweetness of the oranges. Four dining chairs, also intricately carved, sat around it.

A small sitting area, blue velvet sofas and a shiny brass table, was set up in the middle.

Beyond that, a large bed, piled high with crimson velvet comforters and down pillows despite the torpid heat of the car, filled the far end. She could see *him*, with a woman to either side.

Two guards, one awake, one dozing, sat in wooden chairs in front of the bed. Sloppy, so sloppy, and so arrogant. Only two guards in here, and the man in second class? The awake one stood, shouting in Lenarian, as he aimed his gun at her.

She laughed, and held up the chain. "Azcorra!" she cried, keying the spells, and flung the chain deep into the room. It gleamed and spat out sparks as it flew through the air, azural links glowing bright, bright blue. The sparks erupted into lightning that hit everything metal: the brass light fixtures, the sitting area table, and the heating pipes. The gas- and magic-filled pipes.

She was laughing, laughing even as the first bullets hit her, as the car exploded.

Almost a day and a half later, dawn still just a softening of darkness on the horizon, the young newlyweds knocked on the door of 212 Fontana in Az Placeria. They were dirty and shivering and so very tired and scared.

A woman, just a few years older than them, clutching a baby, just a week old, swaddled in a soft cotton blanket, opened the door.

"Jess sent us," the young man said. "She says she loves you." He handed her the azural-inset ring.

Tears welled up in the woman's eyes as she took the ring. She dashed them aside, quickly glanced around, and ushered them inside.

The freedom of metal had begun.

WALKING NONEXISTENT
ROB VAGLE

There's no reason for secrets when you don't exist. There's nobody to keep them from.

Jessie Shaw walked a dark tunnel, the soles of her feet padding firmly on a hard surface that felt like concrete. The air was damp and cool and this reminded her of the relief from the humidity of a Midwest summer whenever she sought refuge in the basement as a child. The memory came sharp and unexpected and she was unsure of where it came from, but that memory was there and it proved she had been somewhere else once upon a time.

She was almost alive.

But the tunnel continued and so did Jessie, listening to the padding of her own bare feet. Inside the walls around her voices spoke, alarms clamored, horns honked. Voices moaned, clocks ticked, and silverware on plates clattered. These noises distracted her and she reached out and touched the wall as she walked, her fingers gliding along a smooth surface that felt like enamel. The wall was cold but her fingers grew hot as she drew them across the wall's surface.

The light at the end of the tunnel drew her closer. The light never seemed to grow bigger. The light was always there, beckoning her.

She thought about her name and the memories—like the one about the comfortable basement—and how they came to her as if they had always existed. They mattered. Jessie lived. There were more memories beyond these walls, she was sure of it. As for the light, she didn't know what that might bring and like the sun it seemed like it would always be there.

As for the walls, the sounds changed, flowed into one another. Music came from there and sometimes the songs took her away, for an instant, inside her head. One song caused her to tilt her head side to side—"Safety Dance" by Men Without Hats—and she was a freshman in high school dancing with someone whose breath smelled like bubble gum.

Sometimes the wall faded in places where people on the other side could see her. She made eye contact with a little boy bundled up in a coat and knit cap with a book bag on his back. When he turned to tell a friend and point at her, the wall grew solid again.

She hadn't had time to put a finger to her lips. To hush the boy. Her existence was fragile. Her existence then had been for his eyes only.

Then the wall faded again and revealed a crowded nightclub and a woman with thick, dark hair and a curl hanging down over her forehead. Jessie caught a glimpse of her between the crowd of backs and shoulders, but once their eyes locked, Jessie felt herself solidify, felt herself planted in the other world with shoes and clubbing attire as if she'd been there all along.

The other woman's eyes were blue and her gaze

remained on Jessie, so Jessie raised her finger to her lips to convey—she really didn't know what she wanted to convey. She only knew she wanted one-on-one, a person to talk to, and then go from there. She was afraid if the woman brought Jessie to the attention of others, Jessie would vanish.

But the woman didn't turn to tell anyone, she was simply drawn to Jessie. They jostled their way to one another until they stood toe to toe.

"Hi, I'm Veronica," the woman said

When Jessie revealed her name, Veronica took her to the bar by a gentle grasp of Jessie's forearm. "Have a drink with me," she said.

The room was hot with pulsing lights and shaking with techno music. Men and men, and women and women, were dancing on the dance floor. Veronica found two seats at the bar, which Jessie found incredible with the large crowd.

They were in a club called Faces. Although it was at least a decade beyond the eighties, this club had Nagel women art prints high on the walls. It smelled faintly of beer but the smell of human sweat, musk, and perfume overpowered it.

Before they ordered drinks, Jessie leaned into Veronica's ear and said, "Don't tell anyone about me. Let's talk. Just you and I. Get to know each other. It's a delicate situation."

"Are you going to turn into a pumpkin?" Veronica asked with a grin and a disbelieving look.

"I'm serious," Jessie said. "This moment is just for you and me. Nobody else."

"I don't have a problem with that," Veronica said.

Jessie relaxed. And the conversation turned.

They talked about themselves. Jessie remembered things about herself as she talked about them with Veronica. Like how she would like to learn how to make sushi, since she visited every sushi place she could find. And how she won first place in her category at the Rock N Roll marathon.

Veronica was a nurse anesthetist, liked going on hikes with her two dogs, and seemed interested in running with Jessie.

Veronica squeezed her hand underneath the bar and Jessie returned the squeeze, their fingers interlocking together. Jessie reveled in the warmth of Veronica's hand.

Bodies pressed against Jessie even as she sat at the bar. But Jessie and Veronica leaned in to one other so that they could hear themselves talk.

Veronica was drinking a beer—it was half gone and she hadn't touched it again for over ten minutes. Jessie was drinking a cocktail, something called a Woo-Woo. The bartender on the other side of the bar—Guido, with his sleeves rolled up on the shoulders and slicked-back hair—fluttered back and forth, gathering glassware and bottles of beer.

"I want to introduce you to someone," Veronica said.

"You can't," Jessie said, fearing the nonexistence. "I told you. Just you and me."

Veronica gave a suspicious grin. "You're too shy," she said.

Jessie hated it when nobody listened to her. They never heeded the warnings. She wanted to grab Veronica and shake her to make her listen. Jessie knew she was too shy to react like that.

But Veronica reached behind her and her arm was lost between the two guys behind them and when she pulled her arm back, Veronica had another woman by the forearm.

"This is my friend, Katie," she said.

Katie had long, flowing blond hair and wore a spaghetti-strap dress. She wore heavy blue mascara and thick, ruby-red lipstick. Her lips glistened underneath the bar lighting.

"Who's this?" Katie asked.

Jessie reached out to touch Veronica's mouth. Veronica easily deflected the reach with her hand.

"This is Jessie," Veronica said. "She's very shy. She's into running marathons and loves sushi."

And Jessie felt a part of her vanish. A small part, but nonetheless the process had started. She was starting to disappear. She wasn't certain of the part. Her senses had dampened and the cocktail no longer lingered on her tongue and cotton seemed to be between her and the crowded club.

"How nice," Katie said.

Then Veronica grabbed Jessie's hand and pulled. "Come on, let's get out of here."

Jessie slipped off the stool, trailing after taller Veronica. Katie ran with them.

"Going to a party," Veronica shouted.

Katie winked at her. "It'll be fine," she said.

Outside where the air was cool and crisp, Jessie shivered underneath a pool of streetlight. The reduction in sound was startling and the honking cars and traffic along the street was unsurprisingly subdued. The night smelled like cigarette smoke and garbage, but the perfume Veronica's friend was wearing covered everything with a flowery scent.

The oaks along the street were bare, with leaves dotting the pavement. She watched as Veronica waved to friends mingling around a dark Ford Suburban double-parked in front of the club.

Now, outside where it was quieter, Jessie leaned into Veronica and said, "Don't tell anybody about me, please. Veronica, tonight it should just be you and me."

Veronica laughed, but she stopped when she saw Jessie bristle.

"You're not going to melt, hon. I just want everyone to know you as I do," Veronica said.

"You don't understand," Jessie said. But she thought: You can't keep secrets, Veronica.

Then one by one, Jessie found herself introduced to each person standing outside the dark Suburban. "Isn't she great," Veronica said, pointing to Jessie. Each time she said something about Jessie—her races, her time living in a small town in northern Minnesota, her college life here in the Twin Cities—a piece of Jessie vanished. She felt numb. Her legs were gone, yet she continued to stand. She didn't know how that was possible.

She pulled away from Veronica, still gripping her hand. "You'll have to excuse me. I need a moment."

"You're okay, aren't you?" Veronica asked.

Jessie wasn't. Her hand either slipped from Veronica's hand because she let go, or because Jessie's hand vanished. She couldn't see her hand in front of her face. The night air grew warm and damp. The streetlights were taken over by fog that smothered light to black.

Then Jessie was walking in that tunnel again, the voices of Veronica and her friends muffled behind the wall. She could hear Veronica call her name, which made it worse. It forced Jessie down that dark hallway towards the light.

She wondered what it looked like in the real world, the existence, when she vanished. Did she literally disappear right before their eyes? Or did they forget about her as if she'd never been there at all?

Jessie felt the years of walking this tunnel. There was enough of her to be real, she thought. Her past would be her future outside of this place if she could find one person through these walls who could keep a promise and a secret.

If she saw Veronica again, would Veronica remember her? It might be naive, but Jessie didn't blame Veronica for wanting to introduce her to her friends, because love did that. Even infatuation, when your curiosity is piqued by another person. You're excited about the discovery and you want to tell the whole world about them. Jessie understood that.

That's what brought her alive and into existence. It was those connections that brought her out of this tunnel before she reached that light.

Jessie walked on.

THE MYSTICAL LIFE OF CAKE

C.J. MATTISON

T he old farmhouse seemed to be holding its breath, as if waiting for permission to slide into permanent slumber. Daylight angled in through the half-closed blinds in the small dining nook, where three dusty and aged brown cardboard boxes rested on the four-person table, the old round dark oak one Dad had bought Mother for a Christmas more than forty years earlier. Under the smells of must and dust and southern Illinois farmland lay the imagined lingering smells of flour and baking powder and stewing fruits.

If Peg closed her eyes, she could see Mother in her blue mom-jeans and a faded red Western shirt with the sleeves rolled up her freckled arms to just under her elbows. She would be circling the kitchen counterclockwise between the white-and-gold laminate counter, the oak table, the white plastic trash bin, and the old blue-painted steel rolling preparation cart, her hands working easily but mixer-fast at each station. They teased her that she always circled counterclockwise like some patisserie cyclone, obeying the effects of gravity and the spinning Earth, driven by steam rising from pots of boiling water.

The mood was broken when Peg's twin, Steve, carried in a fourth box and, seeing not enough room left of the table, pushed out one of the chairs with his gunboat foot and laid the box on the seat. When he turned, he was suddenly Dad standing there, with the dark, lumpy hands and bones of Dad's Algonquin heritage, and a peppering of dark stubble over his chestnut face. She had taken after Mother, petite, her French-Canadian blood running hot and deep from Quebec into the American Midwest via Pennsylvania and the Ohio River.

Steve said in a voice too quiet for such a big man, "I don't think I'm up to this yet."

Peg tested the ache there behind her sternum, relieved to find it still there pushing against her organs, fearing it had left her, too soon after Mother's death to be respectful, a callous retreat. In this pain there was reassurance, that she still held the capacity to hurt enough, to feel enough heartache, to feel her life slamming into a roadblock of loss.

Mother would have brewed her an ironic instant tea, slapped together an irreverent bologna sandwich, and told her to get over it.

She said, "Waiting will make it harder."

He puffed up and said, "I'll get the box cutters." He turned on his heel toward the front door, his jeep, his toolbox.

By the time he returned carrying a shiny metallic retractable, foldable knife, she'd ripped the box open and begun to remove the contents. There was treasure and dreck there, family photo albums and files of old tax receipts, copies of Life magazine from the sixties that might be collectible, vapid romance novels, an old "Vote for

Kennedy" pin, and one for Walter Mondale. Near the bottom, Peg's fingers found a thick book, and when she pulled it out over the open flaps of the box, which were cutting into the bottoms of her forearms, she realized what it was, and carried it to an open space on the counter.

A textured ring notebook with a red-and-white checked cover.

On an index card held by yellowed Scotch tape to the notebook's cover was written in Mother's elegantly simple script:

RECIPES

As she stared down at the tag, Steve's shadow and presence loomed over her like a brooding tree.

He said, "Holy crap. I forgot about that book."

She said, "I didn't. But I didn't know if she had kept it."

"You kidding? She would have been happy if we'd buried it with her." He stepped to the side and brushed the book's surface with his big tapered finger. "But I'm glad we didn't."

She moved his hand and carefully opened the cover. It was a piece of cardboard covered by paper, warped, frazzled on the edges, like Peg felt. She closed the cover again, her mind suddenly seething.

We try to live our lives like this book. Find the recipes that we want to build our lives from, then cook to make those dishes the best way we can, build the layers of flavor and texture, strive for novelty and freshness, yet cling to the old favorites, the ones our lovers crave and our families love.

And yet, time and wear begin to break the whole thing down, peeling the paper, staining the pages, tearing some out, fading some, losing others to friends and family who borrow and never return them.

She and Steve leafed through the pages: heavy corded paper, hole-punched and covered in newspaper and magazine clippings or blue-lined index cards written in blue or red or black ink, some with adhesive reinforcing rings stuck to the holes where they'd ripped through usage. Each recipe was a memory, a wedding, a vacation, a birthday. A death.

They paused a moment, and in an instant of eye contact, a flash of mutual memory coursed between them like an open conduit. The recipe that any of them would choose to define their mother, the unsophisticated, unapologetic, uncompromising leader of their family.

The Cake. Grandma's special cake.

Steve said, "You turn the pages, sis. I'll rip them. Find it."

She continued turning pages, making sure to slide the holes smoothly around the tarnished metal rings. The pages turned again and again, and it wasn't there. The stack moved steadily from the right to the left. She almost missed it, only three pages from the back cover.

She read aloud, "Grandma's Magic Harvest Cake."

Steve said, "Holy crap."

"You said that already."

"You're thinking the same thing I am. After almost fifty years, we'll finally learn her secret."

She covered the recipe with her hand. "What if she was telling the truth? What if the secret really was Grandma working magic?"

"Oh, come on. You can't really believe that."

When she shook her head, she could feel the tension that had suddenly built in her neck.

"No. No, I can't really."

"Then move your hand, and let's find the truth."

They were thirteen.

Steve ran ahead of her through the birch woods, trying to leave her behind like he always did, like a butt. The trunks rose narrow and straight up along both sides of the old walking trail. The green heart-shaped leaves seemed to be stretching out their tips to sense the temperature, wondering if it was time to turn the wonderful bright yellow they would be in six weeks or so, in early October. The path was hard dirt, packed down by human feet for several hundred years, first Native Americans, then early settlers, then immigrant farmers, then generations of bored farm kids. The afternoon breeze was warm and smelled like the inside of a basket that had held flowers and corn husks. Despite the heat, the embarrassing dark hairs on her arms pricked up with the cool of her sweat.

She whispered louder than she intended, "Wait up!"

He paused at the top of a small rise in the trail, then waved her to follow.

He said, "Hurry up! She'll beat us there!"

Peg stubbed her toe, but managed to keep her feet and carried on after Steve's retreating backside. When they reached the point where the trail dumped out into the county cemetery, they stopped to catch their breath. They couldn't see Grandma's grave from where they hid, which meant that Mom couldn't see them either. After their rest, Steve led her in a crouch from the birch grove along the fence line that bordered the cemetery. Three rows down, they cut into the cemetery, then crept to where a huge obnoxious stone pillar topped with a cross dominated that section of the rolling earth.

Steve, having no reverence for the dead, ran between grave markers. He turned as he ran and pressed his finger against his lips to silence her, and scrunched his eyes down mean, but she ignored him. Now wasn't the time to carve into his expanding ego, but she'd take a hack at him when they got back to the farmhouse. He touched his lips again, and jerked his finger off at an angle, toward Grandma's grave. They had just settled behind the ponderous monument nearby when the sound of a car echoed over the cemetery, coming from the old county road that circled the birch wood.

The sound came closer, and then the engine noise stopped. A door opened and closed, then another, and then silence for a while, until quiet footsteps approached. Steve peeked around the side of the mausoleum, then nodded at Peg and touched his finger to his lips again. That finger was doomed when they got back home.

The steps grew close, then stopped. Peg peeked. Mother was just sitting on a stone bench close to Grandma's grave, which was now marked with the bunch of field flowers Peg had helped Mother cut earlier that morning. Next to her on the bench was the bright yellow glass mixing bowl that held the weird thing, the annual ritual treat, the beloved cake batter, the secret blend of flour and eggs and milk and things Mother wouldn't reveal, which would bake into the greatest of her annual rituals—Grandma's harvest cake.

Every year when she was mixing it, they would ask why it was so good, and the answer always came with the reliability of the Sears Christmas catalog: "Grandma puts a magic spell on it."

But now Grams was dead. And Mother sat on the bench

and started talking to herself. But no, after several sentences, Peg realized she was talking to Grams.

Peg whispered, "Wow. Maybe that is her secret. Maybe she does ask Grandma to bless the cake."

"Shh."

She stuck her thumbs in her ears and her tongue at him, and nearly fell over. Rather than laughing, he shook his head.

Mom said, "Well, it's been another year, Mom. I'd like to say it was a good one, but I've had better."

Mother paused, as if waiting to hear something from the long dead and buried person in the casket several feet beneath her. Steve met Peg's eyes, his scrunched up again, but this time in puzzlement.

As if in acknowledgement or reassurance, a breeze kicked up from the still, heavy air and rustled leaves in the trees around them.

Mom went on, her voice less tightly held.

"You were right about them growing so fast. I try to hang on and tug them back like you always told me to, but they run ahead anyway, paying so little mind to their mama. They want to be adults right now so much, and how do you tell them 'No, no, kids, stay children. Being an adult can be a painful thing'?"

Peg's insides suddenly twisted like a stomach cramp. This was a mistake—they shouldn't be there, eavesdropping. But now it was too late, they couldn't sneak away without Mother catching them. Steve leaned forward and cocked his head to one side, turning his head to listen with his good ear, the one that hadn't been damaged by an exploding firecracker.

"They're both ravaged by puberty. You'd probably chuckle over that, but I remember those times of awkwardness with pain. Stevie's started doing that thing boys do when they discover their male body parts. I'm finding stains on his pillowcases."

Peg choked back a laugh. She nudged Steve with her elbow. He hung his head and refused to look at her.

"I asked his father to give him the talk, let the boy know these things are normal. But you know how Tom is. He lets the tough things go, avoids anything uncomfortable. Just let it simmer and hope it goes away."

Mother shook her head, clenched her hands in her lap, her big hands, big for a woman.

"And Peggy, my little raven-haired ball of fire. Too much like me. She may be lucky, Ma. She might keep her clear skin and good looks like you, and not fight the acne like I did. I think she's doing that thing like her brother, like I did at her age. I hear little squeaks coming from under her door at night. If she's like me, she'll have a fire burning down between her legs that she won't be able to put out. And it will get her in trouble. Time for me to have the talk with her, and no delaying."

Heat rose from Peg's chest into her face and she looked at her shoes.

"So much life in my little girl. How do I tell her to stay young, stay innocent? That all the men you love are going to hurt you and then punish you for it afterwards? I know Papa was no different. God knows his son took after him. If Stevie starts acting like his Uncle Peter did when he got to be sixteen, I will smack him so hard."

Uncle Peter was in the drama of his fourth divorce. Peg nudged Steve again, but her brother had lifted his chin and was focused on their mother's words.

"The late-night phone calls are starting again. When it happened last night, I just looked at Tom. He let it ring and said it was over and he wouldn't get involved with that woman again. What they say about good intentions. I just felt that tightening in the pit of my stomach again. And just when I was starting to feel like I wanted him to touch me again.

"What do I do, Mom? Leave him? No. He's a good man, a good father. He's just lost himself in the wild wheat. So I'll tough it out and get on with things. Like you used to tell me." Mother imitated Grandma's voice. "'You can't be like this cake, Meggie. Tough and crusty on the outside, and soft and sweet on the inside. If the outside cracks, you'll collapse all on yourself. You have to be the other way around.' If it was only that easy, Mom. When you're soft and sweet on the outside, people assume the texture goes all the way through and they try to gobble you up. Especially the ones you love most."

Suddenly, Peg felt like her crust had broken and she lay collapsed there on the soft grass. Mom had told her to be kind to others, because you never knew what troubles were rolling around in their heads. But had Peg ever been kind enough to her mother?

Steve tapped her leg. Mother was pushing herself from the stone bench, as if she weighed a thousand pounds.

She said, "Well, I should get back and start dinner. Tom will be getting back from delivering hay, and the kids will be home from school. So, cast whatever magic you can on this cake batter, while I go pick a couple bags of those blackberries. They look about right. And I didn't tell you yet —I found a lump in my right breast."

The breeze blew right through Peg's body. She gripped Steve's leg tighter, until he patted her hand.

Mother went on. "No, I haven't been to the doctor yet, and I haven't told Tom. I want him to stay on his own, and not because of pity. Maybe I'll just have both of my boobs removed, and then Tom will lose all interest in me, as if that makes any difference. But I don't want to go through what you did. I've grown too crusty on the outside, and not tough enough inside."

She stood for a moment, and the breeze tickled her hair around her head.

At last, she said, "It'll be all right, Mom. They're all going to turn out all right. Be back in a minute."

Mother left the gravesite and began carrying her basket toward a stand of bushes in the direction away from them. Steve pointed toward the creek, and then the two of them eased down the bank until they were well out on the trail, and they ran home, neither stopping to talk, as if they were chased by ghosts. Peg's heart pounded, but not from the running. The breeze whipped up, moving the birch branches back and forth, like crazy hectic cooks with green frocks and white pants ringed with peppercorns.

It was the year Father left them, and then returned. It was the year Mother survived cancer. It was the year Peg learned she was going to be all right, just like her mother, and her mother before her. And the harvest cake was especially good.

Now, Steve said, "Mom's secret ingredient. Grandma's magic. What if that really was all there was to it?"

Peg ran her finger down through the list of ingredients, written in flawlessly straight lines in Mother's script, and then read them again. There was nothing unusual there—flour, eggs, sugar, soft butter, vanilla and lemon extracts, berries. And then below these were the steps—beat, mix, fold, pour into a greased and floured pan. Nothing odd. Nothing special. It was all skill. And love.

Steve said, "Nothing. Nothing at all. No magic ingredient, not even liquor. Just really freaking magic. I've tried to make this cake a dozen times, and it never comes out as good as Mom's. Carol and the kids give me no end of grief over it."

"Mine doesn't turn out as good either." She said. She let her eyes play over the list again. "That's odd. Like you said, there's no special ingredient here, but there's something missing."

"Really?"

"Yes, leavening. No yeast, like in the version Mom gave me."

"Hmm. How does that work?"

Peg shook her head and ran her finger down the page. "Nothing. Mix, blend, fold, bake at 375 degrees."

On a whim, she flipped the page over. It was mostly blank, except for a short note handwritten on a piece of white stationary paper with blue edging, taped to the page. It wasn't Mother's handwriting.

Grandmother's?

It read:

The Magic

Set the bowl on the ground near the old cemetery when the wind blows from the west, off the birch forest. Let stand for at least an hour to allow wild yeast to infect the batter. To make sure you get a good leavening, add black berries from the nearby shrubs when their skins are just touched by the white coating of fungus. Allow the batter to ferment overnight to get a good rise.

If not able to visit the cemetery, substitute one tablespoon of store-bought yeast.

Steve said, "It's written like she expected someone to find this."

"Us. Just like you said, Steve. Magic. But it's not Grandma's anymore. It's Mom's. And now it's ours too."

They fell to silence. She turned the page back and forth, reading the ingredients again, envisioning Mother standing there doing the same thing, turning the same page back and forth, then stalking the kitchen with her big woman hands, beating and mixing and folding the batter together with the spoon and the bowl, just as she had all of them, bringing them together. And then from the oven, the sweet, doughnutty smell of the amazing cake as it rose to fill the old red porcelain cake pan. Then the first amazing bite of the caramelly crust, the sweet, yielding middle.

Just like Mother, tough as week-old baguette on the outside, tender and sweet on the inside. Just like her mother before her.

Just like Peg.

Magic. It was all magic after all.

THE BARGAIN
LEAH R. CUTTER

Vanda flipped over the latest English Comp paper returned by that snooty bitch Mrs. Rindahl as soon as she saw the grade she'd received.

What the hell. She'd been certain that she'd finally followed all the instructions, that she'd composed her sentences grammatically. The spell checker had assured her that all the words were spelled right, too.

She hadn't expected a D. She snuck a peek at the grade again.

Shit. Adding insult to injury, it wasn't just a D. It was a D-.

Vanda was going to flunk out of college at this rate. Everyone was going to be so disappointed in her! She was the first one in her family—hell, most of the trailer park where she'd grown up—to not only graduate high school, but to actually find a scholarship to pay for her continued education.

However, that money came with strings. Including a C average.

Which that damned Mrs. Rindahl was about to blow.

Though if Vanda was being honest, she wasn't doing too great in any of her classes. It was her first semester of college, and nothing had gone smoothly. High school had been a lot easier.

Then again, she'd had a large group of friends to help get her through the rough patches, friends who'd share papers and hints about tests. Friends who were all now working, so she never got to see them.

"Vanda, I'd like to see you after class," Mrs. Rindahl added.

Vanda rolled her eyes. Great. Now everyone in the entire class knew she was struggling. She sank lower in her chair. The damned desk, just a chair with an attached desktop, wasn't too small for her, but it still rubbed against her side annoyingly. The black and white leggings she'd put on that morning felt like a bad idea now, chafing her thighs. They were lined, and provided an adequate layer of protection against the Madison, Wisconsin fall, but now felt constrictive.

At least she had on a cute top, a light pink color, the neckline high enough that she didn't feel self-conscious, as though her boobs were sticking out far enough that she would accidentally blind someone by throwing a nipple their way. She wore her dark hair down, not hiding her face but not showing it off, either. She still wore makeup, though less now than she used to, as no one would make snarky remarks if she didn't have a bright enough lip or smoky enough eye, or if the skin of her white face wasn't perfectly smooth, her rounded cheeks contoured to show off what little cheekbones she had poking through the fat.

Some things were better in college than they had been in high school. She could dress to blend in more, now, so people wouldn't be staring at her.

Judging her. Like they were now.

Vanda could barely pay attention to the instructions Mrs. Rindahl gave out, the next reading assignment, as well as the next paper, which was due the following Monday. Vanda was really starting to hate Mondays, turning in a new paper at the start of class, then receiving the previous week's paper at the end.

Damn it, she knew how to speak the English language. Why the hell did she have to study some old moldy poems and write about them? How was that going to help her with a job in business? She needed to write emails and reports. Not sonnets.

Vanda shoved the offending paper along with her notebook into her backpack before she walked sullenly up to Mrs. Rindahl's desk. Bitch wasn't even looking at her, but had turned her back and was erasing the whiteboard.

"Vanda," Mrs. Rindahl started. "I know you're trying," she said as she finally turned around.

Stupid old woman looked like a scarecrow at the best of times. The way she wore her dirty blond hair put up in a messy bun didn't help, along with the T-shirt and vest. Her pinched pale face and pointed nose spoke of a woman who didn't know how to enjoy herself, who probably only ever ate air-fried skinless chicken breasts with broccoli and no dessert.

She didn't understand the lusciousness of buttercream frosting, the silkiness of a smooth chocolate ganache, the perfect mouthfeel of a sablé tart crust.

Not that Vanda had much time for baking anymore, what with all the damned schoolwork and the job she'd taken at the coffeeshop on campus. It was a national chain, so she couldn't even offer to bake some of their goods.

"You need some help," Mrs. Rindahl said.

Vanda bristled. She wasn't some sort of charity case. She didn't need any accommodations, which was just fancy talk for letting poor white trash like her cheat.

"There are open hours at the English Center this afternoon," Mrs. Rindahl said. "And every afternoon," she added hastily before Vanda could point out that she didn't have time today. "I think you can do this, I think you have it in you. A tutor would help."

On the one hand, Vanda wanted to throw it back in Mrs. Rindahl's face that she didn't want any help. She could figure this shit out on her own.

On the other hand, she obviously hadn't figured out much of anything yet.

"Yeah, I'll look into it," Vanda said.

"This week," Mrs. Rindahl insisted.

"Fine, this week," Vanda said, nodding.

She stormed out of the classroom before Mrs. Rindahl could say anything else, could add anything more to her already overburdened schedule.

Maybe college had been a mistake. Except that it had made her mama so happy to have a daughter in higher education. Mama kept talking about Vanda working her way toward being a lawyer or a doctor or something.

But those jobs meant dealing with too many people. No, Vanda wanted to go into business and deal with money. It was something nobody in her family ever had enough of. None of her friends, either.

Vanda could never tell Mama that the happiest place she'd ever been was in the kitchen, working with Aunt Gemma in the pastry shop her husband's family owned. Aunt Gemma might not have been rich, but as far as Vanda was concerned, she had married well.

When Vanda looked at her schedule, she realized she

did have a couple of hours to spare on Wednesday afternoon. Plus, she'd changed shifts with Simone, so she had Wednesday night free as well.

She'd try going to the English Center. See if they could help her get better words onto the page.

Or she was going to lose all her dreams, and more importantly, her mama's dreams, that was for damned sure.

The English Center was located in the basement of the Student Union. Dark, dank hallways led an overly bright office. The blond wood of the reception desk looked slick and cheap, like it had come from one of those warehouse stores where you had to assemble everything yourself. Stained red carpet muffled the sound of Vanda's boots as she crossed from the door to the desk. Today she wore more sensible jeans, boots, and an oversized maroon sweatshirt, all of it warm and dark, so she fit in.

"Can I help you?" asked the surly student standing there. She was obviously in the middle of her own homework and didn't want to take any time to help anyone else.

"I was told there were free hours this afternoon?" Vanda said, unsure of how any of this worked.

"Yeah, there's a signup sheet," the other woman said. She grabbed it off the counter and glanced at it. "Edwardo's available. If you want him."

"Uhm, sure," Vanda said.

The other student shrugged as if that wasn't the smartest idea. But Vanda had told that bitch Mrs. Rindahl that at least she'd try.

The office where Edwardo sat was one of several that

filled the hallway just past the reception area. The door was glass, and large windows made up the wall. Wouldn't be a place where students could sneak off to easily.

A plain desk stood in the center of the room, with uncomfortable wooden chairs on either side. Bookcases lined the other three walls, full of what were sure to be awful dense tomes that Vanda would hate. The lights were horribly bright in here was well, though Vanda supposed that was a good thing, the better to read by. It smelled of day-old fries, despite all the signs that there was no eating anywhere in the English Center.

Edwardo turned out to be a short, skinny Hispanic guy with stubbly black hair and matching dark eyes, dressed in a school band T-shirt and what looked like brand-new jeans. His voice held no trace of an accent as he explained that they'd be going through her last paper, he'd explain what she'd done wrong, and then they could go from there.

He emphasized that he couldn't write her paper for her. Not even for a bribe. Any sort of bribe.

The way his eyes lingered on her curves, Vanda knew exactly what sort of bribe he was looking for.

However, Vanda wasn't interested in men. Or women, for that matter. Her younger sister had had to have an abortion by the time she'd turned sixteen.

Vanda was still a virgin at nineteen, and uninterested in changing that.

Since Vanda could follow instructions (no, really, no matter what Mrs. Rindahl had snottily implied in her latest round of comments), she'd come prepared, bringing not only this week's disastrous paper but a few others as well.

Edwardo insisted that instead of sitting on either side of the desk from one another, they sit next to each other, so that he could go through the paper line-by-line, and they could more easily discuss what he saw. They sat with their backs to the door, no easy route of escape that Vanda could see. Just those awful books surrounding her.

Of course, he sat with his legs spread wide, so that his thigh was constantly touching Vanda's. The first time he brushed his hand down the length of her forearm, she shivered and pulled back, as if she'd been stung.

That just made him pursue her harder.

By the end of their session, Vanda was a shaking wreck. She wanted to go back to her dorm and take a long hot shower, scrubbing all of Edwardo off her skin.

When she told him that she didn't want a second appointment, he looked disappointed.

"But Mrs. Rindahl really wants you to come back," Edwardo said. "The appointment calendar is shared with the English professors. She'll know that you only came in for a single session."

"Maybe that's all I need," Vanda said fiercely. She gathered up her papers and scurried out of the room.

She knew that she should report Edwardo. Though she suspected, thinking back about how the receptionist had offered him up, that others already had.

Of course, nothing had been done about him. Nothing would be done about him.

Plus, Vanda was never certain if her reaction to that sort of thing was overblown. She didn't like to be touched at all, by anyone. Other people didn't seem to mind it. She just wasn't interested in sex. Period.

Vanda could never go back to Edwardo, though. There had to be another way. Some other place where she could learn the damned structures she needed in order to pass Mrs. Rindahl's class. She'd spent enough time on the Internet, even watching YouTube videos. Obviously, that hadn't helped.

There was just something about how her brain worked that she always presented information backwards. It was like racing to the end of a recipe and reading through the instructions before paying any attention to the ingredients.

But that was how she did it. The instructions told her how everything went together. Then, when she went through the ingredients, if she didn't have something, she knew what to substitute because she already understood how it was being used, what its purpose was.

Maybe someone else would be offering tutoring services. She didn't have any money to pay them, but she could offer to bake them things in exchange.

Anything but going back to that damned Edwardo.

Upstairs, in the hallway leading to the large common room where most students hung out, hung a big bulletin board covered with notices. Vanda perused those, writing down the numbers of a few that appeared to be offering English Comp tutoring.

Most were for Calculus, though. Or Comp Sci.

She nearly missed the tiny card tucked into the corner. It looked handwritten, as opposed to almost every other business card stuck to the board.

The cursive handwriting was thin and wobbly, as if the person writing it had hand tremors.

It wasn't offering help in English Comp, though. Not specifically. Instead, it read:

Clear away the cobwebs in your head
Rise up to your true potential
Only serious students need apply

That was what Vanda needed. Something to clean out the distractions and help her rise above everyone else.

The contact information wasn't on the front of the card. She had to tug hard on it to remove it from the board—someone had jammed it in there but good.

At first, she thought the back was blank. She stepped away from the board, into better light, before the light grey writing became visible.

It listed an address, not too far from campus, along with hours that the person would accept visitors.

That was it. No name. No phone. No way of contacting anyone.

She was just supposed to show up, like she had for the English Center. Take what she got.

Vanda nearly put the card back on the board, but she hesitated. This place was open that night, and she did have time.

She'd be sure to tell her roommate where she was going before she went, just so she didn't end up the victim of some psycho serial killer.

However, she was desperate. And while English Comp was her worst subject, she wasn't doing that great in any of them.

No matter how hard she studied, she just didn't seem to be absorbing any of it. Or she studied the wrong things, at least when it came to the tests. Sometimes she just froze when the professor handed out pop quizzes, her mind going completely blank.

Maybe she just needed someone to help her clear out her cobwebs, as it were.

It was only after she'd looked again at the back of the card that she saw the final instruction, namely, to bring the card with her.

Vanda mentally shrugged, shoving the card into the front of her jeans, then racing out of the Student Union. She had an hour or so to eat before this mysterious place would be open for business.

Hopefully, her next appointment would go better than the one at the English Center.

───────

Vanda didn't have a car, of course. That was for the rich kids, the ones who didn't come from the trailer park at the edge of Madison that took three buses to get to. Fortunately, she was used to walking everywhere.

It didn't surprise her how the neighborhood changed from one street to the next. The previous block had been nicer, older homes. Now, she was in student housing, where slumlords charged a premium for shitty tiny rooms that were freezing in the winter and boiling in the summer.

The address on the back of the card turned out to be a house that sat at the back of a double lot. It was dark enough that Vanda couldn't really see the yard, but she imagined that it was full of weeds, the sidewalk cracked and broken. At least it didn't have cars up on cement blocks like modern sculptures, or even discarded washing machines or other appliances, like some of the neighbors.

Vanda walked up the sidewalk slowly, careful not to break an ankle. The house itself didn't look like a place where a serial killer lived. A front porch light cheerily cleared up the gloom. The porch had a rocking chair on it on one side and a porch swing on the other. Tinkling glass chimes hung next to the door. Sun-bleached wood siding covered the walls between the two front windows, both of which were filled with a golden warm glow, as if candles lit the space behind the drawn shades.

An old lady answered Vanda's knock on the door. She barely came up to Vanda's chest, so not even five feet tall. She was slightly stooped, like Grandpa Emery, though her hair was completely black, kinky, and falling over her shoulders. Her eyes were a light color, spooky, like one of those damned Huskies rich people seemed to adore. She had a witch nose, both bulbous and long, while the rest of the features of her face seemed to pull back and away. The long-sleeved blouse she wore had seen better days, the white and blue cotton slightly frayed at the collar and cuffs.

"Yes?" she asked, peering closely at Vanda.

"You had an ad," Vanda said coldly. She pulled out the card and shoved it at the woman.

"Yes, this is mine. And you found it! Interesting," the woman said.

Vanda wasn't sure what she meant by that. She was about to go when the woman gave her a great grin, her flabby lips covering over what few teeth she had. "Come in. Come in."

Vanda stepped into the hallway and looked around. The lights on tables on either side of the door were candles, a whole bunch of them. All she could smell was wax and that musty smell of molding books.

Ugh.

"Please, please, follow me, won't you, my dear?" the woman said, turning and walking farther into the room.

At least the room the old woman led Vanda to was well lit—probably a dining room. A rectangular table filled most of the space, covered with an old-fashioned white linen tablecloth. Sitting in the center of the table was a large round object, covered with a thin purple silk cloth.

Surely that wasn't a crystal ball? And were those tarot cards beside it?

Instead of a serial killer, Vanda was certain she'd just walked into the den of a witch.

The chairs around the table all had tall carved backs with a minimum of padding and upholstery. Vanda sat down gingerly, surprised at how comfortable the seat actually was. Though they looked like antiques, the chairs were very sturdy and could easily hold her weight.

"So, tell me why you've come to see Madam Carlito," the woman said as she sat down on the other side of the table.

At least Vanda could see out the windows behind the witch, the dark night pressing in on the glass.

"I'm having problems at school," Vanda admitted.

"Any specific subject?" Madam Carlito asked.

"All of them," Vanda said, shaking her head.

She hadn't meant to say that. But she suspected that even if she hadn't, Madam Carlito would have known anyway.

"And what do you want?" Madam Carlito said. Her light blue-grey eyes appeared to take on a weird glow.

It was on the tip of Vanda's tongue to talk about the bakery. How much she longed to open up her own store. She'd call it Classy Cakes and Cookies, with the nickname being Triple C. That would be part of her logo and everything.

However, she was in college now. On her way into the business world. Not the kitchen.

"I want to learn business and finance," Vanda said firmly, pushing her dreams to the side. "I need to do better in school for that."

"Are you sure?" Madam Carlito asked, tilting her head to one side and staring at Vanda.

"I'm sure," Vanda said.

"Very well then," Madam Carlito said. "I can help you with that."

"I can't pay you much," Vanda said.

She got another toothless grin at that.

"I don't need much," the old woman said. "Just a single drop of your blood."

"Okay," Vanda said slowly. Maybe she had wandered into the scene where the witch turned out to be a serial killer?

From a basket on the end of the table, Madam Carlito pulled out what looked like a black marble cutting board, the kind you chilled first before rolling out the dough for fancy pastries.

Then she pulled out what looked like a green-covered straw, handing that to Vanda.

It turned out to be a scalpel, sterilized and still sealed.

Huh.

Vanda slowly stripped the paper and plastic from the blade.

For a weird moment, she had the image that she was unwrapping a cloth from an ancient dagger instead. The blade wasn't long and smooth, but rough and square, each edge finely sharpened.

When she blinked, the image of the scalpel came back strongly.

Weird.

"Just prick your finger, and let a single drop of your blood fall onto my plate," Madam Carlito said.

Vanda hesitated, then she went ahead and stabbed her

finger with the scalpel. The blade was so sharp there was no pain, not until afterward. Then she squeezed the tip of her finger with her other hand, pushing out a single drop of blood.

The smooth black marble sizzled when the blood splashed down on it, like oil in a pan. Smoke rose instantly, black and foul.

The effect only lasted a few seconds. Then the stench, like burned sugar, cleared the air.

Vanda shook her head and blinked, suddenly feeling stiff.

She'd only been sitting there a few moments, right?

When she checked later on her phone, she found that she'd been there for thirty minutes, though she couldn't remember anything that had happened during that time.

"When you wake up tomorrow, the first thing you should do is write your next English Comp paper," Madam Carlito said. "The words should be much easier for you then."

Vanda didn't remember telling Madam Carlito anything about English Comp. Maybe it was obvious? Or that bitch Mrs. Rindahl had a reputation?

Quickly, Vanda scurried out of the suddenly overly warm room, back into the cool night.

She stopped walking so fast by the time she reached the corner.

No one was pursuing her. She'd escaped the witch's house.

Hopefully, she'd have more than just a story to tell about it. Though it was a really good story.

The next morning, Vanda did as Madam Carlito had instructed.

The words weren't necessarily easy. She suspected that she'd always have some problem getting things onto the page.

But for once, the structure felt right. She could almost see the breaks between the sections, where she listed her theses, her supporting arguments, her conclusion.

She'd never written a paper that felt solid, as though the base layer of the cake was well baked and could support all the other layers going up.

The rest of her classes that week were also easier. Madam Carlito had cleared away so many of the cobwebs in her head! Vanda wasn't making what she'd always thought of as intuitive leaps, like the other students. For the first time, though, she could at least follow where they were going.

It was exciting to be learning, to feel capable, as if she actually could learn.

Though the paper Mrs. Rindahl returned that morning was another D, Vanda felt so much better about the paper she turned in.

And the next paper that she'd write.

Except that the magic wore off Thursday morning, one week after her initial visit. Vanda initially wondered if she'd come down with a head cold, as it was so difficult to form words and ideas again.

By some miracle, she had Friday night off, and went scurrying off to Madam Carlito's house. It was still just as dark and spooky as it had been the first time. The cold wind blowing off the lake didn't help, with the promise of snow in the air.

Madam Carlito opened the door before Vanda could

even knock.

"Good, good," she crooned as she stepped back, welcoming Vanda back into her house. "I was getting worried about you. Did the spell work?"

"You know it did," Vanda said bitterly. "Otherwise I wouldn't be back."

"Ah, but I cannot make it permanent. I told you that," Madam Carlito said.

Vanda opened her mouth to contradict the old woman, but then snapped it shut when she realized that she did, indeed, know that.

And that she'd have to come back once a week, every week, for the effects of the spell to continue.

They'd talked after she'd pricked her finger. Why hadn't she remembered?

"How much am I going to owe you this time?" Vanda said, unable to keep the fear out of her voice.

"Same amount as always," Madam Carlito said. "It will always be just a single drop of your blood. Never any more."

For some reason, Vanda believed the old woman. All she desired was a single drop of Vanda's blood. Like a solitary gumdrop.

"Then let's get this over with," Vanda said, walking boldly into the old woman's dining room and throwing herself into one of the chairs.

"You do remember the other part of our bargain?" Madam Carlito said as she slowly made her way to the other side of the dining room table. "That this is our secret? That you won't ever tell anyone of me, or the spell breaks?"

Vanda hadn't, but she nodded. "Who would believe me?" she said honestly enough.

That at least got her the goofy smile, instead of the cruel one.

"Of course," Madam Carlito said. She handed Vanda another sterilely wrapped scalpel.

Vanda didn't look at it too closely, didn't want to see the other side of knife she held, the dark cold iron and square blade.

The drop of blood sizzled on the black marble again, smoking and stinking.

Though it felt like mere moments to Vanda, it took about thirty minutes again.

Vanda decided she didn't care.

As long as the magic worked, and kept working, she'd keep the secret of Madam Carlito to herself.

And make all of her mama's dreams come true.

———

It took work, but Vanda managed to pull her average up by the end of the semester. She still had the paper that Mrs. Rindahl had returned with the C+ on it, the first of the papers that she'd written after Madam Carlito. The last one for the semester had actually received an A.

Mrs. Rindahl took all the credit, assuming that Vanda had found a tutor.

It was close enough to the truth. She had found someone who was helping with all her schoolwork.

Vanda hadn't been looking forward to going home over break. Her roommate might have raved about her own mama's cooking, but Vanda's mother couldn't cook worth a damn. Plus, they didn't have the money for all those fancy ingredients to make the kinds of food that Vanda saw on all those cooking shows.

Instead, she'd been looking forward to helping Aunt Gemma out in the pastry shop. She dumped her bag in the tiny trailer home, then raced out again, going directly to the shop.

Once she arrived, Vanda took a step into the shop and took a deep breath, breathing in the scents of sugar, chocolate, cinnamon, and butter. It all smelled divine. The display case at the front was loaded with delectable goodies: palmiers, cupcakes, decorated sugar cookies, spritzed butter cookies, cinnamon rolls, chocolate covered eclairs, and more.

Aunt Gemma raced around from behind the counter and gave her a huge hug, then stepped back. "You're nothing but skin and bones!" she exclaimed.

Vanda looked down. She had lost some weight. She figured it was because the food at the cafeteria was so bland. Plus, she was working, like, all the time.

"Come on back," Aunt Gemma said, pulling Vanda around the counter and into the kitchen.

Vanda looked around, feeling unexpectedly uncomfortable with the industrial mixers, all the piping tips, the pans and sheet trays.

This was her home, though. She was only uneasy because she'd been gone since summer.

Aunt Gemma put Vanda right to work, grating carrots in one of the food processors for a large batch of carrot cake muffins that Aunt Gemma was baking for some corporate event.

It took Vanda two tries to get the food processor adjusted correctly, so the carrots came out the right consistency. Then she had to stop and ask Aunt Gemma again how many she should do. She even had to carefully measure out the cups of carrots because she could no longer trust her eye to know the correct amount anymore.

Only when Vanda tasted the final product did she

understand what else that Madam Carlito had taken from her, besides that single drop of blood.

Her love of cooking and food.

Vanda told herself that it was okay. No, that it was good that Madam Carlito had stolen that part of her. If she hadn't, Vanda would have always been split, always looking at the path not taken as she made her way in the business world.

It was good that she could walk away from the kitchen without terrible longing.

Right?

Vanda was surprised at how slow everyone in her family seemed to be. They couldn't make the connections that she now could. Couldn't see past the bullshit the news was handing them.

Couldn't think critically.

Everyone tried to get her to eat, but Vanda never had any appetite. Nothing tasted good to her, not even Aunt Gemma's homemade apple pie made with the Vietnamese cinnamon and the incredibly flaky, buttery crust.

Even her friends from high school commented on how she'd changed, though she'd tried to fit in with them by putting on more makeup and wearing a baggier sweater to hide her weight loss.

By the end of the evening out with them, she knew that they'd never go out again. Or at least, not with her.

She wanted to share her secret, at the very least with some of her friends. To get them to think in broader, better terms. To understand where they stood in terms of the world at large, and how to improve themselves.

But it was her secret. She couldn't share it with them, no matter how it ate at her.

Plus, what would they have to give up? Would it be worth it to them?

So Vanda maintained her silence, went back to school after the start of the new year, and didn't look back. She spent the summer working as an intern at an investment bank, learning the market and starting her own nest egg.

Come fall, when school started again, no one recognized her. She wasn't as skinny as that bitch Mrs. Rindahl, and vowed to never let herself get that way. She was, however, hardly half the size she'd been when she graduated high school. At least now she could fit into most of the clothes she found at the Goodwill. Cuter than what she used to wear, she'd admit that. Though she still tended to wear her shirts baggy.

And really, was that such a bad price to pay? A single drop of blood every week? The complete loss of taste for food?

She was going places. Doing things that no one in her family had even dreamed about.

They'd all been dreaming too small.

Whereas Vanda vowed to dream big enough for all of them.

She worked hard every summer, getting great references during her interships, so that when it came time, she easily found a job with one of the big international banks downtown. She stayed in what was essentially student housing so she didn't have to go back home.

Or rather, back to the trailer park. It hadn't ever been much of a home.

She learned how to get enough calories into her at the cheapest cost so she didn't turn into mere skin and bones.

And she faithfully visited Madam Carlito every week. She gave the excuse that she was going to see her therapist, an appointment no one questioned.

She got one promotion after another.

She moved her mother into a really cute house in the neighborhood that was closest to their old place. Paid for her sister's rehab in a fancy center. Put aside college funds for her nieces and nephews. Ignored or deflected any questions about her own lack of companionship.

Then came the hard question at the bank. The one she knew was coming. The one she'd been looking forward to and dreading equally.

They had another promotion for her. However, it involved moving to New York, to work at the corporate headquarters.

Would she relocate? The bank would pay for everything.

Vanda said she needed to think about it, but she knew in her heart that she'd have to turn them down. She couldn't fly back here to Madison every week for her weekly "therapy" session with Madam Carlito. The few times when she'd missed her regular appointment, she'd felt her brain shutting down in a frightful way.

With heavy feet, she walked through the neighborhood where Madam Carlito still lived. The tiny house had never changed, along with the weed-filled yard and cracked sidewalk. The neighborhood was starting to see some gentrification, the slumlords being bought out by developers wanting to put fourteen units on a lot that had only held a single dwelling.

Progress. Or so they called it.

Madam Carlito opened the door again before Vanda knocked. She hadn't changed either. Her hair was still black and kinky, her eyes pale and haunting. Vanda wasn't sure what she did for money. Then again, maybe she had other "patients" who paid her more than Vanda, who offered more than just their blood.

Vanda had money now. She'd offered that on more than one occasion. Madam Carlito made it clear that only her blood would do.

"What is it, dearie?" Madam Carlito asked as she drew Vanda into the house.

Candles burned on the tables in the front room night and day. They were the only light allowed in that room. The shades were always drawn as well. Sometimes the smell of something spicy, like oregano, was mingled with the constant scent of wax, though Vanda rarely smelled much of anything now.

"My bank offered me another promotion," she said as she sat heavily in the chair. "One in New York."

"Ah, I see," Madam Carlito said. She glanced around her house, then nodded. "Fine. I will go with you."

"What?" Vanda said, nearly exploding out of her chair.

"You will help pay to move me, yes?" Madam Carlito asked.

"Yes," Vanda said slowly, nodding.

"Good," Madam Carlito said, her grin cheerful. "I've always wanted to live in New York."

Vanda just shook her head. This hadn't been the response she'd expected. Not at all.

She knew how awful it would be once she stopped seeing Madam Carlito.

A tiny, small voice inside of Vanda mourned that she couldn't escape. Not yet.

But that maybe, someday, she would.

Success followed Vanda as surely as Madam Carlito.

As did the haunting sensation of impostor syndrome.

Other people just had false beliefs that they weren't worthy of what they'd achieved.

Vanda didn't have any doubt.

It wasn't until interviewing for a piece about "important women in the banking world" that Vanda had any pause. The interviewer, another woman, kept harping on Vanda, asking who her role models were, who'd helped her out of the trailer park.

Who, besides Vanda, was actually behind her success?

Vanda couldn't tell the interviewer about Madam Carlito. Not only would no one believe her, everyone would think she was crazy.

Plus, if she ever talked about Madam Carlito, the spell would be broken. That secret was more important to her than anything else.

So Vanda made up a bullshit story about Mrs. Rindahl, her English Comp teacher, who'd pressured her into getting a tutor. After that, Vanda had had a series of people who'd helped her, but really, it was all Mrs. Rindahl's fault.

Let the skinny bitch suck on that.

She was pretty sure that Mrs. Rindahl wouldn't even remember Vanda. Or if she did, she'd be happy to take all the credit for Vanda's amazing turnaround.

However, weeks later, the question ate at Vanda as she spent yet another night alone in her penthouse apartment overlooking the lights of the city. She didn't mind being alone, not really. She had enough companionship during the day with her backstabbing co-workers.

When asked, she'd always laughingly joked that she

was married to her job, that she couldn't see anyone else. Given the crazy hours she worked, it wasn't far from the truth.

Besides, in addition to taking her love of food, Madam Carlito's spell had also emphasized Vanda's need to be alone. She wasn't still a virgin at thirty-eight, but it had only been the one time, and she'd had to be pretty drunk to go through with it.

Vanda had amazing protein drinks that gave her all the nutrients she needed without ever having to worry about cooking. She could afford them. They all tasted like nothing, but then again, no food tasted good. She was actually kind of grateful for that, as she'd seen too many people along the way become addicted to one thing or another.

Vanda's addiction was to money.

The night grew quieter around her, though the city never properly slept. Vanda wrapped herself in a soft blanket and sat in her chair, watching the lights blink out.

It was at times like these that she questioned her bargain. Was her success worth what she'd given up? Worth carrying the burden of her beginnings? Worth the secret that burned inside her, sizzling like the blood that dripped from her finger onto Madam Carlito's black plate?

A few months later, when Vanda discovered that the energy drinks no longer worked, that no matter what she took she was always too tired, she finally went to see a doctor.

And found the cancer that was eating her up inside as well.

During her chemo treatments, Madam Carlito volunteered to come to Vanda, to her penthouse, in order to continue their "sessions." It was odd to see the old woman out of what had been her natural habitat. The apartment the old woman stayed in had retained the feel of her house, with the constant candles, the smell of wax, the old books and older, ratty furniture.

In Vanda's brightly lit apartment, the old woman was like a dark cloud. She moved hesitatingly, as if feeling her true age, whatever that was. (When Vanda had looked up the deed for the house Madam Carlito owned in Wisconsin, she'd found that the Carlitos had owned that land since before there were proper records. Madam Carlito hadn't bothered selling it, but still kept it, after she'd moved.)

After opening the door and letting Madam Carlito in, Vanda went back to the nest she'd made for herself on the couch, with blankets and soft pillows. She was always cold, now. She'd hired a nurse to come and look in on her, as Vanda didn't have any friends or relatives she could call on.

And she doubted that she'd care for Madam Carlito's bedside manner.

The old woman scooted closer to the couch, taking one of Vanda's cold hands in her warm ones. The skin on the back of Madam Carlito's hand was wrinkled, covered in age spots and veins. The fingers couldn't straighten all the way out, but remained slightly bent like claws. Her yellowed nails were broken off and dirty.

Still, Vanda found that she could tolerate the witch's touch more than anyone else's. Particularly since the only other touch she got those days was from doctors and nurses, poking and prodding.

She watched with glazed eyes as the woman pulled out the too-familiar dagger. The sight seemed to wake something in Vanda, though she much preferred the illusion of the sterilized scalpel.

"What else do you take? Besides the blood and my love of food?" Vanda murmured.

She didn't expect the old woman to answer. She'd asked before, she was certain of it. But Madam Carlito had never replied.

Until that day.

"You were supposed to give me your sex drive," the old woman said, chuckling as she precisely pricked Vanda's ring finger. "But you didn't have one. So I took the only other thing you loved."

Vanda nodded. That made sense, actually. Madam Carlito lived off Vanda's passion.

"Did you give me the cancer?" Vanda found herself asking. It had been the most pressing question she'd had since the diagnosis, though she hadn't been able to ask it before.

"No, dearie," Madam Carlito said. The blood sizzled on the black plate as always.

This time, Vanda actually watched Madam Carlito hunch over, breathe in the smoke, her eyes glazing over as the rush hit her.

Madam Carlito grew younger before her eyes, her skin filling out, her eyes less rheumy, turning more blue than grey. Even a few of her teeth grew back.

The effect wouldn't last long. By the time the thirty minutes was over, Madam Carlito would be back to her old self.

But that brief hit would be enough to give her life for another week. Or more.

Why was Vanda able to see Madam Carlito and her ritual? Was it because for the first time, Vanda hadn't handled the knife? Hadn't been the one to make herself bleed?

Madam Carlito sat back, looking satisfied. "Your life was never going to be that long," she said, chuckling. "You would have died of a heart attack long before now if you'd stayed on your old course."

"And now?" Vanda asked, fascinated. Would she remember this conversation? Had they had it before? Or would it fade, like always, the time compressing until she thought only seconds had passed?

The old woman shrugged as the color already started draining from her cheeks. "You'll live as long as you can," she said. "I cannot prolong your life. Or cure your cancer. Don't even bother asking."

Vanda nodded. Madam Carlito's magic was selfish in nature. That she could help other people when she used it was an unexpected side effect.

"I want out," Vanda heard herself saying. A deep stabbing horror filled her core, worse than the diagnosis of cancer or the removal of the huge tumor that had taken over her unused womb.

Cackling, Madam Carlito started gathering up her plate and dagger, wrapping it back up in the green cloth that bound it. "You know how to break the spell," she said as she stood. She looked so much stronger now than when she'd come in. More like a storm cloud. "All you have to do is to tell your secret. Let the world know that your success isn't actually yours. You cheated to get here. You don't belong here. And you know it."

Madam Carlito turned to go. "See you next week, dearie," she said triumphantly, letting herself out of the penthouse.

Vanda slumped back into her nest, feeling weaker than

ever.

Madam Carlito was right. Vanda didn't belong here. She'd cheated. Taken a shortcut. Given up her dreams to support a vampiric witch.

Triple C. She still remembered the name of the pastry shop that she'd always wanted to open. Classy Cakes and Cookies. Now, she was faced with cancer, cheating, and something else. Perhaps complete idiocy.

Was this to be her legacy? She'd played the system long enough to know that without Madam Carlito's help, she'd lose her place quickly. The job promotions would stop coming. Along with all those lovely perks.

And yet…there was still that tiny voice inside her that longed to be freed from the witch's spell.

All she had to do was to tell her secret.

No one would believe her.

Worse, she'd lose her position. HR would put her on a "temporary" hiatus until she came to her sense. Or could be quietly let go.

People in the hallways at corporate would stare at her. Vanda had always wanted to be the power behind the throne, not the face of it.

There had to be a way out.

Triple C, that quiet voice reminded her.

Cheating, Cancer, and Connections. That was the key to this mess.

The next morning, Vanda started putting together her plans, calling in favors and setting up trusts. No one questioned her motives—particularly not if they knew about the cancer. She was just cleaning up some loose ends as far as other people were concerned. Covering eventualities if the chemo and radiation didn't work.

Then, the night before Madam Carlito was supposed to

return, Vanda made her final call.

She rang the private number of the woman who'd inter-
viewed her about "women in banking." She left a long,
rambling voicemail about how she'd lied, coming clean
about Madam Carlito, confessing how she'd cheated the
system.

When she hung up, Vanda felt lighter than ever before.
She slept dreamlessly that night, finally comfortable in her
own body again, having reclaimed herself.

All her brain was gone by morning. She could barely
even read the email that the interviewer had sent her,
asking her to verify what she'd just said.

Vanda did gleefully, though words were now difficult
again. She gave excuses for herself, that she had "cancer
brain" (which she did) and hormone issues (which she also
did, from the medical menopause).

By the time the piece came out, Vanda was long gone,
back to Madison.

She still couldn't taste worth a damn. She wasn't sure if
any of the abilities she'd given Madam Carlito freely would
ever return.

But she was going to live her dream, finally. Open the
Triple C. Hire a staff to help her recover.

Only once did she drive through the old neighborhood
where Madam Carlito's house stood.

The lot was empty. Never developed, according to the
papers she'd found.

How many other people had Madam Carlito sucked
dry? Vanda would never know.

Hopefully, the others had found their own way free of
the witch, told their secrets, and retaken their lives.

She could only live her own life, now.

For as long as she had left.

STRANGER TO A LITTLE GIRL
PATRICK MAMMAY

The little girl danced across the field, spinning and twirling so free. She stopped from time to time to grab a flower or spot a bird or a bee. The field was large and surrounded by trees, and as she danced and leapt among the grass, and flowers, near the trees, someone took notice, someone hidden, someone mean.

Mister Tumault saw a little girl in the field where he stood, but he could not be seen, not by a human with eyes so blind, no, he could not be seen, not even by the wind, the sky, the birds, or the trees. He watched her dance and twirl in her little blue and white dress with red lace seams. Her golden skin, her almond-shaped eyes, long, black braided hair, and her smile, her smile as big and bright as the sun, as she laughed in the warm afternoon air.

Mister Tumault was caught, so happy to see this little girl, this little girl for him to see. He must get closer, but how to approach her, surely she knows the danger of strangers, but to get closer he must be seen. What shape, what form should he take, there must be one that won't scare her away, this little girl, this beacon, this treat.

Meili bent to pick a flower to smell it; she inhaled deep. When she opened her eyes, a man she did see. He was tall, but not the tallest, and thin, but not the thinnest, perhaps young but much older than Meili. His eyes were blue and his hair yellow, and he smiled a thin smile at her, so it seemed. She looked around, but no one else was to be found, so she knew he was looking at her.

"Hello little girl, how about a wish? For a secret and a kiss, I can grant you your wish!"

With a flourish the man flashed gold in his hands, then a bird with colorful tailfeathers, then a bouquet of flowers as pretty as pretty could be. He was flamboyantly dressed, in tan pants and a white shirt buttoned down the middle, flamboyant here, but traditional garb in a world so far away, in another time another place.

"A wish?" said Meili.

If the man was a stranger to Meili, then Meili was a stranger to the man. If the danger was there, surely he would know it, too, therefore they must not be strangers and there must not be danger. The man was not scared and neither was she. She was intrigued, for she had a wish, oh she did.

"Yes, a wish. I am Mister Tumault and I can grant a wish, but I must receive a secret and a kiss. That seems like a fair trade to me."

Her hands dropped, loosely clinging to the flower they held, as she looked up to the strange man.

"I'm Meili. I would like a wish, I can give a kiss, but I don't have a secret to speak."

He rolled his head with a smile. He was so close he could taste it, and it was Meili. She would be his feast, once he had that secret and a kiss. A little trick.

"Oh, I'm sure you do, I'm sure you do. Tell me something no one else knows. It doesn't have to be yours; it doesn't matter whose."

Meili smiled at the idea, that bright smile so tasty.

"I don't know what a secret is—do you have one? Maybe if I heard it would make sense."

Mister Tumault paused with a thoughtful finger to his lip. A secret was expensive, a very expensive gift, a gift with risk, but this little girl was not something to be missed.

With a breath and a hmm, he said, "Sure, okay, I guess. A secret is this. This is not me that you see. I'm not a man. I'm a different being. It's true, it's a surprise, but because I have a wish to gift, I must hide."

Surely that helped, at least that is what he felt.

Meili smiled a great big smile. "I have a secret to tell, but first my kiss." She closed her eyes and puckered her lips and leaned forward, but still far from his.

Mister Tumault could barely contain his excitement. First the kiss, then the secret.

He leaned down and placed his lips on hers, a gentle peck. Her eyes popped open and she grabbed his neck. She pulled him near and whispered in his ear; she told him a secret without fear.

His smile grew large as she started to speak. Her fingers on his neck grew tight as she whispered, "I have your secret and now your kiss, tell me what you wish before I eat you, like this."

MACHIAVELLI'S PEARL
MICHÈLE LAFRAMBOISE

T he scents of mineral oils and varnishes battled with the dusty smells of the little atelier in the Santissima Annunziata monastery. Each color had its own odor, greasy like the Prince's lips, earthy like my father's homely face, or acidic like the insides of my roiling stomach.

The venison from yesterday's feast threatened to surge upwards, spilling onto my clothes. Bile was already building up inside my mouth.

It was all I could do to grab the armrests of the rose-wood chair I was supposed to sit and look decorative on. I thanked the Lady that the painter my father had hired had not arrived yet. I couldn't risk being seen in such a disheveled state.

The room had one narrow window dispensing a greyish daylight. From the plaza beneath it, shouts, clanking armor, and angry voices rose from the scattering crowd. Of course, they had discovered the Prince, his body in a state of disarray far more advanced than mine.

I put the painter's tardiness to good use, combing my

hair with my fingers, straightening my veil, and trying to calm my fluttering heart.

At fifteen, I was quite limber, but the unexpected exercise had taken its toll on my calves. The soles of my feet hurt so much I was certain there was a florin-sized hole under the heel.

The bells of the Santa Maria del Fiore cathedral were still tolling, their deep voices echoing through the city. I rose to look out the window. One pigeon flew by, its arrow-straight path a telling sign it was carrying an urgent message. Men in arms wearing the Medici colors patrolled the piazza, stopping every passerby and merchant.

The whole city was in shock. News of the murder and theft had spread to all lips in the time it had taken me to get here, holding my robe with both hands.

Two militia guards had stopped me in front of the monastery. My well-behaved lady's dress did not have any pockets, so the space between my small breasts was the first place the less well-behaved guard had searched, not without feeling the merchandise.

I kept silent during the humiliating procedure, my lungs on fire. I pumped air in short puffs to catch my breath, which amused the men. Eventually, they released me along with a few rowdy comments. I flew up the stone stairs to the door.

An old monk opened it, clad in a rough fabric robe. He led me to the studio, his bark-soled sandals clop-clopping on the tiles. He made no comment on the poor state of my clothes, the dust on my leather slippers, or the absence of my mother. Maybe he had made a vow of silence.

My thoughts went back to the previous day, when my life was simple, and my worries revolved around my siblings' antics, the silk merchants' dealings with the

Medici, and mother's insistence that I behave like a lady instead of giggling all the time.

The Previous Day

The city-republic of Florence was a proud mix of towers, castles, churches, and monasteries all vying for dominance with arches, spires, and glazed windows. The people of Florence were a similar mix of merchants negotiating, shopkeepers haggling, nobles parading with (or without) a retinue.

I had put on my best dress, a dark green silk gown, with a pleated neckline gilded with golden lace, from which sprung the yellow sleeves of my linen chemise, like a symbol of spring. A gossamer-thin shawl, fixed to my hair by a copper pin, flowed like a dark river around my shoulders. The delicate gown had caught the gaze of several merchants on the Ponte Vecchio, prompting Mother to pull the shawl over my bright feathers.

Since our house lay on the south shore of the Arno River, we used the covered bridge to get to the center of the city. Musicians sat, beating on drums and playing flutes, the music filling the enclosed space. Ladies flit their fans in a teasing manner as they strolled from one vending table to another.

We crossed Piazza del Duomo, where the cathedral of Santa Maria del Fiore stood tall. I slowed down to peer at the works there, small histories encased in rock. There were so many that I always found a new one.

Standing close to this sanctified place, I felt exposed despite the filmy veil wrapped over my shoulders and hair. My mother didn't mind the exposure, but she shoed away both pigeons and urchins, the latter drawn by our luxurious clothes.

We continued north to the Piazza Santissima Annunziata, where we arrived at the entrance to the monastery.

Mother imperiously rang the bell at the main door. The porter opened, annoyed at the disruption, but his frown dissipated as she slipped a florin in his palm. The monk led us to a room on the upper story.

I was presented to a twig-like man in his thirties, the severe squinting lines of his face softened by a gentle smile. His eyes reminded me of the midday Mediterranean sky, a washed-out blue. He wore dark clothes, an oddity here in Florence. He was visiting from the city-state of Milano.

"Don't move, please," he had said.

He had looked and looked, under my mother's severe scrutiny. He used a fine coal to draw a few lines on paper made from cloth.

Mother had waxed on and on about how Francesco di Bartolomeo would be a good match for me. A silk merchant, he was older; he wanted to see something of me beforehand.

When the painter lay down his coal, he said it was only a first draft. My mother's lips were pinched as he dismissed us.

"We pay him by the hour," she said, grumbling.

As we exited the monastery, I saw a tall, robed monk accompanying a grey-haired man with a perpetual sneer imprinted on his lips. Behind them walked four guards clad in the gaudy red and black of the Medici.

Mother almost fainted. The Magnificent Lorenzo de Medici had resisted everything coming his way: bouts with illness, various poisoning attempts, the French invasion. Only the Mad Monk had forced him to flee. But the

Prince allied with Pope Alexander VI to put an end to this "unfortunate intermezzo" (my father's words) in the year 1498.

The Prince's velvet doublet sported silver ornaments and bracelets, but the most arresting feature was a dark, eyeball-sized marble dangling from a gold chain. Many men wore baubles to show off their status. But my gaze was drawn to the marble, curiosity and fear mingling in my stomach.

It was as if a third person were present, and not a person I cared to know better.

The monk beside the Prince noticed me gaping and smiled. Despite his plain clothing, he was handsome, with an intense gaze under straight dark brows and short hair. No, he wasn't a monk after all: his hair was shorn short without a tonsure.

Monk or not, he had smoldering black eyes, his gaze peeling off all the layers of my clothing. I felt blood heating my cheeks.

Mother grabbed my elbow.

"Do not look at him," she said, pulling at my sleeve.

Only when she had put the whole piazza between us and the men (who had by then disappeared into the monastery, visiting who knew whom) I turned to my mother.

"Who is the man with the Prince?"

"Why, his secretary, Machiavelli."

I had heard the name before, pronounced in angry or envious tones by men, or in sappy, simpering tones by other girls.

Niccolò Machiavelli was a brilliant negotiator, too brilliant for his own good according to Father. Maybe they went there to have their portraits made, too. Nevertheless, I felt an unease, like a too-tight bodice; the marble came back to my mind like an ill-intended guest.

"What is that stone the Prince is wearing?" I asked in a meek voice.

Mother adjusted her filmy veil against the sun. Her gaze darted this and that way, like a mouse scenting a cat nearby.

"It's a pearl," she whispered. "Signor Machiavelli found it in Savonarola's tunic."

"The Mad Monk?"

Mother signed herself so fast her white hand was a blur. I was a child then, but I remember the clashes of broken crystal wares, my mother's tears. The monk's disciples had forced Father to turn in all our mirrors for a vanity bonfire.

Girolamo Savonarola had been a formidable orator, drawing crowds to his sermons. He convinced Charles VIII to spare Florence in exchange for power. He turned Florence into a severe theocracy, using young men to patrol the street and beat sinners. After four years, his iron rule prompted the Pope to excommunicate him.

Savoranola was later hanged and burnt in the main piazza with two disciples, thus ending Florence's "unfortunate intermezzo."

"Some say that pearl had helped him sway his followers," Mother said. She smiled under her veil. "Sad that poor Niccolò couldn't keep his treasure."

And now, the Prince wore it as a bauble. We left, each small lady step adding distance between us and the power-hungry men in the Sanctuary.

The next morning, on the day everything changed for me and Florence, I had put the pearl away from my thoughts. I was supposed to return to the painter for my portrait, but it was one of those days when Mother did not feel well.

"Go with your father," she said from the mass of silk pillows propping her up. "And behave."

I trailed after my father as he parted the flow of people, due to his girth but also to the parcels he was carrying on his back and under his arms. The best samples of fine cloth were rolled in tight cylinders, and spices in their glass flagons were tied together and clanking softly.

Father had arranged to meet the Prince's secretary at the Palazzo Vecchio, where the council directed the affairs of the city. The stupid war (his own words) started against the Pisa Republic had blocked his latest convoy of goods. The spices and rare oriental herbs would wither if they stayed any longer in the carts under the pitiless sun.

Alas, midway, he found out he had forgotten a document at home, a safe conduct pass that would let him go to Pisa and take possession of the spices.

Burdened as he was, he couldn't get home and back here in time. I offered to run and get the missing papers for him. His weary face softened.

"Cara, ladies do not run."

"I will walk fast, Papa," I said. "Tell me what to look for, and where to find you after."

I hurried to our house on the other side of the Arno river, passing though the covered Ponte Vecchio and resisting the urge to stop and admire the wares displayed on the merchant's tables.

Thanks to my good leather shoes, getting to our house and retrieving the small wooden box with the safe conduct posed no problem.

The Palazzo Vecchio looked like an old man's weathered face, all done in pale gray stones. I skirted the vast Piazza Signoria where Savonarola had met his fiery end, keeping to the walls to cool myself after my exertions. The stern finger of the watch tower seemed to chide me.

My father was not waiting at the door. He must have already gone inside.

I rushed through the palace's two inner courtyards with their imposing columns, then, remembering my father's whispered directions, took the stairs to Machiavelli's office. The handsome monk was not in the room. A younger man rose, frowning at my presence or my sweat-stained dress, the result of my scurrying through the Ponte Vecchio.

I explained my business, my eyes darting to and from the heavy columns. The secretary's assistant looked down his nose at me. He snatched the box from my hands, sniffing as if the contact had soiled him.

"Wait here," he said, pointing to a low wooden stool in a windowless corner. He disappeared into the corridor.

I did what I was told, of course. I hoped my father would be satisfied with his dealings and his safe conduct.

It was dark in the office, despite the lighted candles. The palace walls themselves seemed to press in around me. I noticed a beautiful ink pot resting next to a pile of papers, and wondered if the secretary's long fingers had caressed its curve.

I chased those unworthy thoughts away and recited a rosary, praying to the Lady of the Flowers.

There were no flowers here, except those painted on the inkpot.

Suddenly, my heart beat louder than the street musician's drums at the Ponte Vecchio. My heart felt so heavy I was afraid it would fall through my belly, ripping through my insides. I breathed in and out, to no avail.

I felt someone entering the room, emitting a coppery scent. Like blood on a bonfire.

I twisted on the chair. No one was here. But the oppressive presence stayed close, about to crush me in invisible arms. A faraway man's voice echoed, sniggering like a drunk carnival reveller.

That did it.

Father or no father, I fled the room.

The stifling impression receded as I raced down darkened galleries. I met no one, which was strange for Florence's main seat of power. I was not familiar with the place (no women were) and got lost in no time.

At last, I heard voices coming from a stairwell going down to some cellar. Hoping to find my father, I walked down the stairs.

The voices grew louder and louder. The dizzy feeling returned, blurring my sight. I heard a half-laugh, sniggering mixed with angry shouts. None of these voices was my father's, but he often kept silent in a loud-mouthed group.

However, I didn't need him to guess those negotiations were not going well.

A guard passed by me. He would have seen me if he had looked up the stairwell, but he was minding the bottle of Tuscany wine he carried. The guard disappeared through a recessed door in the dimly lit corridor. The palace was a seat of justice, and the lower rooms would mostly hold prison cells.

As I approached, a smell of dust and cinder wafted from the hidden room. The guard had left the door partly open. Holding the trailing hem of my robe, I looked through.

It was a low-ceiling room. My view was blocked by a closed casket. Candles on a table cast a wan orange light on the stone angels lining the wall, leaving deep shadows. It was a crypt of some sort, holding a saint's relics. A row of stone chairs, for meditating, lined the wall behind the table.

A smell of cinder and decay permeated the place.

"Put it here and leave us," a rich voice said.

The guard obeyed, setting down the bottle next to four copper goblets.

I crept into a cavity between the casket and the stone wing of a lamenting angel. Moments later, the guard walked out, closing the door behind him.

A silver bowl held burning incense, releasing blue threads of smoke. But, despite the attempt to purify the air, the rotting stench persisted.

"Our offer is unconditional."

The Prince had a low, growling voice. He sat on a stone bench, his silver brows knotting, his dark jewel dangling from the chain. I averted my gaze from the pearl, afraid the foul presence hidden inside would detect me.

Next to the Prince stood Florence's archbishop, laden with jewellery; his gold cross alone must weigh twenty pounds. Of course, Signor Machiavelli was on the Prince's other side. He was well positioned to see me huddling next to the stone angel, had he not been preoccupied with the negotiation at hand.

"You would be wise to sign," Machiavelli said.

The man facing them had his back to me. A merchant's gold-embroidered tippet was draped over his shoulders. He was thinner than Father, and less calm. A state of frenzied anger emanated from his jerky gestures, his dark hair waving side to side.

There was no one else present. I pulled my robe's hem

tighter to make a retreat. As my hand reached the latch, an angry shout froze me in place.

"I won't sign!"

The envoy seized the paper, covered in exquisite scripture (probably from Machiavelli's hand), and tore it in two pieces. The sound sent a shiver down my spine, as if I were the one being ripped in two.

The Prince chortled, a high-toned hee-hee! that grated at my nerves.

"Then I will take Pisa as easily as I pick a ripe apple," he said, his fingers mimicking plucking a fruit, then crushing it.

The visitor spat on the table, missing the goblets by an inch.

"Pisa will never surrender to your...witchcraft!"

Machiavelli remained as still as a stone angel. His hand covered the hilt of his dagger. The archbishop advanced, stooped under the weight of his golden cross.

"Please," he said, laying his ringed stick fingers on the table. "The Prince cannot be insulted by a mere messenger!"

The visitor advanced toward the diminutive archbishop.

"A mere messenger? I am the envoy of Pisa, from the high Council!"

Pushing the archbishop out of his way, the visitor pounced toward the Prince, his hand curled around the handle of a short dagger. Machiavelli pounced as well, but he was on the Prince's other side.

A smile creased the archbishop's lined face as he put his heavy ornaments in order.

The Prince's veined hand touched the pearl. My own

heart pounded, as if a fist had closed over it. The oppressive presence I had sensed grew to fill the entire room.

The envoy paid no attention to the dark marble on the silver chain.

Before the point of his dagger reached the Prince's doublet, green flames erupted from the pearl.

The flames, short and mold-green, ran over the man's whole body.

The messenger from Pisa let out a high-pitched shriek as his clothes took fire. His dagger clattered on the stone slabs. I did not understand how a man could burn like that, without first being covered with mineral oleum.

Soon, his flesh bubbled, forming angry boils as he writhed on the floor, howling. I was reminded of the roasted beef our father had served at our latest carnival feast.

I put one hand over my mouth, lest I add my own screams to the pitiful man's. Despite Signor Machiavelli's inclinations for women, the Prince would never let me live.

Neither, I realized, would the archbishop. He would have me tortured and burnt as a witch, like he had burnt the Mad Monk.

Closing my eyes on my tears, I prayed to Our Lady.

Santa Maria del Fiore, please carry this poor man's soul to a quiet place, far from the fire.

I don't know how long I prayed while the invisible presence swirled around me. Was it Savonarola's soul? The hissing of flames subsided. The agonizing screams had, mercifully, ceased.

"Hee, hee! A foretaste of Hell!"

"Don't use that word, my Prince!" Machiavelli said.

I squinted though my tears at his harried voice. Despite being reportedly jaded, the Prince's advisor looked a little pale. Father said Machiavelli was more apt at plotting than killing.

On the floor, a black outline remained, like a dark carpet shaped like a hunched body. The archbishop's golden slipper emerged from the pristine robes to push at the cinders, sending up wisps of black powder. I was not mistaken: nothing remained of the man who had defiantly stood there.

"Powerful," the archbishop said. "It could serve the Church, producing miracles, burning heretics! So, Signor Machiavelli, tell me how this marble came into your hands," he said.

"After the execution, I searched the monk's discarded habit. Under his cowl, I found a hidden pocket."

The archbishop licked his lips.

"The pearl was there. Beautiful and white," the advisor said. "And...potent."

He took one goblet and poured wine into it.

"I learned that Savoranola had bought it from a merchant in Venice," he said. "The pearl may have originated from the deep ocean in the East Indies. That fool monk used it to sway an entire city. I wondered if I could to do the same."

The Prince chuckled.

"Hee, hee! So, Niccolò has decided to be generous with the Church."

Machiavelli pursed his lips.

"I prefer to convince men with my own power of reason, not with magical help. It had seemed the best way, to keep that pearl on holy ground."

He tasted the wine, then offered to fill the Prince's goblet.

"Besides," he added, "I could need a favor later."

The magnificent Lorenzo burst in laugh.

"It has cost me enough to buy it back!" he said.

Sour lines dragged the archbishop's papery face down. I wasn't sure he had agreed to that deal. If gambling hadn't been declared a mortal sin, I would wage ten florins the Prince had forced the archbishop's frail hand.

"Remember, I was the one who understood the potential of the pearl, attuned to the person wearing it," the archbishop said, his hooded eyes sparkling.

The old Prince stroke his sparse beard. He closed his hand on the dark marble and sighed with contentment, like Father after a good, fulfilling meal.

"We could set the entire Republic of Pisa ablaze."

Those words shocked his secretary.

"My Prince, you want people to admire you," he said. "They can't do that if they're dead."

Niccolò Machiavelli's practical words held a tiny drop of compassion. The Prince dismissed his suggestion.

"My dear Niccolò, you talk like that poor deluded Savoranola. We will march on Pisa and burn half its populace. The survivors will pay tribute!"

As the Prince rose from his seat, the stone shone a beautiful white, as if Our Lady Herself had taken residence in its translucent depth. Except none of the men seemed to notice the radiant light. I crossed myself, unable to take my eyes from the shining.

The men—with the light—filed out. The Prince did not spare a glance at the black smudge that had once been a man.

I pressed myself closer to the wall next to the weeping angel, lest the hem of my robe showed.

As he swished close in his robes, the archbishop's odor nearly made me gag, despite the lingering scent of incense. The stable boys must have been right, then: the priests never washed, considering bathing a sin.

Staying near those cinders was out of the question. I rose from under the angel's wing and pushed against the door the men had closed behind them.

To no avail. It was locked from outside.

I squatted near the stone angel. What the Prince intended to do was beyond evil. I remembered my father's desire to go to Pisa. My tears rolled down as I realized he would be killed along his prospective clients.

Then, the lock clicked. The heavy door swiveled, like an answer to my prayers. I scrambled in my robes and raced outside.

A hand grabbed my hair. I was pulled into a powerful embrace and pushed back in the room. A stench of wine mixed with lower body odor made me dizzy. The cursed pearl pressed against my bosom, filling me with dread.

"I felt your presence," the Prince said. "Don't worry little one, this will stay between us, hee, hee!"

Mother had warned me, over and over, about keeping my virtue. I was to be as pure as a white dove before my marriage. She had also told me about the Borgia women, about men taking privileges.

And no man was more privileged than the one who pushed me against the table, his greasy lips searching my own. The stone angels looked on, their eyes empty.

I twisted like the snake under Our Lady's feet to evade him. I fell on the hard floor, the Prince of Florence tumbling over me.

Oh, Santa Maria del Fiore, protect me!

As I was writhing like the poor messenger before me, my fingers touched metal.

The envoy's dagger had rolled under the table, forgotten. I grabbed the handle and pushed the point upward, into the embroidered doublet, meeting no resistance. The Prince's elation veered into a surprised gasp.

"Witch!"

He pressed his side, one hand still clenched on my arm.

"You will burn like him!" he cursed, blood seeping through his fingers.

Without thinking, I grabbed the pearl. No greenish flames engulfed me.

The Prince kept cursing and calling for help, but his voice and his hold on me were weakening. As I burst free, the pearl detached from its receptacle.

Once outside I turned, expecting to see my dress soaked in blood.

It was intact. Not a single spot.

"Evil can't hurt you," a feminine voice whispered. "It feeds on ambition, cruelty, neglect. Take the pearl, hide it. Alone, it is innocent. When you can, cast it in the sea it should never have left."

I looked into the pearl and saw inside a pale woman with a kind smile.

"Go, my child. I will protect you."

Pigeons scattered from the Signoria Piazza in a rain of huroo and droppings as I ran out.

The little birds had brains enough to recognize evil. While the humans, even the archbishop, only wanted this power at their beck and call! The pearl was smooth and cold against my palm, as pristine as when it had been plucked from an oyster.

Fingers closed around my sleeve.

"Here you are, cara!"

My father pulled me aside.

"Where were you? I got the safe conduct, but then Signor Machiavelli had to leave in a hurry...and now, it's like a hen house in the palazzo."

The tower's bronze bells pealed in mad chimes.

I presumed my father had lingered in the third courtyard while I was waiting in the office, and I went on my fool chase before he came back. Behind him, red-and-black-clad guards were pouring out of the Palazzo.

Signor Machiavelli was shouting to search everyone in view, his dark robe waving about.

I closed my hand around the pearl. I could never give it back, not to another prince, the archbishop, or even to mild-mannered Signor Machiavelli.

What any ambitious condottiere would achieve with it filled me with dread. The burnt crisp body of the envoy would be joined by hundreds, thousands more as the next prince's warring schemes blossomed into poisoned fruit.

I vowed to return the magical object to the sea where it came from.

"Papa, I have to go to the painter!" I said.

He smiled.

"You're right, cara," he said. "We are paying him by the hour!"

I fled to the nearest street before the guards reached my father. I heard him protest as the eager men began searching his bags.

I rested under a portico, hands clutched on both dress and pearl. My feet hurt as if I had walked on hot coals.

A low boom rose, followed by another, as the bells of the Florence cathedral started to answer their sisters at the Palazzo. Surprised people ran to and fro, hearing the alarm, thinking another city-state was attacking.

If I had been a boy not hampered by robes, I could run faster than armed guards. As it was, they would catch up with me soon. I prayed to our Lady, asking for her protection.

My frock had no pockets. I hid the pearl in the most logical place and took to walking straight and slowly, like a proper lady.

As I emerged in the Piazza Santissima Annunziata, beggars and merchants ran every which way, scattering pigeons, overturning vegetable stands.

A faint trace of smoke still lingered when the guards caught me. The first guard did not mind as he searched my pocketless garb, while the other plunged grubby fingers in the valley where more-endowed ladies carried small items.

Wary of another encounter, I rushed to the monastery, relieved to find the silent monk opening the door for me. When I entered the little studio, the painter was blessedly absent. I took the time to arrange my clothing and hide my smoke-smelling hair under my veil.

The portrait had progressed in my absence.

The fabric of the green gown was rendered so well that I could almost caress the pleats with a finger. The shawl was completed, the background—he had taken some liberty with all that shrubbery!

At last, the portraitist came in, his grey hair in disarray. His outraged expression told me he had been searched.

"Has everyone gone mad?" he raged. "To think me a ladrone!"

He noticed me, sitting demurely on the chair.

"At least, you are here!" he said.

He fumbled with his brushes.

"Now, only your head remains, and the light will not last long."

He positioned me this way and that way.

"Now, look at me, and smile."

I managed a closed half-smile, like a prim lady being forced to be polite.

The artist sighed. Well, he hadn't witnessed horrid flames burning a man to a crisp.

"Shy, aren't you?"

Before I could answer, steps echoed on the wooden stairs leading up to the small room. An angry fist pounded on the door. I blanched, struggling to keep my position.

The master cast his brush aside. He threw the door open before the hapless man could pound on it again.

"What is going on? Can't you see I'm working!"

"We, er, the Prince, is..." the man babbled, puffing under his iron helmet.

"If the Prince wants his portrait done, he will have to wait! La signorita is first."

Then, a face I recognized appeared, its patrician features suffused with purple.

"Ah, Signor Niccolò," the artist said, "to what do I owe the pleasure of your company?"

The secretary bit his lips.

"The Prince is dead," he said.

"Long live the prince," the artist responded in a droll tone.

"A pearl of great price was stolen an hour ago from the Palazzo! We must find it!"

Whether it was for his own ambitions or those of the next Medici prince, I had no idea.

Men entered the small studio. They threw coffers and boxes open, made me get up from the chair, checked under the drapes. Rude fingers felt under my veil and, again, down my little valley.

"Your men have already searched me," the artist said. "The monks can attest to my presence at their holy office."

So that explained where why I had seen so few monks about.

"Signor, there's nothing here," one guard said.

The guards left, their rapiers scraping against the door jamb. Machiavelli followed, then turned, his intense gaze encompassing the artist and me.

"Perdone," he said.

I heard—or imagined, like a simpering girl—a sincere apology. Perhaps, Niccolò Machiavelli, intent on avoiding a bloodshed, wanted to bury the pearl far from the clutches of the archbishop or another prince.

Perhaps.

I bowed, as any well-educated woman should do. My father's hired artist closed the door behind him.

He stroked his grey beard while he drew. He worked in

silence, for which I was grateful. I was in no mood for small talk.

The pearl grated against my molars, its salty taste on my tongue. Despite the Lady's soft reassurances, I feared the pearl would blaze its way through my bowels and roll to the sea by itself, leaving only my clothes intact.

An economy my miserly mother would probably appreciate.

While the portraitist worked, I heard the crash of furniture being turned over and Machiavelli's ragged voice shouting orders. I prayed to the Lady.

Give me courage. Give me strength.

An image of a blue-green sea rose in my mind. The sea, calling the pearl.

"Your noble mother had not told me you were so shy."

My noble mother couldn't care less, I thought.

The artist's expression grew softer.

"Naah, don't worry, child!" he said.

Through the wall behind him, the clang of broken wares and muffled curses continued. Despite the things I had seen, I couldn't help finding the whole situation funny.

Here was Signor Machiavelli fuming about the disappearance of his pearl, overturning furniture one hall away, while the nice artist from Milano stood an arm's length from it!

I did my very best not to spit out the treasure, laughing inside.

"Why, Lisa!" the artist said, peering at me. "With your eyes sparkling like little stars, you have such a wonderful smile! Oh, that dimple in your left cheek, per-fecto!"

Master Leonardo made a kiss with his lips and fingers. Then he set to work, while the sun sank in a sea of clouds as red as Signor Machiavelli's complexion at that moment.

THE WALL
ANNIE REED

The morning had turned out unseasonably warm for November, even for Northern Nevada, with not even a hint of a breeze from the foothills to the west. Veteran's Day should be cloudy and cold with the possibility of rain, but the day had dawned sunny. A perfect day for Stan to spend time outside with his grandson in this quiet park just a few miles from the high rises at the center of the city, just like he had when the boy had been little.

Or it would have been if sweat wasn't already trickling down the back of Stan's neck. The small of his back beneath his golf shirt and windbreaker was damp with it. His hands were shaking and his chest felt tight like he couldn't breathe, and he wasn't anywhere near the memorial yet.

He hadn't planned on this visit to the memorial. He wasn't sure he even wanted to be here, not if being here was going to upset him this much. He didn't need to touch the smooth black granite and trace Timothy's name with his fingers to remember the man who'd meant more to him than life itself.

He'd only come because his daughter had asked if he

wanted to take Jonathan to visit the Vietnam Veterans Memorial while it was on display in the park. In her round-about way, what she was really asking him was to get the kid alone and see if he'd open up about where he'd gotten the bruises and cuts on his face and the scrapes on his knuckles.

Not that Jonathan wanted to be here either since he was currently dragging his feet getting out of Stan's car.

Stan could relate. He could always take the boy to breakfast instead, but it felt disrespectful somehow not to at least go look at the memorial now that he was here.

He sighed and tried to get a handle on his emotions. He wasn't normally such a foolish old man. Timothy would have teased him, would have reminded him that the memorial was just a hunk of stone, nothing to get upset about. Vietnam and the war and the ambush where Timothy had died were more than fifty years in the past.

Stan stretched his shoulders and tried to distract himself with mundane things, like whether he should leave his windbreaker in the car. He'd put it on that morning more out of habit than anything else. Golf shirt, wind-breaker, and khaki pants with a thin leather belt. Old man clothes. That was his uniform these days. Far removed from the uniform he'd worn for his country.

A car door slammed behind him, and he heard Jonathan scuff his way across the parking lot.

At sixteen, Stan's only grandson was already half a head taller than Stan and skinny as a rail. Not that Stan was all that tall. In his prime he'd never been more than average height, but age and gravity had stolen precious inches along with the flexibility of his spine. These days he felt small, especially standing next to Jonathan.

"Is that why we're here?" Jonathan asked as he stopped next to Stan on the concrete sidewalk encircling the park.

His head was tilted to one side, something Stan thought the boy did to keep his lanky hair off his face. Jonathan squinted and then held one hand up as if to shield his eyes from the sun as he looked toward the center of a large swath of lawn where the memorial had been installed.

The sun was at the boy's back, only a couple of hours above the eastern horizon. The unnecessary gesture was another teenage protest at having to get up and actually do something with his grandfather this early on a school holiday.

The memorial they'd come to see was a half-size replica of the Vietnam Veterans Memorial in Washington, DC. The replica was made up of black granite panels erected side by side to form two long black wings. Just like the memorial in DC, the highest point of the replica was the center. From there, the two wings stretched out at an angle from each other, each wing decreasing in height until the far ends looked like they dug into the wide expanse of lawn where the replica had been erected.

And just like the memorial in DC, the replica's black granite panels were covered with tens of thousands of names of the dead.

Stan had never been to the original wall. The Moving Wall, as this replica was called, had been created to travel from place to place so that people who couldn't go to the original memorial still had a way to honor soldiers killed in Vietnam.

The memorial looked like a slash of nothingness against all that winter-brown November grass, but it was far from nothing. No matter how much Timothy might have teased him, Stan couldn't deny the power of all the accumulated grief and loss etched into those black granite panels. It stole Stan's breath even half a football field away.

"That's it," he finally made himself say, his voice gruffer than he'd intended.

If Jonathan noticed, he didn't mention it. Most of the time he affected a don't-give-a-shit attitude, but Stan knew better. Teenage boys gave a shit about everything.

The bruise on his grandson's left cheek just below his eye had turned a mottled greenish yellow with a few spots of dark purple where rough knuckles had dug into the kid's face. The scrape on his chin and the cut across the bridge of his nose were healing nicely—he might not even have a scar. At least not one people would be able to see.

"So, what do we do?" Jonathan asked. "Just go look at it?"

If Stan could bring himself to get that close to it. He hadn't expected the memorial to affect him this way.

"That's the general idea," he said, and somehow he got his feet to start moving.

Just like he had all those decades ago.

Keep marching. Keep walking. Keep slogging through the jungle, one foot after the next, and never let yourself wonder if the next step would be your last.

The guy at the head of the patrol, a tall black kid from Michigan by the name of Jamal Watkins, took the first bullet.

The NVA ambushed them from the trees, shadows in black pajamas hiding in the deeper shadows of the jungle. One minute Jamal was grinning at something the new kid in the company had done, some misstep the kid had made because he was the FNG and didn't know any better, and the next minute blood was gushing from a round that blew through Jamal's right shoulder, taking muscle and bone with it as the jungle around the patrol erupted with the rapid fire of automatic weapons.

Timothy yanked Stan to the ground as mortar shells fell around them sending great gouts of dirt and splintered trees and shattered bodies into the air. A fallen tree gave them the barest amount of cover, but it wasn't enough. A ricochet hit Stan in the upper arm, and his entire arm went numb.

Soldiers shouted instructions to each other and screamed as they were hit. The jungle filled with smoke and gunfire and explosions, and the smell of blood and shit and piss filled the air. NVA dropped from the trees, dead and dying and merely wounded, but they just kept coming and coming.

The enemy knew the jungle, knew how to use it to their advantage. Jamal had been born in fucking Detroit, Stan in Queens. What the hell did they know about jungle warfare? Timothy had been born in Montana, but the jungles of Vietnam were nothing like the pine forests of his home.

The patrol's medic had been among the first to die. Rounds ripped a jagged line through his chest, and he was dead before he hit the ground.

The FNG picked up the medic's kit and tried to help Jamal, but Jamal bled out before the evac helicopter got to them.

Jamal with his wide smile and good heart wasn't the first of their company to die, and he wasn't the last.

Timothy had been the last.

And Stan had been holding Timothy's hand, their fingers intertwined, when the light went out of his eyes.

The park had been a working ranch back in the days when the handful of buildings clustered near the river could hardly be called a town. As the city grew and the demand for land became intense, the rancher's descendants deeded the ranch to the city on the condition that the city keep the land intact and turn it into a regional park, including a museum honoring their family's contribution to the area.

The city had kept up its end of the deal. The acres and acres of old pasture land had been planted with grass and trees and landscaped with jogging paths and flower gardens and a meditation area with Japanese maples and dogwoods and a koi pond. The ranch house had been renovated and turned into a museum dedicated to the history and accomplishments of the land's original owners. The north side of the ranch house had been expanded into a high-ceilinged exhibition space for special events.

When Jonathan had been a toddler, Stan had taken him to a dinosaur exhibit in the ranch house. Jonathan had been fascinated with the full-size animatronic T-Rex. Stan had tried to read all the informational placards in the exhibit to the boy, but like any headstrong two-year-old, Jonathan had just wanted to be picked up so he could get closer to the dinosaurs.

That visit had been the only time Stan had ventured into the museum side of the old ranch house. The first two rooms were stuffed to the gills with memorabilia from the ranch—old tack and restored furniture and guns, lots and lots of guns—dating back to the late nineteenth century. A short movie honoring the family's part in establishing the city played on a continuous loop in another small room.

Jonathan hadn't wanted to stay and watch the movie. He'd wanted to see the animals.

Dozens upon dozens of big game trophies from Africa and the Arctic and North America filled the rest of the museum. Apparently the rancher had been a big game hunter in his later years.

All the dead animals with their glass eyes only made Stan sad, especially a mountain lion mounted to a tree limb that appeared to be growing out a wall. The lion had been posed in mid-snarl, its expression fierce and menacing.

Being fierce hadn't been enough to save the lion's life. There was always someone bigger. Someone with a better weapon. Someone who didn't play by the rules or give a shit about anyone's life but their own.

Vietnam had taught him that. The war and the fallout from the war he'd lived through after he'd returned to the states had left him believing the only way to survive in the world was to blend in, so that's what he'd done for fifty years. Lived his life the way everyone expected him to. One wife, one kid, one grandson, and never a mention of Timothy or the war beyond the fact that he'd been wounded overseas.

The memorial had been set up on the lawn to the west of the ranch house. Maples and oaks, their branches winter bare, lined the edge of the lawn where it sloped down to a marshy area that was the remains of an old irrigation ditch, but no trees shaded the memorial.

Dry grass crunched beneath Stan's shoes as they made their way across the lawn to the wall. The closer they got to the memorial, the more he felt like the world was pressing down on him.

It almost felt like he was buried beneath all that black granite, weighed down by each of those thousands and thousands of names inscribed on the stone. They'd died while he'd survived. He thought he'd come to terms with his survivor's guilt years ago, but now he wasn't so sure.

More people than Stan had expected to see this early in the morning were clustered near the memorial. They stood on the lawn in front of the wall, some by themselves, some in small groups. The Vietnam war was ancient history to most people like his grandson. Stan had thought the memorial would attract only a few older men and women who, like him, had survived their time in country or who'd lost loved ones to the war. But a surprising number of middle-aged men and women, some with children younger than Jonathan, had come to pay their respects.

A few people were holding sheets of thin paper against the wall and rubbing crayons or bits of graphite over the paper to make an impression of a name etched in the granite. One young woman only slightly older than Jonathan lay sprawled on her stomach so that she could trace a name close to the ground.

Some people were crying, men and women alike, but Stan's eyes were drawn to a dry-faced man not that much younger than himself.

The man held a toddler with one arm, a blond-haired little boy of no more than two. The man had his other hand on the wall, and the toddler leaned forward to touch the wall next to the old man's gnarled hand.

The toddler's expression was as solemn as the old man's. No tears, no fussing. Just touching the wall with the flat of his hand with something approaching reverence.

Stan couldn't remember ever seeing such a mature look on such a young face.

"Holy shit," Jonathan said, his voice barely above a whisper. "Those are all names."

Over fifty thousand names, Stan didn't say.

"I thought..." Jonathan sucked in his lower lip. "From far away, they just look like lines in the rock. I thought that was pretty stupid, you know? Just a bunch of black rock with a bunch of lines. What kind of a memorial is that? Even tombstones are engraved, but this..."

He shook his head and shoved his hands in the pockets of his jeans. He was far more handsome than Stan had ever been. Stan had never understood what Timothy had seen in him.

Jonathan cleared his throat. "Are you here to see someone?"

Stan had never talked about Vietnam with Jonathan. He'd barely talked about it with his wife, much less their daughter or her husband. He'd been surprised when she'd first suggested that he take Jonathan to the memorial, but then he'd realized she had an ulterior motive.

The fight. Jonathan wouldn't tell his parents what had happened. Stan wasn't sure the boy would tell him either. But Stan's daughter had always been a bulldog with a bone once she got an idea in her head, so he'd agreed.

And now Jonathan was asking if Stan was here to see someone.

He couldn't just turn his back on Timothy and walk away, even if the only part of Timothy that was left was his name on the wall.

Was he here to see someone? "Yes," Stan said.

He was here to see the only man he'd ever loved.

Vietnam was a shock to the system. Loud and hot and steamy, locals constantly trying to sell him booze and drugs and sex. Jostling against him, shoving him and screaming obscenities at him when they thought they could get away with it, and little kids always trying to pick his pockets.

For a kid who'd grown up in Queens, it had been too much.

Even for a kid who'd screwed up his courage once and gone to Stonewall after he got his draft notice and realized that he might die without ever once being kissed like it meant something, Vietnam was too much.

Timothy rescued Stan from that chaos.

He introduced Stan to the pleasure of letting a good book take him to a quieter, better place. Before that, books had been something Stan had to read for school, and that shit was over. Timothy taught Stan chess and how thinking three moves ahead could save him on the battlefield.

"It'll keep that skinny ass of yours alive," Timothy said.

He told Stan stories about growing up in Montana with his dad and older brothers, real mountain men, he called them.

"You weren't?" Stan asked, fascinated with the idea that someone like Timothy, with his deep blue eyes and features that were almost but not quite delicate, might be a mountain man.

Timothy laughed. "I read and I play chess. Sometimes I fish, but that's it. What do you think?"

They became inseparable, the best of buddies. Timothy looked out for Stan when they went into the jungle on patrol. He taught Stan all the things boot camp hadn't, like how to spot NVA hiding places in the tall trees and how best to pack his gear for long treks through the jungle.

And somewhere along the way, Stan realized that they weren't just buddies anymore. The first tentative touches were almost inevitable. Quiet stolen moments where no one else could see.

Decades before don't ask, don't tell, they had to be so very careful. Never saying the words, never letting anyone see what they meant to each other.

Stan had never told Timothy he loved him. Not even when Timothy lay dying in a hot, stinking jungle so far away from his Montana home.

It was the biggest regret of Stan's life.

Timothy's name was on the third panel from the end on the right-hand side of the wall, in a row slightly below shoulder height. If this had been the full-size wall, the name would have been far over Stan's head.

He touched Timothy's name with the kind of gentleness that Timothy had used the first time they'd been together. He traced each letter like the mere touch could bring back the man so Stan could finally, at long last, tell Timothy what he'd felt. What he still felt.

He didn't realize that his face was wet until Jonathan spoke up behind him.

"Grandpa? Are you okay?"

Was he okay?

No, he was far, far from okay, but he had to say something.

"I think you would have liked him." Stan glanced at Jonathan. "He would have liked you."

Jonathan had his hands stuffed in the pockets of his jeans. His don't-give-a-shit expression was long gone.

"He saved my life, you know," Stan said, turning his attention back to the wall. "More than once, but that last time…he got me on the ground, got us both behind cover when all hell broke loose. Saved my fucking life."

Mortars and automatic gunfire and the smell of blood and dirt and jungle rot choking the air, Stan's arm on fire as blood soaked his uniform sleeve. Timothy told him to stay down, just stay the fuck down, but he didn't take his own advice. The radioman had taken a hit, his leg half blown off, his guts shredded by shrapnel.

"I have to call it in," Timothy told Stan. "Call in the evac or we're all going to die out here. You understand?"

"Let me go," Stan said. "You stay here. I'll go."

He tried to get up, but Timothy pushed him back to the ground. "You can't call in the coordinates, you don't know how."

Stan saw the truth of it in Timothy's eyes, and they shared the kind of look men shared when they know their tomorrows aren't guaranteed.

"Just don't die," Stan said.

"Never," Timothy said.

But he had.

He reached the radio, still strapped to the dying radioman's back, and called in their coordinates. Called in a strike and an evac while blood ran down his back from wounds he might have survived if not for the last bullet that blew through his thigh.

Stan saw Timothy go down. By the time he crawled to where Timothy lay, the ground beneath Timothy was soaked with bright, arterial blood.

Stan tried to stop the bleeding, but it was too late. Timothy reached out to Stan with one weak hand, and Stan held it, their bloody fingers threaded together, until long past the time Timothy was gone.

Standing in front of the wall, Stan told his grandson every last detail that he could remember of that firefight. He owed Timothy that much. "That evac saved the rest of us," he said.

Jonathan didn't say anything for the longest time, but something was going on behind his eyes.

Had Stan said too much? He didn't know.

"He wasn't just another soldier, was he?" Jonathan finally asked.

Stan heaved a deep sigh, his heart beating heavily in his chest. He turned back to the wall and touched Timothy's name. He wasn't about to deny what they'd been to each other. Not here. Not now.

"No," he said. "He wasn't."

The dry grass rustled as Jonathan shifted behind him. The quiet murmur of the other visitors to the memorial blended with the sound of traffic passing by the park a half mile away, but Jonathan said nothing.

The silence between them grew uncomfortably long, but Stan didn't want to break it. Jonathan needed to come to terms with something he'd probably never imagined about his grandfather. If he was anything at all like Stan had been when he'd been sixteen, Jonathan probably didn't like to think about his parents, much less his grandfather, ever having sex.

"You loved him," Jonathan finally said. It wasn't a question.

Stan couldn't deny that either. "Yes," he said. "I never

told him, but I think he knew." He hoped Timothy had known.

"Is that...was he the only...?"

There'd been kissing at Stonewall, groping in the back room and sweet release at the hands of a stranger twice his age, but that hadn't been love.

"Yes," Stan said.

Timothy's name was so small on this wall. All the names of the dead were, but to Stan, Timothy had always been so much larger than life. It didn't seem right that his name was so small.

Jonathan stepped closer to the wall until he stood next to Stan. He touched the wall, his fingers not quite on Timothy's name. The scabs on his knuckles stood out against his pale skin.

"Did Grandma know?" he asked.

Stan started to shrug and made himself stop. "I left that part of my life behind in Vietnam. Walled it up, told myself it was over. If she knew, she never said. She never asked, and I never told her."

His own version of don't ask, don't tell.

Somewhere in the distance, a dog started barking, high angry yipping barks, and more dogs took up the cry. A slight breeze had just started. It lifted the lank hair that had flopped over Jonathan's forehead.

"Why did you bring me?" Jonathan finally asked.

"It was your mother's idea," Stan said. "She was hoping you'd tell me what happened."

Jonathan had come home late from school a few days ago, his cheek already swelling and threatening to turn into a black eye. He'd flat out refused to tell his parents what had started the fight or even who had been involved.

"It was just a stupid fight." A deep frown creased the boy's forehead, and he sighed. "I don't like bullies."

Stan nodded toward the wall. "He didn't either," he said. "He enlisted, can you believe that? We were being drafted left and right back then, and he enlisted."

Jonathan turned his head to look at Stan. There was no disgust in his eyes, no judgment. "Tell me about him," Jonathan said. "Not the soldier stuff. Tell me who he was."

So Stan did.

As the sun rose higher in the clear November sky, Stan told his grandson all that he could remember about the man he'd loved. The words spilled out of him as more and more memories rose to the surface.

He told Jonathan about how Timothy had grown up with his brothers in Montana. How he'd loved to fish. His brothers loved to hunt but putting worms on the hook always made them squeamish, so whenever their dad took the boys fishing, they always made Timothy do it.

About how his brothers played football, but Timothy went out for track. He'd won medals at district matches, and he wore his letterman jacket with as much pride as his brothers had worn theirs.

About how Timothy never kept his preferences a secret from his family, but he'd kept them hidden from the Army, pretending an interest in women that he didn't feel so that he wouldn't be dishonorably discharged.

"Do you think..." Jonathan paused, clearly trying to figure out how to say what he wanted to ask. "If he had survived, do you think you'd have stayed together?"

That wasn't a question Stan had expected. When he'd been in Vietnam, when their love had been new, Stan had dreamed of a life together after the war, a life where they wouldn't have to hide and lie. A life where they could be themselves. Even then, he'd known it was only a dream, but the dream had kept him going, right up until the day Timothy died.

Stan had been so lost after that, it was a wonder he'd survived. The only reason he hadn't walked in front of an NVA bullet was the knowledge that Timothy had given his life so that Stan could live.

"I don't know," he said. "It was a different time back then. Men like Timothy—men like we both were..." He paused, realizing that was the first time he'd actually said something like that out loud. "Times were tough back then."

"It's not all that different."

There was a dark current of anger in Jonathan's voice. Stan wondered if that was what the fight had really been about, but he wasn't going to ask.

Jonathan would talk about the fight when he was ready. And if he never was? The boy was growing into a man, and men kept secrets. Stan's daughter would have to learn to live with that.

More people were in the park now, filling up the space in front of the black granite panels. A middle-aged woman carrying a white rose crossed behind Stan and Jonathan. When Stan glanced at her, she nodded at him.

"Thank you for your service," she said.

Jonathan frowned after her. "How did she know?" he asked after she stopped before a low panel two away from where they stood.

Stan had no idea. Maybe it was simply because he was the right age range.

While he appreciated that people felt a need to thank soldiers for their service, the men and women who'd died in Vietnam had been so much more than soldiers. Jonathan had asked him about who Timothy had been as a man. Who he might have been if he'd survived. It had been the kindest thing Stan's grandson had ever done for him.

Timothy would always be so much more than a name on a wall. Stan didn't need to stay here any longer. He'd paid his respects to Timothy, and the grief he'd felt when he'd first come to the park had lifted. He could breathe again.

Stan took a step away from the wall. "How about I buy you breakfast?" he asked his grandson.

Jonathan raised an eyebrow. "You're ready to go?"

Yeah, he was. Timothy had lived on in Stan's memory. Now he'd keep living on in Jonathan's.

"I thought I'd tell you a few more stories," Stan said. "Unless you're all listened out."

For the first time that morning, Jonathan smiled. It was the kind of indulgent smile parents give small children, but Stan would take it.

"No, I'm good to go, Grandpa," Jonathan said.

As they walked across the lawn toward the parking lot, a breeze kicked up from the foothills to the west. The breeze brought a chill with it that felt more like November, and for the first time Stan was glad he'd dressed in his old man's uniform, right down to the windbreaker.

Timothy would have made fun of him if he'd seen Stan in this getup. He might have called himself a mountain man, but Timothy liked fine clothes, and he had a wicked sense of humor.

"Remind me to tell you about the time Timothy put together costumes for his brothers for the school play," Stan said.

The football players had appeared on stage in drag— that time-honored tradition of football players dressing as cheerleaders. According to Timothy, his brothers had been the best dressed cheerleaders in the whole world, thanks to a little judicious altering of their costumes.

Jonathan chuckled. "I can just imagine." Then he scrunched up his nose. "Does Mom know?" he asked. "I don't want to screw up and say something if she doesn't."

No, she didn't, but did Stan want to keep hiding this part of his life from her?

"Let me talk to her when we get back to your house," he said. "I don't want you to have to keep my secret."

He didn't want anyone to have to keep his secret. Vietnam was half a lifetime ago, and it was long past time to let this secret go.

He owed it to himself.

Most of all, he owed it to the man whose name was engraved on the wall.

UNTRUSTWORTHY

ROBERT JESCHONEK

One minute, I'm standing in a frozen ballroom, shivering as a giant spider-thing made of ice—a creature with the face of a little girl—skitters toward me. The spider screams and breathes fire from its lips, charging so fast there's no way I can outrun it.

The next minute, I'm back in the bathroom of a boarded-up roadhouse in the middle of a hot summer's night in rural Louisiana, flicking a little black spider off my right hand.

Bending over the filthy sink, I splash cold water on my face, trying to snap myself all the way back to reality (whatever *that* is, these days). Then I make the mistake of looking at myself in the cracked mirror, and I cringe. Even in the dim moonglow streaming between the rickety wall boards, I look awful.

Without makeup, without sleep, the creases in my dark brown face seem deeper than ever. My dark eyes are blood-shot, double bags sagging under them with the weight of worry and exhaustion. My salt-and-pepper hair, hastily hacked short on the road, is coming in frizzy and wild. It's hard to believe I was considered quite attractive all the way through my thirties.

Now I'm a haggard fugitive in my mid-forties who looks like hell warmed over.

That's what thirty-two days on the road, on the run, will do for you. That and a lifetime spent carrying other people's darkest secrets in my head.

I'm a specialist—what they call a *Secretive*. Paperwork can be stolen, computers can be hacked, but a properly trained human mind with photographic tendencies can store secrets in perfect security. God help you if the system breaks down, though; then you've got two choices: get killed or go on the run. *Then* get killed.

I've chosen option two. The fact is, there's someone I badly want to see before I get to the *killed* part.

I brush my teeth with soap residue from the ancient bulb dispenser and my index finger, then straighten my T-shirt as best I can. I'm glad it's black, so the blood spatter doesn't show up so much. My blue jeans are another story, but those are the breaks.

I have to keep moving. I needed five minutes to get my shit together here after the fight in the parking lot, but I can't afford to piss around any longer. Gotta get to where I'm going before *they* kill me...where I'm going and who I'm going to see there.

"Come on, Ashanti Virago." I take a deep breath and let it out slowly, gathering my strength. Gotta face it, gotta get out there, can't be a coward.

I flick the hook latch and turn the doorknob. Ease open the bathroom door and step outside like I own the world.

Then I walk across the parking lot, stepping over and around the bodies as if they were nothing but dog turds or speed bumps. One, two, three, five.

Six. Every last one of them beaten into unconsciousness by my hands or feet or both.

Make that seven. One last body's on the hood of my stolen silver Honda Accord. He flops off easily enough when I back up suddenly, though.

Then I bolt off into the night, leaving all those bodies like anonymous humps in the moonlit shadows of the Spanish moss–laden trees.

Half an hour up the road, my breath turns to chilly mist, and I feel myself going away again. I barely have time to jerk the car off the road and throw it out of gear before I'm gone.

This time, I'm back in that vast, icy ballroom, feeling the freeze right through to my bones—though my shivers aren't just from the cold.

As many times as I've been to this Memory Mansion of mine, I'm still not sure what to expect next. Will it be a giant spider with a little girl's face, or something else?

I have no idea, and I'm the one who *built* this place.

"Hello?" My voice echoes in the huge chamber, but no one answers. I walk in a slow circle, gazing at the glittering ice pillars and chandeliers.

This was always my special hideaway, the core of my talent...the key to the secrets I kept.

I was a Secretive in title and practice alike, brought in to store clients' greatest secrets—the code to a vault, a password to a Swiss bank account, the location of a dead body —and keep them safe from those who covet them. I also had to make them available to their owners at a moment's notice, which is where the Memory Mansion comes in.

It was here, as required by my employer, that I constructed mnemonic devices pointing the way to each memory, giving me easy access to the voluminous library of secrets in my head. Need to recall the hiding place of some stock certificates? I just find the ice sculpture of a ticker tape machine, give it a tap, and the answer blazes into my mind like the morning sun.

At least that was how it worked before the Alzheimer's disease started. Now my mansion isn't predictable at all.

And I've never needed it more in my *life* than I do now. I've never needed to *find* someone more than I do now. At least the secrets to lead me to her, gathered during my time on the run, are still in there—though the mnemonic constructs to access them are no longer easy to control. My subconscious seems to bring them up when I need them, but I can't get all the information I need with a simple tap.

Even as I think that, a giant cobra grows out of the icy floor before me. It flickers its crystalline tongue as its head bobs from side to side, staring.

Hsssssssss.

The creature does *not* look friendly, but I need to try anyway. "Where is Serendipity Virago?"

Hssssssss.

Just as the cobra lunges, I dart out of the way. As I sprint, I hear it slithering after me, its massive body rustling over the ice rink floor.

I'm almost to the grand staircase when something else thrusts up from the ice in front of me. This time, it's an alligator, its long, jagged maw opening wide as I slide straight for it, unable to stop.

That's when I see the same little girl's face in the gator's crystalline throat, glaring at me. She opens her mouth, too, and I see it's lined with teeth like a shark's, jutting in concentric rings.

I'm just about to plunge inside when I snap back to the real world. The Memory Mansion is gone; I'm sitting in the front seat of the Honda again, safe and sound.

I wipe the drool from my chin with the back of my hand, then grab the paper map on the seat beside me. I unfold it to the index on the back and scan the list of towns and cities.

Cobra. Gator.

When I see a name that fits the latest clues in my Memory Mansion, my hands start to shake. I find the matching location on the map, trace the route, and pull back onto the road. Then I stomp on the gas.

Somewhere out there in the darkness of the bayou, the town of Cobra's Gate awaits.

"Mother, you're fired."

This is what it's like to develop Alzheimer's after a lifetime of having a flawless photographic memory and working as a Secretive. One day, you're sitting at a café on the Isle of Capri in Italy, enjoying an espresso...

...and your son, Marcus, sits down across from you and tells you you're a dead woman.

Actually, he says you're "fired," and he's not your *biological* son—but things are a little different in Sub Rosa, the international organization I work for. *Used* to work for.

"You made The Mistake." Marcus shook his head sadly as he said it. The bright Italian sun glinted on his dark brown skin. "The dead client's wife wanted the combination to his wine cellar, and you got it wrong. Entering the wrong code tripped the security override and flash-fried millions of Euros worth of vintage wines in seconds."

What kind of employer kills you if you make a single mistake? Especially if that mistake comes after a lifetime of sterling service as an *elite* Secretive, one of the *best* in the world?

Sub Rosa, that's who. The same lovely group that strips you of any biological children you might have when they discover your potential, sending them away to limit distractions from your work...then eventually assigns other "children" (in their twenties) for you to mentor. Marcus falls in that category.

"Thanks for everything, Mother, I really—"

I didn't let him finish his sentence that day. It was clear what would happen if I didn't take immediate action.

Leaping up, I drove the table at his chin, stunning him, knocking him backward. Then I scooped up a butter knife and drove it into his rib cage with practiced ease, hitting just the right spot to disable but not kill him. I might have forgotten a few things lately, but I damn well remembered my martial arts training well enough to do the job.

Marcus howled in pain. Blood seeping from his wound, he tried to fight back, but I wouldn't give him an inch.

"Stop!" he shouted. "They'll just send someone else!"

Teeth clenched, running on instinct, I twisted the blade.

"You can't hide! You have no secrets from them!"

One more twist of the blade in his bloody chest, and I let go. "That's where you're wrong. I have a *few* secrets."

Marcus's eyes glazed over. Was he in Audit mode or just going into shock? "A few secrets? I don't know...don't remember..."

"But only one of them truly matters." I spat on my "son" and jumped up. The *polizia* would be there any minute, and Sub Rosa would not be far behind. "One secret is all *anyone* needs in this life."

The sun rises as I roll into the town of Cobra's Gate. Everything looks quiet and still, but I know it won't last. In situations like this, Sub Rosa pools its Secretives to track the runner; you might be surprised how easy your movements are to predict based on the secrets from multiple sources intersecting with your life.

In other words, the name of the game here is get-in-and-get-out-*fast*.

You might not think that would be a problem. After all, Cobra's Gate is a tiny town. But the person I'm looking for —the one who'll lead me to my final target—doesn't *want* to be found, at least not by Sub Rosa's death squads.

As I drive down the main road through town, I watch the trailers and shacks for some kind of telltale marking or sign. It's a challenge. Escapees like her don't usually put out a red-and-white-striped barber pole to show you where they are.

But that's good, right? Because when you finally find her, you'll know she's the real deal and hasn't been compromised. You *hope*.

Suddenly, a skunk waddles onto the road, and I slam on the brakes. As I watch and smell it pass, I close my eyes, triggering a visit to the Memory Mansion the way I used to do before the involuntary zoning-out started.

I breathe in hot, humid air and breathe out icy mist. Just like that, I'm back in the frozen ballroom.

Before some hostile beast can rise up from the ice and attack, I focus my thoughts on harnessing the power of this place. I feel it resisting, pushing back as I fight to sink my fingers into it and make it work to my liking.

Just then, I hear a muffled growl and see the ice ripple a few feet away. Might be a clue in the form of a raging monstrosity...or might not.

But that's not a game I want to play right now. Pouring on the juice, I exert my will with all the strength I can muster.

And the growling stops. Instead of a creature, the floor extrudes a cube of ice as tall as I am.

When I touch the cube, its outer layers melt away, revealing a shape like a sculpture within a slab of marble. A ray of light streams in from one of the high windows, making the object glitter and gleam. I take a good look at it.

Then I pour on the willpower again and manage to snap myself back to reality on the road, with no sign of the skunk in sight (though the stench of it lingers).

I let out my breath and relax my tight grip on the wheel. For once, the Memory Mansion worked the way it was supposed to; I recognized the object in my vision, and it opened a secret like an oyster in my mind when I touched it.

The object was a *tire*. A tire with a big smiley face on the tread.

Jo's Tires doesn't look like much. It's just a rusty corrugated metal building with three garage bays and tires piled every-where. If you saw it along the road on your way some-where, you'd forget it as soon as you passed and never think of it again.

Unless you were me. Unless you knew it was part of an

underground railroad for Secretives whose time is about to run out.

"Hello?" I get out of my car and walk toward one of the bays. "Is anyone here?"

No answer, though I see a light glowing dimly in a corner of the garage.

Carefully, I continue forward. "I'm a Secretive, and I understand you might be able to help me."

Looking over my shoulder, I worry that Sub Rosa will appear at any moment. I hate to think they'll ruin this place for others who need it, though I guess that's why it's—

Suddenly, I hear running footsteps and turn to see the source. Before I can get a good look, the woman in grey coveralls sprinting toward me takes a swing at my skull with a tire iron.

I duck back away from the swing and leap into action, unleashing a vicious kick at my attacker. The kick catches her in the gut, knocking the wind out of her, and I follow it with a jab to her throat.

She reels, nearly dropping the tire iron...but it's a feint, and she comes up swinging. This time, the iron makes contact, clipping my left side hard enough to launch a bloom of pain there.

Pissed, I erupt in a flurry of moves—spinning, kicking, lunging, punching, hacking. They're some of the same moves I used to knock out seven men at the boarded-up roadhouse last night...but they don't work as well this time. The coveralled woman loses her weapon and reacts with rapid-fire moves of her own—a punishing series of blows and kicks that land more often than not.

I probe for a weakness but don't find any. She deflects everything I throw her way and responds with double the force at double the speed.

Finally, I put together a combination that has an impact, hammering her with a barrage of strikes to the upper body that are mostly just feints before a whirlwind kick to her left leg.

She goes down on that knee, and I take her the rest of the way with a single rabbit punch to the chin. Unfortunately, she takes me down with her, latching onto my sleeve and yanking me off my feet.

Next thing I know, we're on the gravel, four feet apart with blood on our faces. It's only then that I get a good look at her—pale skin, round face, green eyes, black hair in a ponytail with a sprinkling of grey. My guess is she's Japanese or Korean, though I'm not sure.

And she's grinning.

"Good fight," she says. "Now what's the good *word*, hon?"

She wants the password that proves I'm with the underground, and I don't blame her. I think hard; a rebel Secretive gave it to me early in my journey. I locked it away in my mind...but it eludes me now, when I need it the most.

It's in there somewhere, though, I *know* it. I think back to the Memory Mansion three visits ago, and the thing that ran me down in the icy ballroom. The thought of that creature has a gravity that attracts me.

I almost say "spider" but then I catch myself. Not "tarantula," either. Something that *sounds* like it.

"Tarantella," I tell her.

"Good to meet you." She gets up on her elbow and reaches over to shake hands. "There's always help here for condemned Secretives."

"Thank you." I push myself up to a sitting position. "I'm looking for someone."

"Who's that?" asks the woman.

"My daughter," I tell her. "My baby girl."

"When was the last time you saw her?"

I wipe blood from my face with the back of my arm. "Twenty-three years ago. And God help me, I can barely remember her."

The woman, whose name is Maginot, offers me tea in a chipped white cup. Sitting on a dirty stool in one of the bays, I sip the steaming brew, relishing the hot liquid as it slides down my throat.

"How long you been on the run, Ashanti?" Maginot produces a flask and offers it to me.

I can't afford the slightest buzz to dull my senses, so I wave it off. "Thirty-three days now. All the way from Capri, Italy."

"On your own?" Maginot looks impressed. "That might be a record, hon." She sips from the flask. "So how did you find out about me?"

I scowl at the ripples in my tea. "Followed the trail through my Memory Mansion...one secret linked to another."

Maginot leans against an oil-soaked workbench, tilts her head to one side, and stares. "But where did you *first* learn about me? And the railroad?"

"Someone told me on my travels, but I don't remember who." I point at my right temple and shrug. "My memory's failing."

Maginot nods. "But not your *fighting* skills, obviously." Another swig from the flask, and she returns it to the pocket of her coveralls. "And now you want to *kill* your *child*, is that right?"

My hands clench around the cup, nearly breaking it. "I want to *find* her!"

"Same difference," says Maginot. "You know Sub Rosa's closing in, don't you? They *always* find runaways. What do you think they'll do to *her* when they catch up?"

My heart thunders in my ears as I glare at the thought of it. "I'll kill every one of them who tries."

Maginot shakes her head and pushes away from the workbench. Grabbing a tire from a rustbucket Chevy on the lift, she throws it on a balancing rack and sets to work on it.

"This is the part where I talk sense into you," she says. "How old was your child when they took her away?"

"Three years." It's a guess. As often as I see her face in my Memory Mansion, I don't always remember much else about her.

"Assuming she's still alive..." Maginot pauses and shoots me a meaningful look. "Assuming that, she is *twenty-six years old* now. She might not even *remember* you." Again, she pauses. "So ask yourself, what do you hope to accomplish by showing up in her life all of a sudden?"

"I just..." My heart's racing. "I just want to *see* her before I...before they..."

"But is that *fair* to her? Is it any more fair than them taking her away from you in the first place?"

I get up from the stool and put the teacup down in my place. Something bends inside me, straining to give way— then straightens and stiffens again. "Are you going to help me or not?"

Maginot turns on the spin-balancer and lets it run for a moment. When numbers appear on the digital readout screen, she switches it off. "No one can truly *help* you," she says sadly. "But yes, I will do what I can to see that you reach your goal."

Relief floods through me. "Oh, thank God." My next step, I'm ashamed to say, might have been to torture her for the answers I require. "How can I ever thank you enough?"

"Shhhhh." She holds a finger to her lips. "It will be our secret, Ashanti."

Just as Sub Rosa uses its network of Secretives to pool their secret knowledge and track down who or what they desire, Maginot relies on a network of *ex*-Secretives. She communicates with them via secure mobile apps, tapping their collective insight in search of revelatory fractal patterns.

It's a miraculous system, and it gets results fast. Within an hour, we're in her black extended-cab pickup headed northwest, racing toward the city of Shreveport.

I'm so full of anticipation, I'm ready to burst. "Tell me about her. What's she like these days?"

Maginot's face is aloof behind her aviator sunglasses. She steers the truck with two fingers at the bottom of the wheel, texting constantly with her free hand between us. She texts so much and so energetically, I wonder how she even keeps control of the pickup. "What did you name her back in the day?"

It's on the tip of my tongue. "Why? What's her name now?"

"Married name is Delacroix."

My eyes light up. "Married? Do I have grandkids?"

Her phone warbles then, and she spots a fresh text on the screen. "Not sure yet." Then, she looks up at the rearview mirror and drops three consecutive F-bombs with a vengeance.

"What is it?"

"Hold on." She throws the pickup into higher gear. "We've got a tail."

Looking back, I see a white BMW SUV hurtling toward us, gleaming in the afternoon sun. I feel the pickup swerve and accelerate, bolting away from our pursuers.

Then my breath turns to mist, and I'm standing in the Memory Mansion again.

"No!" There's no reason for me to be here now. I focus hard, trying to regain control and jump back to the car chase.

But the icy floor just ripples and gives rise to an unexpected form. This time, it's not a giant spider, cobra, gator, or even a smiley-faced tire.

It's a *little girl*. More than that, it's *my* little girl. The one whose face inhabits so many of the constructs in this icy place.

When she speaks, her high-pitched voice echoes through the cavernous ballroom, pronouncing two words with absolute clarity:

Don't stop.

Then *whoosh*, I'm back in the cabin of Maginot's pickup, and the back window's blown out, and she's shooting over her shoulder.

The BMW behind us suddenly veers left and crashes into a speeding tractor trailer that blasts it into bits.

Maginot looks over at me. "You can't control it anymore, can you? The Memory Mansion?"

I don't answer the question. "How much farther?"

"Not far." Maginot grabs her phone and thumb-types a text like a lunatic. "But we've got another tail. We should probably abort."

I glance back. "But we're so *close*."

"I thought you'd say that." Again, Maginot rattles off a text. "That's why I've arranged for some people to meet us."

"People?"

"A few friends, that's all." Maginot stomps on the accelerator, and the pickup surges forward. "*Dependable* friends."

As much as my memory's been failing, I still get flashes of the old days now and then. I remember holding my baby sometimes, and the smell of her head. I remember changing her diaper and feeding her from a bottle. I remember her crying, and me crying too, being a single mother with no one to help me.

Sometimes, I even remember the day they came for me and took her. I remember fighting and being beaten. The last time I saw her howling face as they dragged her away.

Sometimes, it feels so real that I can't help screaming. The pain is so fresh, it's like they stole her only yesterday.

And sometimes, it seems so long ago, and the memories are so incomplete, it's as if it never happened at all. As if the Alzheimer's is taking even *that* from me.

The certainty of my own remembered pain.

Thank God no one's walking or riding a bike on the street when we barrel into the trailer park outside Shreveport. Pretty sure Maginot would mow them down, she's driving so fast.

Not that slowing down is a good option. The sooner we

get to my daughter (and grandkids?), the better chance we stand of keeping them safe from Sub Rosa.

"Which trailer is it?" I gape at each one as we fly past, as if I might recognize the daughter I haven't seen since the age of three.

"Dead ahead." Somehow, Maginot's still calm and collected, driving with the same two fingers and texting nonstop. "Good news. My gals are here already. They're all ex-Secretives I've helped in the past, so you know they've got no love for Sub Rosa."

She slams on the brakes and spins to a stop in front of a dumpy trailer with dirty white siding and decaying black trim. Another pickup and two cars are already parked in front of it, angled like barricades.

I'm out before Maginot and looking around frantically. I see six women hunkered behind the cars, all carrying assault rifles, but no twenty-six-year-old African American woman who used to go by the birth name...the birth name...

It rushes back to me, and I shout it at the trailer. "*Serendipity!* Are you in there, Serendipity?"

"Ready, people!" Maginot might carry only a tire iron, but she acts like she's in charge of the gun-toting crew. "Let's give those bastards a welcome *they'll* never forget!"

"Serendipity!" Even as my allies prepare for battle, I run to the side door of the trailer, determined to rescue my flesh and blood. "Come on out, baby!"

I try the handle of the door, but it doesn't budge. "Open up, honey!" I pound my fist on the weathered panel. "It's Mama! Open the door!"

Just then, I hear one of the defenders shout a question. "Where the hell *are* they? I thought they were right behind you!"

"I don't know," says Maginot. "They *were* close behind."

Suddenly, the door handle moves, and the door swings inward. It takes me by surprise, and I let go, tumbling back into the stubby, unkempt yard.

That's when someone finally emerges from the trailer —but not whom I expect. I see no twenty-something black woman or beautiful grandchildren running out of there.

Instead, men in gleaming black helmets and body armor storm out of the place brandishing fully automatic rifles. They bolt down the single step from the threshold, coming up behind Maginot and her defenders, who are all looking the other way, expecting oncoming vehicles full of armed Sub Rosa killers.

It's like a shooting gallery. Before any of those women can turn and even think about getting off a shot, the armored men open fire on them. Rifles chatter, staccato bursts crackling with measured force—and the bodies of six women drop as one.

At that exact moment, against my wishes and will, my breath turns to mist in the midday Shreveport heat. The Memory Mansion takes hold again, snapping me back to the ballroom of icy desolation.

And I am faced with the ice sculpture figure of my daughter once more.

"Serendipity?" I shake my head hard, but it's full of fuzz. "I can't...I have to get back. My friends, they're...oh my God, they're..."

Bring it on in, Mommy. The ice child spreads her arms wide and waggles her fingers, inviting a hug. *Bring it on in right here.*

The thought of embracing that icy form makes me shiver...but she sounds just like my daughter. Her voice is exactly the same.

I think. Frowning, I reach deep for the memory of it, but it slips away like a fish wriggling through a murky pool.

I'm right here for you, Mommy. The ice girl glides toward me, arms still spread wide open. *I love you with all my heart and soul.*

"What's *happening?*" Panic gathers and churns in my belly. Something, *everything's* wrong, and I've known all along but only now am I able to glimpse the actual truth of it. Only now am I aware of the vaguest outline of the single most important secret that's been lurking within me all this time.

Thank you, Mommy! Serendipity continues her graceful approach. *Thank you for finding me again!*

"Again?"

Suddenly, I'm back on the ground at the trailer park, sobbing as I stare at the bloody corpses of Maginot and her friends.

Two men are talking. The barrels of their rifles dangle on either side of me.

"...the tenth cell of traitors she's rooted out so far," says the man on my right. "We ought to have a party for her or something. A cake at least."

"Why bother?" The man on my left laughs. "She'd only *forget* it in the morning!"

The man on my right chuckles, too. "That leaky memory of hers is a real *gift*, isn't it? *Ten* times she's run off in search of her kid, and it always ends up like *this*, and she *forgets* it ever happened."

"Which she blames on her 'Alzheimer's,'" says the man on my left. "As diagnosed by a doctor working for Sub Rosa, of course."

"It's a genius setup." The man on my right snaps his fingers. "Ashanti here doesn't remember shit, except she wants her little girl back. All it takes is Sub Rosa nudging her in the right direction here and there, exposing her to the right suspected Secretive subversives, and she picks up the right clues to lead us to the underground's cells and safehouses."

"Friggin' brilliant, if you ask me." The man on my left crouches beside me, smiling. "That brain damage from the accident really paid off, didn't it?"

I can't stop sobbing as I listen, and then my breath turns to frost again. This time, back in the mansion, the ice child is only inches away, smiling.

Will you always save me, Mommy? Serendipity stares up at me with ice crystal eyes. *Will you always protect your baby girl?*

"What accident?" I back away from her. *"Tell me what accident!"*

Mommy? Mommy, don't go!

Then I'm back in the steaming heat with the armored man smiling at me.

"That first time, you almost pulled it off, didn't you?" he says. "It was *your* idea back then, going AWOL to rescue your kid, and you went for it. Found a guide through the web of secrets...got her to lead you to your kid in a Sub Rosa lockhouse...broke her out and ran for the hills."

I gape at him like he's speaking a language I don't understand. My mouth hangs open, pregnant with screams, but nothing comes out of it.

"Too bad you flipped the getaway car when they ran you down. But hey, things have a way of working out."

The man on my right crouches, too, and reaches over to pat my shoulder. "Your kid died, but at least the brain damage led to a second career."

Finally, the screams break free. I feel myself falling into endless clouds of frigid mist.

Only to be caught by my baby in the mansion.

Mama, she says. *I've got you. Don't worry, Mama.*

Her arms are cold around me. My tears freeze as they fall, pattering to the floor as tiny ice cubes.

At least we still have each other, Mama, she says. *Isn't that enough for you?*

I look at her crystalline face, glittering in the sunlight streaming in through the icy walls. I find a memory of her, the real her, a teenager then, sitting beside me in the car as we ran away, holding my hand tight. Blood pumping. Just before.

Just before.

We were almost free, almost safe. I remember feeling something I haven't felt since...or have I? Would I even remember what it felt like if I felt it again?

Then I wrap my arms around her and hold her tight. My skin sticks to the ice of her body, it's so cold.

"It's enough." What was her name again? "It *has* to be enough."

Then I remember, as the two of us turn slowly on the rink of the floor, propelled in little circles by the force of our hug. I remember what that feeling was, because I feel it again. It turns out it's not such a big secret after all.

Happiness. That's what it was.

THE AGINCOURT SAINT

C.H. HUNG

Holy mother of God. It hurt like hell, but Nicholas Cordonnier was finally bleeding to death.

He could barely breathe, smashed as he was between the oppressive weight of a steel-armored knight sprawled atop him and the thick, hoof-churned mud of the dying battlefield beneath his back. But maybe that was a good thing. That unique mélange of the soldier's life assaulted him with every breath—the stench of blood and entrails, of rain-drenched muck and rusting metal, of road-worn leather and unwashed, sweaty men. A jumble of bodies, the dead and almost dead, piled around him in uncaring chaos.

A few voices moaned piteous prayers or pleas. All French. All men that Nicholas had eaten with and slept with and marched with and, in the quietest hour of the darkest night, fed from. And through them all threaded varying heartbeats, loud and soft, slow and fast, hammering against Nicholas, reminding him that he hadn't fed properly in far too long.

He couldn't move his arm to clutch the brass medallion

hanging from a strip of worn leather around his neck, but he prayed anyway. He prayed that this would be the last time he'd bleed, that he could lie down to rest for all eternity after spending the last half-century in sin. Today had been a good day, one devoted to a good cause and a good man. He would be glad to die this day.

The nicked artery in his leg pulsed. Another few minutes, and it would all be over. Not even the unholy disease in his blood could bring him back from this, thank God.

"Allez," the knight slurred. "Remuez-vous et foncez à l'attaque..."

The voice roused Nicholas from his euphoria. He knew that voice. He had followed that voice here to this hellhole.

Nicholas pushed against the steel weight pinning him down. "Marshal," he gasped on a shallow breath. "Are you all right?"

"Who is this?" The steel moved, well-oiled leather hinges making no sound as its owner shifted. Nicholas winced against the extra pressure to his groin. "Le cordonnier?" the marshal Boucicaut asked, his gruff baritone sounding clearer and more incredulous with every syllable.

"Oui, marshal."

The marshal of France, Jean le Maingre—more commonly called Boucicaut—groaned and heaved himself up. Bodies tumbled. A stray hand from an unknown corpse smacked Nicholas in the teeth as it fell over, leaving behind the taste of death and dirt and dried blood, and then suddenly, he was squinting up into the late afternoon sky, wispy with clouds and fringed with the edges of a beech and ash forest. For a moment, Nicholas was a child again, racing through those same trees with the carefree freedom of innocence and promise. Then a dying man's moan shattered the past and he blinked the sticky mud from his eyes.

The mud he'd slathered all over his skin protected him from the sun's rays and camouflaged him when he'd fallen. Broad golden and rust leaves hemmed them in on the east and west, forming a channel into which the English had rained arrows down upon them earlier, like sheep being herded into a pen. And like stampeding sheep, the French army had churned the once-beautiful fields of Agincourt into slick, impassable mud as they fell in droves, outmatched by the archers' miraculous range. If his mistress knew what had happened here...

Fear stabbed through Nicholas, sharper than the arrowhead that had pierced his artery. Of course she knew. She always knew when this much blood spilled. And if she found him again, he'd be lost.

He must not be found.

Please, God, he prayed, let me go toward the end I have earned. I am ready to meet my eternal fate.

A shadow fell across his vision and his memories.

"We are fortunate, Cordonnier," Boucicaut said. Blood trickled from his elbow through the gap in his plate armor as he rested one gauntleted fist on his hip, trailing red rivulets down the length of his vambrace. He scanned the bodies littering the open field, then the horizon. "Not only because we still breathe, but because it appears the enemy has moved on. Rise and let us search for others as fortunate."

Nicholas struggled to obey. He managed to prop himself up on one elbow, but his injured leg had gone numb and refused to move. His medallion swung like a lead anchor around his neck, mocking him for his weakness when he should've been nigh immortal.

"I cannot, marshal," Nicholas said with some regret, thankful that weariness masked his relief. "I am not long for this life. Please, get away and save yourself before they come back to finish us off."

Boucicaut surveyed him. His mouth thinned into a grim line, and then he knelt into the mud, drew off his gauntlets, and began tearing fabric from the nearest fallen soldier.

A wave of dizziness from blood loss overwhelmed Nicholas enough for him to collapse back into the muck with a wet splat. "No, marshal, you are far too important to risk for someone like me," he protested, batting weakly at Boucicaut's competent hands.

But the marshal ignored him and wrapped the makeshift tourniquet around Nicholas's thigh. Nicholas felt the noose tighten around his leg. The blood slowed, then stopped. Torn flesh began mending, unbeknownst to Boucicaut. In another few minutes, the artery would close up and Nicholas would be whole enough to walk again.

Goddammit, he thought. So close.

"Why?" he asked, too tired to worry about offending his better.

"Because we are all God's creatures," Boucicaut said calmly as he helped Nicholas to his feet. "And because, sometimes, it is in saving the least among us that we in turn save ourselves."

The English captured them an hour before dusk, before they reached the safety of the castle walls at Tramecourt. Besides Nicholas, Boucicaut had found and patched up four other men from the fallen, and the ragtag remnants of the marshal's men-at-arms had been beating a straggling retreat southeastward, toward the relative safety of Arras. Had they been Orléans's men, they would not have dared venture into Burgundy territory.

But none of that mattered now. Now, the five soldiers were roped into the prisoner line corralled in the shadows of the Agincourt château while Boucicaut had been stripped of his armor and led away into the heart of the English encampment.

Hundreds of grime-streaked captives lashed to a long rope strung out along the huge, grey stone walls of the château. English soldiers patrolled the line, prodding the unruly into place with long spears or a swift kick of their boots.

Sweeping a glance over the neat rows of tents and sleeping rolls as they'd marched in, Nicholas guessed that perhaps the encampment hosted more French prisoners than it did actual English soldiers. Odd that his countrymen weren't regrouping for an internal revolt. Their chances now couldn't possibly be much worse than their chances on the battlefield, when arrows struck out of nowhere and broke the cavalry line, and pain-crazed horses trampled their own men-at-arms.

The drying mud on Nicholas's skin itched like crazy, but he didn't dare scrape at its protective layer. With the return of his life, la faim in his blood had also strengthened and now asserted its will to live, overriding Nicholas's will to die. It was what made him loathe living so much, if he could call his existence such—the fact that he couldn't trust that all of his desires were his own anymore.

Just another secret to this hellish afterlife that his mistress had kept from him to get him to say yes.

The grass for a thousand meters from the wall had been crushed down by the Englishmen into wet earth, creating a slick, firm surface like tightly woven thatch, useless to him. He needed more mud if he were to stay hidden here, out here in the exposed open. As night fell, Nicholas breathed easier, but he still didn't scratch at the itching. Campfires rose and threw shadows and smoke all around them. The men bunched closer to share their warmth and ward off the chill of night, including Nicholas, even though he didn't feel the cold. He moved purely to conceal himself in the herd.

He recognized some of his fellow prisoners, all of them common men-at-arms, but many more were strangers. He'd heard from earlier whispers that the few remaining knights were taken captive and cordoned off elsewhere, probably where Boucicaut had been taken. The combined French armies had numbered in the tens of thousands up against the pitiful few thousands of the English, but some-how, those devil dogs had made their numbers count.

"I told the monsieur," one of the prisoners muttered. Firelight glinted off the crowned triple fleur-de-lys of the House of Orléans over his left breast. "Their archers were set too far back to be human. We should've brought a sorcière."

"Shush," another prisoner hissed, also an Orléans man. "That kind of talk will get you burned at the stake, no matter which side of la mer you're on."

Nicholas lowered his head, trying to make himself disappear into the prisoner ranks. The back of his neck prickled with a sense of impending danger that had nothing to do with the English and everything to do with the nervous scowl darkening the second prisoner's expression.

"It wasn't the archers," a third prisoner replied, "it was the bows. They were taller than any we have."

"And you think a mere man could've drawn those strings?" the first prisoner retorted.

"I've seen them," the third said, "and I've heard them talk of it. They call it the longbow, and it is a new invention from a country they call Wales."

This prisoner wore no coat of arms that Nicholas could see, nor could Nicholas tell by the man's vague, bland accent which region he might've hailed from. But many of the troops didn't wear the arms of their houses if they couldn't afford the livery, so that in itself wasn't unusual.

Unusual, though, that the prisoner understood English well enough to know about the new bows that had demolished their army, as none of them were nobility with the means to study foreign languages. Nicholas studied the man out of the corner of his eye. Fair, weathered skin, but not too fair. Smoother, too, than he had noticed at first, therefore much younger than he'd thought. An olive undertone beneath the grime. Straight, clean teeth and dirty, mud-brown hair.

It was the teeth that gave the man away. Whoever this unmarked prisoner was, he hadn't tried hard enough to hide. Nicholas hunched further into himself, glad that he'd taken the time to stain his own teeth with red wine. Lots and lots of wine.

"See," the second hissed again. "Not magic. Never magic. It does not exist. Don't speak of it again lest you bring a curse down upon us."

The first prisoner looked as if he might argue, but snapped his mouth shut and huddled with the others as a pair of English soldiers approached, marching down the line with menacing purpose.

"Quiet down over here," one of them barked in their guttural, bastard language.

Nicholas, unfortunately, had had to learn it years ago at his mistress's insistence. He kept his expression blank so that he didn't give himself away.

But the third prisoner did respond. "Apologies, kind sirs," he said in fluid English. The Frenchmen started with surprise, and a few sidled away from the man. Nicholas feigned a similar reaction and took the opportunity to shift farther away from all of them.

"My brothers are merely lamenting their thirst," the prisoner continued. "Perhaps it would help if we could have some water?"

The soldiers shared a glance. Evidently, they hadn't expected their prisoners to understand the words as much as their tone.

"We'll see," the one responded cautiously, in a way that meant they most definitely would not see.

"Thank you," the prisoner said diffidently, completely at odds with the quiet confidence he'd exhibited earlier about the bows.

The soldiers left and the French dissolved into furious whispers among themselves, carefully leaving out the unmarked prisoner. Nicholas weighed his options and decided he didn't like any of them, but that the stranger would be the least risky. He'd bet the tattered remains of his humanity that the stranger had as much to lose as Nicholas did.

He made sure their area was clear of English soldiers first before asking the stranger, "What other languages do you speak?" He played it safe with French, in case he was wrong about the stranger.

"What are you doing?" whispered one of the Orléans men. "He's English. A spy. You shouldn't talk to him."

Nicholas ignored the Orléans man. The stranger raised

a brown eyebrow and studied Nicholas with inscrutable brown eyes. "Greek," he said finally. "Latin. Italian. Spanish, of course, and Portuguese."

The Romanic languages were out. Too close to French. And Nicholas would rather leave Latin to the holy men.

"You are not one of us," Nicholas said, his native musical cadence softening the rapid-fire edges of his Greek. Silence fell over the prisoner line, and then the French murmur rose up again, this time pointedly ignoring them both.

Well, it couldn't be helped. The idiot sheep could either get over their fear of the unknown and do something about their predicament, or not get over their fear and die when the English finally got smart enough to realize they were all worthless ransom-bait, since none of them were nobles. Nicholas had lived long enough to know the latter was the far likelier outcome.

The eyebrow rose even further. "And you are not just a soldier," the man replied, his own Greek syllables more clearly pronounced but coming much slower, like the Peloponnese. Not like the more traditional and popular Athenian Greek. Likely not tutored. The stranger's fluency had been gained through first-hand immersion. "I cannot imagine that many soldiers would be so well-versed in the classics."

"I've had time to study."

The other eyebrow shot up to join its mate. "How much time?"

At that, Nicholas smiled. His teeth were stained, certainly, but they were straight and he had all of them. Not even mad King Charles, God bless his poor soul, could boast that much.

Nicholas knew what his perfect teeth would mean to

the stranger, and he knew for sure now that the stranger was not wholly human, if at all. An everyday human would not think to ask specifics about time.

The stranger sucked in a breath, then released it slowly. "Not witch," he said, "nor daemon. Lycan or hemophage?"

Nicholas bared his teeth further. Now he could narrow down the possibilities on how he could best use this stranger to his advantage. The fact that the stranger ruled witches and daemons out so thoroughly meant he was one of them. They all had some means of sensing each other, although Nicholas wasn't quite sure how. His mistress had never explained.

"Does it matter, monsieur?" he asked. "We are in the same basket, you and I."

The stranger smiled. "On our way to Hades," he said cheerfully, although he still watched Nicholas with care. He flexed his hands within his rope bonds, his brown eyes going distant for a moment. "Call me Leo."

"Nicholas." He supposed he should've eased Leo's worries, as Leo probably wondered if he'd just found himself tied up to a rope with an enemy. The witches were centuries deep into a secret war with the werewolves, with daemons and vampyres switching allegiances often and without warning. But Nicholas had learned the hard way not to give up any more information than strictly necessary.

Leo nodded toward the brass medallion hanging around Nicholas's neck. "The archangel Michael? Or Saint Christopher?"

"Neither." Nicholas shrugged. "Crispin and Crispinian."

"Unusual," Leo commented, "especially for a soldier." He left a wide pause for Nicholas to fill, but Nicholas didn't feel like obliging.

Instead, he mused out loud, slowly and deliberately, "Surely we two could put our heads together and discover a means of escape. Common captivity is no place for the likes of us."

More importantly, he needed to get moving. Get out of this death trap before his mistress arrived. These men would know no mercy if she perverted the situation to her own cruel motives.

The memory of her sly, laughing smile that he echoed now sharpened his hunger so swiftly that his heart beat harder against his chest. Blood flowed sluggishly through his veins. La faim had eaten through most of his body's remaining blood in the effort to mend his spurting artery. He would need more to replenish all that he'd lost today to both la faim and to his leg wound.

"Surely we could," Leo agreed, watching the English patrol. The prisoner line fell silent as the patrol swept past, glowering at them all. It was the same pair who'd promised to look into the water situation for Leo. As Nicholas had expected, no water materialized.

"They captured the duke," Leo continued after the patrol ranged out of earshot. "And the rearguard is still at large. With the duke held hostage, the rest of the army—as inexperienced as they are—will fall back and regroup, and come back for him."

He must've meant Charles, the Duke of Orléans, nephew to the king and the highest ranking nobleman on the field. Nicholas realized after a moment that Leo had not wanted to say Orléans's name or title out loud and pique the curiosity of the Frenchmen. He nodded to let Leo know he understood.

"When?" Nicholas asked.

"Soon." Leo's eyes flicked to the two who'd been

arguing about the bows and magic. "Dawn, perhaps, when there is enough light to tell friend from foe, French from English."

And innocent men from the monsters who hunt them in the night.

Nicholas thought of the marshal he served. A man of honor, rare these days, who'd earned the nickname "Le Boucicaut" for his bravery, as his father had before him. Their captors would've kept Boucicaut near Orléans. If the French came for Charles, they would regain their marshal as well.

And if his mistress came for Nicholas, she would lay waste to the entire camp to find him, no matter who else was there. The shadows flung onto the walls behind him by the campfires seemed to dance along their own, independent of the flames that birthed them. Their sinuous movements reminded him of how leisurely his mistress liked to hunt. He shivered and wished it were from the cold and nothing else.

Nicholas offered up a quick prayer. He would never see Boucicaut again. One way or another, Nicholas Cordonnier would die tonight and move on. The least he could do to honor the marshal was to make sure his countrymen had a fighting chance to rescue their noblemen.

In the meantime, he couldn't wait until dawn. Despite his best efforts not to disturb the mud caking his skin, it was already flaking off in dusty bits, exposing his pale flesh underneath.

He was thinking through plausible excuses to get Leo to act sooner when the man flexed his hands again.

"I think for you, friend Nicholas," Leo said, "dawn may be too late, hmm?"

Nicholas narrowed his eyes. "What do you mean?" he

asked, stalling to get Leo to reveal how much he'd guessed. The prickling along the back of neck traveled down his spine, setting all of his senses on fire.

The hunt draws nearer than I feared.

Leo spread his hands, palms up, in a placating gesture. "I can see more by starlight than the keenest eyes of a wolf," he said gravely. "But you are no wolf, are you?"

Starlight magic. The flexing had been Leo drawing on his eldritch magic, knowing Nicholas wasn't one and therefore couldn't sense the pull in the currents.

Leo was a witch. Worse, he was Astral—his magic used for support and tacticians, less for battle. Nicholas couldn't hide from his kind. Not entirely. And Leo would be nearly useless in a fight.

"No," he said, and once again, his regret was real. "But it doesn't matter now. You're as dead as I am."

Leo frowned, his fingers curling against his palms. "What do you mean?"

The dancing shadows stepped from their walls and enveloped the men, muffling their startled cries and cutting them off with eerie sharpness.

Nicholas closed his eyes. "My mistress is here," he whispered. "And she will slaughter you all to make sure I don't run away again."

When Nicholas opened his eyes again, the pile of corpses before him rose higher and taller than he had ever seen before, stacked haphazardly against the stone walls of Château Agincourt. Unseeing eyes stared up at the stars from atop the jumble, several meters above Nicholas's head. Gold-threaded fleur-de-lys mixed with the crimson

Lancaster rose, tumbling one over another, until Nicholas couldn't tell where one dynasty ended and another began.

He sank down to his knees and into the thatched mud, clutching at the yawning pit of his stomach. No heartbeat sounded from the pile of what must've comprised at least a few hundred bodies.

"Why?" he asked dully.

The voice that answered him was as different as Boucicaut's in every human and inhuman way possible.

"Because, mon petit chou," purred his mistress into his ear, in soft, sultry, dulcet tones meant to lull him into compliance but instead brought a rush of bile to his throat, "you are my creature, and it is far past time for you to learn that your actions have consequences." Her voice hardened, sharper and more brittle than glass, as she circled soundlessly behind him and whispered into his other ear, "That you cannot save anyone, much less yourself, from my wrath once you've incurred it."

He threw his head back and screamed in frustration. "But they were just innocent men!" he shouted.

She completed her circle and stood before him, as cold and unruffled as a marble statue. Long, straight hair darker than midnight flowed down past her shoulders and over her bosom to her wide waist. White, chiffon-like fabric wrapped the ample curves of her body in stark contrast to the rich brown of her smooth skin and the deep black of her starlit eyes.

"Then don't disobey me," Nyx said coolly. "It really is that simple."

Nicholas stumbled to his feet and lurched toward her, hands outstretched and curled into claws. "I'll kill you," he snarled. "I swear to God, I will kill you, or die trying."

She danced out of his reach and laughed. "Honestly,

chouchou, what do you hope to accomplish by this silliness?" He lunged and she dodged him again without effort. "You can't even die. Not that easily, anyway. My little pets make sure of that."

She meant la faim, of course. Her creation, as much as Nicholas had been her creation. A cursed spirit of unceasing hunger that lived within his blood like an evil spirit. His own birth parents had merely provided the vessel.

At the faded memory of his birth family, Nicholas stopped and swayed in place. He clutched at his father's brass medallion and lowered his head, praying for strength.

Her voice was almost gentle when she said, "You have a choice to make, mon petit."

"I'm surprised I have one at all," he spat out.

She ignored his bitterness. "You can choose to save yourself. I will honor your request and take my pet back, and let you die the natural death you earned so long ago."

Nicholas froze. Surely, this was too good of an offer to be true. He thought through her words but could find no fault with them, no loophole that she might slip through to renege.

Except that she hadn't yet spoken of other options.

"Or?" he asked, cautiously.

Nyx smiled, a tiny, fierce little smile that sent chills down his spine. This was the smile he dreaded. The one that told him he never had a choice after all except for the one to run.

"Or," she said dramatically, sweeping an arm off to one side, "you can save those pitiful creatures. I will spare them all the fates of their brethren. You decide."

Nicholas saw the rest of the men then, a mob of a thousand or more, penned in by inward-facing spears and stakes as sturdily as sheep in the center of the camp. Boucicaut stood front and center, arms crossed and head thrown back in defiance as he glared at Nyx, tracking her movement with eyes as intense as a wolf's. Just behind him, Charles of Orléans peered nervously over his shoulder, having to stand on tiptoe to do so. Several meters down the line from the nobles, Leo stood watching Nicholas, one arm cradling the other, broken at an awkward angle, both of his hands still and quiet. Surprisingly, he was flanked by the two Orléans prisoners who'd snubbed them earlier.

And if he were not mistaken, there stood the English king, Henry of Monmouth, and his brother Humphrey, the latter sprawled unconscious in his king's arms, also penned in with the French. Henry hovered over his injured sibling like a mother bear, snarling off his attending generals who tried to carry the burden of Humphrey's limp body for him.

There they all gathered, French and English mingling, nobles and commoners alike, no one jostling for position, no one brawling the other. For the first time in nearly a hundred years, the two kingdoms stood side by side quietly, without warring.

Nicholas gripped his medallion even tighter, trying desperately to hold on to the memory of the man who'd given it to him, who'd given him first life. Of the boy who'd accepted it, and now drew on it for strength and guidance.

His family had thrived here once, decades ago, earning a hard living cobbling shoes in the small, relatively unknown town of Agincourt. He'd grown up here on this very battlefield, when it had been fields of tall grass waving gently in the breeze, and not the blood-soaked graveyard it had become overnight.

What would it matter if Nicholas did choose death tonight? He had determined, after all, that he would die, one way or another. This way would be the surefire method. No chance circumstance or happy Samaritan to luckily step in and save him, as Boucicaut had done with the tourniquet.

But Nicholas had chosen to serve Boucicaut because the marshal of France was the most chivalrous and honorable knight in the kingdom, bar none—worthier than even the English's so-called Knights of the Round Table. Nicholas had defied his mistress to join this war, to join Boucicaut, because he believed in the marshal's unswerving faith that it was their honorable duty to expel the bastard English from their land, to protect it for their king and country.

And Nicholas had done it all to atone for his first sin, the one that had started him down this path. Of being too cowardly to die, when the black plague had taken his body and almost taken his life. Of bargaining away his eternal soul in exchange for eternal life on Earth. He'd been a coward for only a moment, but he would pay for much, much longer. In Boucicaut, Nicholas had seen the man he should've become, that he wanted to become. That he hoped, with all of his soul, he could still become.

He met Boucicaut's gaze now, and the marshal nodded once, slowly. Boucicaut saw only one path out of this conundrum, and he would expect Nicholas to take it. Because that was the path the marshal would've taken, had it been his choice to make.

Nicholas was right. His mistress hadn't given him a choice at all.

Small victory for him then, that he was no longer too cowardly to die.

He turned to face his tormentor, his creator and his damnation. She read his decision on his face and smiled, this time her sweet smile, the one that she wore when she won. She wore this one often.

"Your pain has taught me so well that I am entirely yours," Nicholas said, every word costing him a piece of his resolve. "Dying to serve and please you."

Her smile widened into a feral grin. "Why, chouchou," she murmured, "perhaps you should've been a poet."

She pressed a kiss to his cheek, and where her lips touched his skin, the mud fell in a shower of dust, revealing a rough expanse of days-old, dark blond stubble. The expanse radiated outward, sloughing off more dirt, until Nicholas stood bright and shiny and clean, his dirty blond hair ruffling in the breeze. "You know where to find me when you're done here," she whispered, and then she was gone.

Shadows gathered along the wall of stakes and spears, umbra black and just as impenetrable. The darkness slithered like smoke, carrying away with it the barriers that had contained the imprisoned. For a moment, the tableau remained frozen as the prisoners blinked at each other, then at Nicholas, swaying unsteadily on his feet.

Boucicaut ran toward him and caught him before he fell. "Careful now, Cordonnier," the marshal said. "Breathe easy. We've got you now." Gingerly, the marshal propped Nicholas up with a beefy shoulder until Nicholas felt steady enough to stand again on his own. To the gawking bystanders, the marshal roared, "Bring me some water!"

Leo hurried forward, wincing as the steps jostled his broken arm. Boucicaut made to block Leo's approach, but Nicholas reached out and grasped Leo's good hand in his own. With a grumbled caution, Boucicaut subsided.

"Friend Nicholas," Leo said, breathless and urgent, moving close so that they could not be overheard even by Boucicaut. Behind Leo, the crowd had surrounded them, although the marshal's rumbling baritone kept them at bay, for now. "Who was she? What do I tell my people?"

Nicholas knew Leo wasn't asking for the humans, who had no idea that creatures such as the witches and the daemons, the werewolves and the vampyres, all existed in secret side by side, factions warring with each other as intently as the French and the English had these past hundred years. No, Leo was asking for himself, as a witch, and for the rest of his brethren, whether this was the start of a new war, with new enemies and new alliances.

Whatever the case may be, it was far above his responsibility now. He'd done what he could, for who he could.

"Give them the name Nyx," he said wearily. "Your elders will know her. She is a creature as old as time, and just as ruthless, as you've seen."

Leo nodded and squeezed his hand, then stepped back and melded into the crowd.

As he did so, light from the breaking dawn caught the brass medallion around Nicholas's neck, bathing his newly cleaned features in golden light and gleaming through his blond hair. Unprotected, the sun's rays burned into his skin, flushing his face and making him as rosy-cheeked as painted cherubs.

Someone from the crowd gasped. "An angel!"

"A savior," another said, "who saved us from the she-devil."

"A saint created this very day," a third cried out, and suddenly the chant spread like wildfire through the mob. "Our saint of Agincourt!"

He was as far from any of those entities as he could possibly be, Nicholas thought with wonder, surveying the men's rapturous expressions. And yet they all believed in him. Believed that he'd saved them, when they didn't know the truth—that if Nyx hadn't killed them, he might have, because he, too, had an internal drive to survive that he couldn't ignore. He, too, was a monster and a devil.

But perhaps he was a little less of a monster today. Perhaps a thousand souls less. As Nicholas allowed himself to be surrounded by the press of grateful men, a pile of humanity warm and comforting and welcoming, he felt a renewed sense of purpose filling his veins with hope.

He'd lost so much, never to be recovered. So much more had decayed as he grieved. He wearied of mourning. It was time to move on.

Agincourt's once-beautiful fields would recover, one blade of grass at a time. Just as his soul would recover. One life at a time.

THE GOOD PATH
PHILLIP MCCOLLUM

"Hardy, get in here."

My fingers kept tapping the keys, filling in address and emergency contact info, while my brain tried to ignore the call. The woman next to me, Maude, was about my mother's age—somewhere in her carly sixties with straight silver hair down to her shoulders and a pair of large-rimmed glasses. A small white towel was wrapped around her neck. The smell of sweat radiated through her grey sweatshirt and sweatpants.

She'd just been through her second free spin class and was ready to commit to a full year's membership. I was excited to have her come on board as it was the end of January and she was at the tail end of the New Year's resolution crowd, most of whom were already dwindling away by the day.

Maude seemed committed. It was five-thirty a.m. on a Monday morning and she was so gung ho. I admired a woman like her. That level of dedication was nothing to sneeze at.

"Hardy!" came the voice again.

I kept my eyes on the screen, but craned my neck a little. "I'm with a customer," I said loudly.

I smiled at Maude and she shifted quickly from looking slightly uncomfortable to flashing a smile of her own.

We were seated at one of four desks just to the left of the tall, well-lit lobby where members would walk in, use the fingerprint verification system to check in, and commence their hour or two of voluntary torture. Just outside through the large-paned windows, the yellow lamps of the parking lot were joined by the occasional headlights of arriving members.

"Okay, Maude. We're almost set. I'll just need a credit card—"

I stopped as I literally heard my boss, Sgt. Jeremy Closs, marching out of his office. I took to calling him "Sarge" in my head even though he was no longer a sergeant. Yet, when he introduced himself to others, he insisted on the title. His rubber-soled tennis shoes somehow found a way to clap steadily against the thin carpet lining the office area. It was like magic. A cold, hard-edged magic.

Both Maude and I turned to see him standing uncomfortably close behind us. He stood at a slight five-eight and maybe hit 160 pounds on a good day, but he was pure muscle. Through his short-sleeved, moisture-resistant, collared shirt, his arms showed no signs of fat; only tight flesh and knots of twisted veins beneath. Last week, I'd seen him squat five reps for five sets of 315 without even warming up. Wherever he found the Samson-like strength to do what he did, it certainly wasn't in his hair—he hadn't changed his buzzcut since he'd been discharged from the Marine Corps twenty years ago.

He flashed me a look that could have killed any number of people if they hadn't been inoculated against it.

Then he turned to Maude, wiping me from his reality for the moment.

"Hello," he said. The sudden smile on his face lined up with a scar that ran down his right cheek so that it looked like someone had tried to extend it at some point in his life. It couldn't have been from combat because when he was enlisted, the only action going on was brief flare-up down in the Congo. I also doubted it was from a drunken bar brawl, because I can't imagine the man ever touching a glass of alcohol in his life.

"I see you're signing up for our discounted yearly membership at Sound Body Fitness..." he said, peering over my shoulder at the screen. "...Mrs. Givens. It's a pleasure to have you in our ranks."

It was like someone flipped a flaky switch with his voice, trying to turn from drill sergeant to soft-voiced therapist, but not quite completing the transition.

She nodded quickly, the smile now seemingly stuck to her face with superglue.

"You're making the greatest investment of your life," he continued. His gaze turned to the wall opposite the parking lot, where there were more glass panes through which the rest of the gym could be seen—men and women of all shapes and sizes gathered around various contraptions built of iron and black vinyl, chatting between workout sets. Some were puffing away vigorously on elliptical machines with headphones pulled down over their soaked heads, while others kept a slow and steady pace on the classic treadmills.

Sarge puffed up his chest. Sniffed the air like a predator. Then he took in a deep breath as if he'd just scaled Mt. Everest and was sucking in the purest air his lungs had ever had the pleasure of experiencing. I was barely aware of the years of built-up sweat combined with bleach permeating the walls and floors, but I knew it was there. It was a sour smell that had stopped being noticeable after my first month of being a personal trainer here.

"De la Cruz!"

Our newest team member, eighteen-year-old Vincent De la Cruz, stood up from behind the front desk in an almost-salute. He was a part-timer, earning extra cash to help pay for classes at the local junior college. "Yes, sir?"

"Assist Mrs. Givens with the completion of her application."

"Yes, sir!" Vincent replied, practically running over.

If there was a hint of a grin forming on Sarge's face, it shut itself down before it even had a chance to manifest.

His hand came down just below my neck like a vise grip. I already knew to tense up my traps. The first time he'd done that, I'd spent some of that week's pay on a deep-tissue massage.

"My office, now," he said.

Without a further word, he turned and marched back. I followed, though with a little less rigid cadence in my steps. I could have swore Vincent smirked as he passed me by and took my chair, finishing up with Maude.

Sarge held the door open for me and when I entered, he closed it gently. He then drew the venetian blinds so that the place became a tiny box of its own. There was a metal folding chair in front of his desk, but I knew better than to sit down before he had invited me to. Another rookie mistake I'd learned to avoid after the first week.

His chair was a simple wooden stool. No back. No cushion. Comforts made you weak, he said. Ruined the posture. "What kind of example would that set?" was a favorite rhetorical question of his.

I stood with my hands behind my back, trying to avoid eye contact. Behind him were various plaques, trophies, and framed photos of him in uniform. Even as a younger man, he'd had a permanent scowl plastered to his face. I'd often wanted to take a closer look at what he'd exactly won as the plaques and trophies were too hard to read from here, but when the sergeant wasn't around, his door was locked. Even if I'd gotten ahold of the key, I hesitated to think about the consequences of him finding me skulking around his office.

"Take a seat, Hardy."

I saw he'd done so already, so I let out the breath I'd been inadvertently holding and sat. Even though Sarge was shorter than me by half a foot, the stool he sat on was tall enough so that he slightly looked down on me while seated.

He said nothing for an uncomfortable amount of time, but again, "Do not speak unless spoken to," was another familiar refrain.

"Explain yourself."

Great. It was going to be a day of guessing games.

"Sir?" I said.

His tone softened a little. It took on more of a guidance counselor tone. "I know what you've been doing, Hardy, and I want you to explain yourself."

I was at a loss for words. "Is there something specific you're referring to, sir?"

More uncomfortable silence before he exhaled sharply, opened a drawer in his desk, and pulled out a white three-ring binder. Slipped inside the front plastic sleeve was a familiar color printout: Sound Body Fitness Bible.

Every new hire is given a copy, paid for out of the first paycheck, of course. It was about thirty pages long, filled with sections and subsections and sub-subsections, mainly containing odd screeds and proverbs Sarge had written down. Largely, it contained his views on life with a smaller section on how he ran things at the gym. For some reason, as he held it in his hands, it was the first time I'd ever noticed a wedding ring. It was a plain silver band, dulled from all the scraping against weights and pull-up bars, but it stood out as his white-knuckled hands gripped the bible like it was a winning lottery ticket. I wondered who would ever marry this maniac.

"Quote for me chapter five, verse two," he said.

I tried to recall what that might have even possibly been. It shouldn't have been difficult, as Sarge would often pop-quiz us during staff meetings or even when I was doing something as simple as picking up used towels from the locker room.

Still, my mind was drawing a blank.

"Seems you're due for a refresher," he said. He threw the binder toward my side of the desk.

I pulled it into my lap.

"Read," he said.

I started reading.

"Aloud," he said.

"'We are all examples'," I read. "'What we say, what we do, what we think—these are paramount to living our lives toward their ultimate end and guiding others toward the good path.'"

Sarge's hands were now resting interlaced on the desk. He leaned forward.

"Explain yourself."

I racked my brain.

"I'm sorry, sir. I'm trying to understand—-"

"I know about the doughnuts, Hardy."

The doughnuts?

"Yes, the doughnuts," he said, as if hearing my thoughts.

It all came together. Now, I realized what he was talking about, or so I thought. I had picked up a box of doughnuts last Saturday when I visited my parents, but the fact is they lived two hours north of here. How could he have...?

"You're wondering how I know," he said. "Don't bother. It's irrelevant. What's important are your actions."

Sarge rose from his chair and placed his hands behind his back. He looked over his various awards as if he were inspecting Van Goghs at a museum.

"Do you feel that by purchasing disgusting, sugary, oil-laden sweets that pass for breakfast, you have guided people toward the good path?" he said, talking to the wall.

"Sir, I only—"

His back remained facing me.

"Answer the question."

I could tell that he wasn't going to let me out of here until I confessed my sins. A large part of me wanted to toss his little bible on to the floor, grind into it with my tennis shoe, and tell him to shove this job. But, given what he knew about the doughnuts, it didn't seem a wise tack to take. Sarge was a popular man in this town. He knew a lot of people and was active in the local Chamber of Commerce. From what I'd seen of him the past few months, if I thought things were bad now, he could make a lot more trouble for me if he wanted to.

So, I relented. "No, sir."

"'No, sir,' what?"

I tried to regulate my breathing. Tried to hold back a frustrated exhalation. I gritted my teeth.

"No, sir. I don't think that purchasing the doughnuts set a good example and guided people toward the good path."

He finally turned around. There was that scar-connecting grin now. Slight, but there.

"Discipline must be maintained, Hardy. Without it, there's no hope for any us. Just as you kept this little secret from me, withheld the truth, I'm going to have to withhold a portion of your next paycheck." He looked down at me like I was something his dog just puked up. "Those sugar-bombs have obviously affected your posture, a result of junk calories. You look to have gained a couple of pounds. I'll have De la Cruz verify your weight. Once you lose the two pounds, you can receive the pay which I've held back."

"But, sir—-"

"Or maybe it's ten pounds. Do you think you gained ten pounds, Hardy? Maybe indulged in a second or third maple bar?"

Now my own knuckles were whitening, gripping the sides of the folding chair.

"Understood, sir."

"Good," he said.

I tossed and turned that night, waking up in a cold sweat after seeing myself being whipped into submission at what I presumed was Sarge's house (I'd never seen the place). He had me doing push-ups in his basement with his scummy, oversized boot on my back the whole time. Every time my face came down, my nose crashed into a plate piled with frosted doughnuts.

Eat your pig food, piggy. Eat your pig food.

He kept repeating it over and over until my tears blended in with vanilla icing, leaving a slimy trail running down my cheeks to my chin.

It was one a.m. and I lay on my back now with the sheets thrown off, wondering just how he could take money away from me like that. I wasn't exactly living a life of luxury as it was. I would be hurting for a bit if I didn't get all of my paycheck. It would be store-brand peanut butter and no heat for at least a couple of weeks.

Sarge didn't pay his staff any more than absolutely necessary. He probably spent hours poring over every penny noted in his ledger, making sure not a one went to waste.

After futilely trying to sleep, I decided there was no way I could continue working under the damned little dictator.

Screw the job.

Screw the consequences.

I still wanted to train, still wanted to get people feeling good and healthy, but there were towns all over America where I could do that. I'd just move somewhere far, far away from that a-hole.

With my mind made up, I begin to feel an urge to go out with a bang. I got out of bed, threw on warm clothes, and ran some errands.

Most of the lights were off at the gym. It wouldn't open for three hours, which meant Sarge would be there in two, followed soon after by brown-nose Vincent. But, a few strategic lights were turned on around the entrance and the path to Sarge's office. It was so the cameras could pick up anything suspicious, only that didn't worry me—the cameras were only decoys because Sarge was too cheap to actually pay for the recording system.

I headed straight for his office, but of course the door was locked.

It probably would have busted open easily enough—it was only a simple lock on the knob—but I didn't want to leave any mark that shouted I was the cause of all the things that were going to soon piss him off.

I wasn't looking to do anything blatant. Just tiny things that he would catch eventually. Things that would drive him slowly nuts—a market-fresh trout that I would place as far behind the file cabinets as possible; one of those electronic beepers that would sit inside the drop ceiling, going off at random intervals throughout the day; and then for the coup de grâce—I was going to take some of those stupid, smug military photos of his and Sharpie the shit out of them with mustaches, devil horns, and black eyes.

But first I had to get in the door.

It was a simple knob lock and I wondered if the old credit card trick would work. If it didn't, I'd think of something else.

As the door slid open and my library card fell to the floor, I said a silent prayer of thanks—both to the little old lady who'd given me the thing and to Sarge for being a cheap bastard.

It took me about ten minutes to take care of the fish and secure the beeper in the panel to the right-rear of the room. Then I dug around Sarge's desk drawers and found a ten-dollar bill with a yellow sticky note on it:

Good recon work, De la Cruz.

I wasn't surprised, but I slammed the drawer closed, which rattled the entire desk.

I turned and faced the back wall. I pulled out my Sharpie and inhaled its heady scent like it was apple pie fresh out of the oven.

I went to work. First I pulled down a framed photo of him and three soldiers standing on a dock. A grey destroyer or something like it floated in the background while the men put on their best don't-eff-with-me faces. I laughed as the intimidation effect sort of went away when Sarge wound up with oversized sunglasses and a joint hanging from his stiff lips.

Next up was a photo of our illustrious leader crawling prone in the mud beneath a field of barbed wire, which probably would have been a whole lot easier if he didn't have a hot dog sticking out of his ass.

I stepped back, wondering what else I could deface.

I glanced at a yellow certificate behind a plate of glass —an official Marine Corps discharge. I almost moved on to the next object, but something about it struck me funny. Like it was a little off-center. I pulled the frame down and looked closely. The paper inside was folded at the top.

I undid the backing and the paper fell onto the floor. I picked it up. Indeed, the top was folded. I flipped it open and my heart skipped a beat.

Then I smiled and said another little prayer of thanks.

I'd swapped out the stool for the folding chair and I was leaning back precariously on two legs with my shoes scuffing up Sarge's desk when he came to a stop. He stood in his office doorway, his dark green gym bag hanging from his shoulder while he gave me a silent, icy stare for what seemed an eternity.

Behind him, I saw Vincent stroll into the lobby, piping his head in our direction.

Sarge threw his bag onto the floor and gyrated his head on his neck like he was getting ready to go ten rounds.

"Don't know how you got in. Don't care. You're fired. Now get out before I throw you out."

"Now, Sarge," I said, "is that any way to speak to your star employee?"

Veins popped out along his crimson neck like tree roots running crookedly through the ground.

"You have five seconds," he said, walking deliberately toward me.

"Or what? You'll discharge me?"

He seemed to slow a little, but kept coming around the desk.

"I don't know, Sarge. Seems pretty...dishonorable."

Six inches from pounding my face in, he stopped moving and glanced up at the back wall. Everything was there. Maybe he even saw some of my custom artwork, but his eyes were drawn toward the slightly off-kilter frame holding the bright yellow piece of paper.

"What did you say?" he said.

I'd only seen the man's eyes bulge as much as they did when a pair of middle-aged women came in one time, asking if he offered meditation classes.

"I'm sorry," I replied. "What do you mean specifically?"

This was getting to be too much fun. I noticed Vincent was a little closer now, acting like he was turning on the computers just outside the office.

"Never mind," he said, staring back down at me again.

"Now, are you going to get out of here or are you going to make this old Marine get nasty?"

I put the chair back on all fours and removed my feet from his desk and raised my hands in defeat. "Okay," I said. "I'll get out of your hair."

As I stood, his nostrils were still flaring but his breathing began to steady. I walked toward his office door. Vincent wasn't even trying to hide it now—the smirk on his face was a mile wide.

I turned. Sarge had his hands on the suspect frame, inspecting it. "Hey, Sarge, I'm going to get back to work now. I have a client coming in at six a.m. By the way, have I ever told you how glad I am that you invested in a copy machine, even if it only works half the time?"

He spun back to face me and said nothing.

"You could copy all sorts of things with that. Flyers. Motivational posters. Even stuff that might really interest the local paper. Or folks in the Chamber of Commerce," I said. "Who knows?"

Sarge worked his jaw muscles back and forth. There was no piece of skin left on him that wasn't some shade of maroon.

"So yeah, thanks for that. And, gee, I almost forgot... thank you so much for the fifty-percent raise! That was a wonderful surprise. You didn't have to do it, but I'm not gonna turn it down, either." I laughed and smiled back at Vincent, who looked like he'd just crapped himself.

Sarge probably could have bitten off the end of a piece of wrought iron if I shoved it in his mouth, which I may have wanted to do at some point, but moment by moment, I was feeling so much less hostile.

I started back toward my desk, but stopped one last time.

"Oh, and Sarge?"

He ground out something that sounded like, "What?"

"If you look behind the front desk, I brought in some doughnuts to celebrate. I left you a couple maple bars. But let's try to stay on the good path, okay?"

ACROSS THE OCEAN, FAR FROM HOME

DAYLE A. DERMATIS

"Please, Florence, I beg of you...save my baby."

My sister's plea resonated in my head as I entered an alley in London no respectable woman should ever enter, and probably never had. The low heels of my walking shoes rapped on the cobblestones, echoing up the brick walls on either side. Dark here, away from the streetlamps—most of which hadn't worked on the streets, so my eyes had already adjusted. Eyes that watered from the stench of urine that grew stronger the farther I went.

Something scrabbled in the heap of trash in the corner. A rat, probably.

I shuddered, swallowed against a dry mouth. I wanted nothing more than to flee, out of the alley, out of this section of the city, back to the safety of my brother-in-law's (questionable though that was). At least there, the dangers were a known quantity. Only Mabel's words, choked with tears and rough with desperation, kept my feet moving forward until I reached the rough wooden door, a holdover from the previous century, or maybe a century or two before that.

I adjusted my cloche hat more firmly on my head, and then laughed grimly at myself. As if my respectable appearance would protect me somehow.

The people here were no doubt just as likely to turn me away, slam the door in my face, as they were to beat me, rob me, do something unspeakable to me. Or kill me.

"Save my baby..."

Save Mabel's daughter—my niece—three-year-old Clara, from the hands of Mabel's husband, Reginald.

It hadn't been a marriage of great love. Mabel's fiancé hadn't come back from the Great War, and Reginald's wife had been lost when influenza swept the nation. As had mine and Mabel's parents, leaving us very wealthy young women.

No one had any illusion that that wealth hadn't made Mabel even more attractive than she already was. Reginald had a minor title, but the family fortune had floundered; Mabel sought security, and brought money to the agreement.

I had simply been another part of the agreement. As the elder sister, at twenty-five I was already a spinster, and was grateful for a roof over my head because it kept me close to my beloved Mabel. Our parents had left us both generous trusts, enough to live well on for our entire lives if we continued to invest judiciously. Still, a relatively young woman living on her own in this day and age was frowned upon...and once I saw the darker side of Reginald, I swore I'd stay to protect Mabel and Clara.

But Mabel was right. That was no longer an option. It was no longer possible.

I raised my hand to knock a second time when the door was yanked open from the inside.

The man was older, unshaven, his hair roughly cut. He

was in his shirtsleeves, suspenders hanging down over brown corduroy trousers worn shiny at the knees. A toothpick dangled from the corner of his mouth.

His blue eyes raked me from head to toe and back again. He didn't leer, but his expression was far from welcoming all the same. I squared my shoulders, held my ground even as he said, "Yer in the wrong place, luv."

I'd worn my plainest outfit, to minimize the truth that I was a woman of means, but I knew the cut of the cloth—and even the cloth itself—spoke volumes. My stockings were fine, and had never seen mending. My bob was the latest fashion.

"I was told..." My voice wavered, and I tried again, putting all the firmness I could muster into my speech. "I was told someone here could help me obtain certain papers."

The splinter of a toothpick in his mouth shifted from one side to the other.

"Did yer, now." He grunted, eyed me again, holding firm to the door with one hand, to slam it in my face.

I swallowed again. Leaned a tiny bit closer, composing my face so I didn't react to the sour smell of him. "I can pay," I said quietly—as if there were anyone in the alley to hear my words.

He grunted again, stepped back. "Come on, then."

I followed him down a dark hallway—the gas lights were out, and the building apparently hadn't been wired for electricity yet—and into a room.

I'd interrupted a card game, and drinking. Chipped glasses of amber liquid, a fistful of bills in the center of the small table. A cot along one wall, a small stove with a kettle atop it in the opposite corner, shelves with a few dishes, a simple wooden wardrobe. He must live in this one room.

The three other men, still seated, stared at me, smoke curling from cigarettes between their fingers.

I clutched my pocketbook, stared back, and prayed to the heavens that my knocking knees weren't visible beneath my ankle-length skirt. Prayed, too, that I wouldn't die here this night.

The first man jerked his thumb. "Business," he said, and the other three scraped back their mismatched stools. They looked closely at the table, no doubt memorizing the placement of the cards and money so the first man wouldn't take advantage of their absence.

They left, and the first man indicated a chair. I sat, feeling the legs wobble a bit beneath me, and told him what I wanted.

Fake papers for myself and Clara. Different first names, a different but shared surname.

"Yer have photographs?" the man asked.

I nodded, undid the clasp of my purse, drew out a brown envelope. "All the information you need, I believe," I said.

He didn't even open the envelope. He just tapped his fingers on it, surveyed me one more time, and named a price.

It was easily twice what I'd been warned to expect. I wondered what he'd do if I bargained, or refused.

"I can pay half that now," I said. "That's all I've brought with me." It was the God's honest truth, and if that wasn't enough for him, or if he chose to simply take it from me and toss me back into the alley... "The rest I can promise when you're done."

To my great relief, he named a date two weeks from now, and I agreed. What else could I do?

I stood, my knees still as weak as the chair legs seemed

to be. I could only hope he wouldn't take what I was handing to him now and vanish.

I wasn't sure Mabel, or Clara, had the time it would take to start this process over once again.

The ship's side loomed high, high, higher than I had expected. I'd seen these steamers at the docks only from a distance before, and it wasn't until I was close up that I realized how far back I had to tilt my head, straining my neck, to see the top of it.

Dark and scratched riveted metal sides, even though she was one of the top in the royal fleet. Then again, she'd been built before the Great War. A metal gangplank sloped upwards to a door that seemed tiny in the massive wall of the ship. A gull sat unblinking on the railing, surveying the mass of people jostling for a place in line to board. It looked braver than I was. The ship nestled impossibly close to the dock, but that was a good thing: if the gangplank had been longer, I might have lost my nerve.

Up the slope, into the bowels of the ship...that was the chasm I had to cross. The steps that would change my life forever.

The air stank of fish and brine, and of the people crowded too closely. Over the din of good-byes and the shouts of sailors, I heard another gull cry harshly, somewhere above us. I was too hot in my wool coat, but if I took it off, I would have to carry it.

Our trunks were already on board, and I had no one to assist me.

I shifted Clara—no, Mary now, I must remember that, must never slip up—in my arms. She was already almost too heavy to carry for long, but I think it gave her comfort to be held. It was all I could do not to keep glancing nervously behind me. At any moment I expected to feel a heavy hand on my shoulder, strong fingers squeezing and digging into the soft flesh beneath my collarbone because Reginald enjoyed causing that sort of pain.

It was soon after the marriage vows had been taken that Reginald had made his reasons for marrying Mabel clear: he expected a steady production of sons, and no complaining about it, or about anything else. Her job was to be the perfect wife and make him look prosperous and smart.

It took several tries for her to carry a baby to term, and when she did, the result was Clara (Mary now). Reginald had been apoplectic. He'd refused to see the baby, blamed Mabel for being weak, for being willful, for disobeying him.

When Mabel became pregnant again, it gave her a respite from Reginald—he knew better than to lay a hand on his wife and risk the life inside her, the life that could be the son he craved.

That baby survived the early, dangerous months—survived to be born—and this time, Mabel had done her job and given Reginald a boy.

Which turned Reginald's attention to the problem of Mary.

He had already alluded, when sloppy with drink, that Mary would soon need schooling in being a proper woman, obedient to her future husband, because her only worth was to marry well and thus bring more fortune to the family.

The irony was not lost on any of us.

The alarm we felt only grew. Reginald's ideas of how to properly school a woman were clear.

Mabel felt she could not leave, no matter how hard I begged. No one would believe he was a monster at home; he was a fine, upstanding, respected man in the eyes of society. Reginald had too many friends, too much influence, and his standing, she said, would be ruined if she divorced him. He would never allow it. She believed—and I agreed, however much I didn't want to—that he would rather see her dead.

His cruel treatment of her, she swore, had lessened since the birth of the boy. I didn't believe that would last.

"Save my baby," she begged me. She could not escape from Reginald, but Mary could.

Reginald might not have cared for Mary, but he would care that she had been taken from him. That would be an unforgiveable slap in his face. Our plan hinged on him not realizing immediately that she was gone, giving us time to get to Southampton and board the ship.

It wasn't until the ship was well away from the port that I truly felt safe. I couldn't see any way Reginald could find us now. I hadn't even told Mabel our new names, to be safe, and she hadn't wanted to know them. We both feared the vicious ways he would try to get her to tell him anything he wanted to know.

Mary must have sensed my relief, or maybe she was just exhausted by the excitement and confusion of the day, because she fell asleep as soon as we were in our cabin.

It was then, only then, for the first time that I allowed myself to weep.

I wept from relief, yes, but for so many other things.

I wept for Mabel, who would bear Reginald's wrath, and I prayed he would spare her the worst of it for the sake of their son, prayed that she would survive.

I wept for Clara—Mary, curse it!—torn from her

mother and left with this poor imitation of one, and I prayed she would find some comfort from me.

And I wept for myself, and the knowledge I would never see my country again, and I prayed for the strength to carry on.

By the time Mary woke, my tears were dried. I had resolved never to let her see them. For better or for worse, I was the only family she had now, and I had to present a brave face, showing only strength and love.

At Ellis Island, I handed our papers to a smartly uniformed man about my age. He was handsome, and he smiled at me, but I couldn't think of flirtation. I stood before him in deceit. The forgeries had gotten us out of England; now they had to be believable enough to grant us access to America, where we could finally disappear.

"Frances Williams," he said, peering at the photograph, and then at me. "And this must be Mary Williams."

"That's right," I said, not too cheerful, not to nervous, not too anything. I was sweating but chilled, expecting shouts and accusing fingers at any moment.

"T'isn't my name!" Mary, on my hip, pulled out the three fingers she'd stuffed in her mouth in order to make her horrifying declaration.

My heart stopped. I was sure I'd drop stone dead right then and there, and all was lost. We'd be arrested, deported, cast back into the hands of Reginald, and then we might as well be dead.

The man's sandy eyebrows raised. "It's not?"

I couldn't speak, even if I'd had an inkling what to say.

Mary didn't notice my panic. "No. It's Froggy!" she

cried, delighted, throwing her hands in the air and then croaking.

I nearly lost my balance, my legs weak from relief. It was a game we'd played aboard the ship. If I put her down, she'd no doubt start hopping right here and now.

"Well, Miss Froggy," the immigration man said, tapping her on the nose with our papers, "welcome to America."

And so we joined the masses flooding into New York City, to become lost in the crowd and begin our new lives on a new continent, an ocean away from home.

We spent the first few nights in a hotel; not the best, but a decent one, safe enough for a woman alone with a small child. I knew we couldn't do that for long, for money was too dear. I hadn't been able to make many plans for fear Reginald would cotton to what was happening, which meant I could receive no letters in the post, and thus could not arrange accommodation ahead of time.

A few days later I rented a bedsit in a decent enough boarding house in a brownstone on a shady street. Mrs. Leary, the middle-aged widow who ran it, softened when I said I, too, had lost my husband, and she was charmed by Mary.

Still, Mary woke more nights than not, crying for her mama, and it broke my heart to soothe her with whispers that I was her mama and that she was safe. Lies built upon lies. I prayed she was young enough to eventually forget.

Although I was extremely careful with money, I swiftly realized my savings wouldn't last nearly as long as I'd hoped. I had never come close to spending my yearly allowance; I'd always been frugal, and living with Mabel and Reginald meant I hadn't had many expenses, just clothes and toiletries and books. Mabel had given me what she could before I left, too.

But the money left behind in my trust was lost to me now; there was no possible way I could draw on it without Reginald finding out, and using that information to track us down. Nor could I invest some of what I'd brought with me, not as a single woman.

I sold my finer dresses, getting a fair price even though they were a season or two out of date, and my jewelry. It broke my heart to part with pieces that had been in my family for generations, but where would I wear it here? And while a few pieces brought a tidy sum, it would still only last me so long.

I would have to get a job.

I was not averse to the idea; I'd never been one for idleness, and believed women possessed the same mental faculties as men.

Father had taught me how the family estate was run, even, despite some ribbing from his cronies. I couldn't have inherited, but I could have assisted a future husband with the business side of things. I understood finances and bookkeeping. My penmanship was excellent, and although I had never used a typewriting machine, I was confident I could learn. I was confident in my abilities and my brain.

I applied first at banks, and my confidence was immediately dashed.

I had no papers, no certificates to show I had taken courses in anything, and no references. And that was all on top of me being a woman.

I could pay for falsified papers again, but I had no idea how to find someone suitably disreputable in New York City, nor did I want to take the chance on spending such a large sum again. The more I spent, the longer it would take me to earn it back.

I could probably talk my way in to a nanny position—having a child of my own gave me experience there—but most of those jobs required me, and thus Mary, to live in someone else's house. Perhaps I suffered from paranoia, but I felt the more we were around other people in close quarters, the more likely we were to make a mistake, slip up, reveal some detail. Plus I wanted to keep Mary safe, not thrust her among strangers.

In the end, I accepted the only option that seemed to be available to me: I put on my oldest clothes and took a job cleaning other people's houses.

I suppose I could have railed against it, against the idea that I, who once had servants at my beck and call, now acted as one of them, but that would get me nowhere. I gritted my teeth as my hands stung from lye, as my back ached, and I did my best.

It turned out my best was surprisingly good, once I learned the tricks I'd had no reason to have knowledge of before. (After all, a good servant is rarely seen.) My understanding of how things in a proper household should be, from the perspective of someone who'd checked the work of the servants, who knew the whys and wherefores of the tasks, gave me a unique edge.

Mrs. Leary was kind enough to watch Mary for me until Mary was of school age, and she charged me almost nothing. She saw our situations as similar, and in some ways they were. I changed the subject when she inquired about my late husband, giving only a few vague details. She was as close to a friend as I dared myself have, and still I couldn't bring myself to be honest with her.

New York shared with London its cultural center as well

as its rough areas, and we lived on the fringes of it. The brownstone was in a respectable enough neighborhood, albeit one a little rundown around the edges, and my work took me to better neighborhoods. On the weekends, Mary and I explored our surroundings, and spent many days in Central Park, a space that astonished me.

Hyde Park, Regents Park...they were all so manicured and civilized. Central Park had similar areas, but also areas wild and untamed. It seemed to me that was part of its American-ness.

I settled on a bench, watching Mary run and hop and laugh with other children—she had organized them into a game involving frogs, it seemed. I smiled. She was strong-willed, but she was so good-natured that she got away with it. It was a beautiful sunny spring day, not yet too hot, a few puffy clouds high in the pale blue sky.

When I closed my eyes, if not for the accents, I could imagine I was back in England, enjoying an afternoon respite before stopping somewhere for proper tea. Oh, how I missed tea. I missed Mabel, and my friends, and the London I'd called home far more, but at my lowest, some-times I thought oh, if only I could have a proper cup of tea, the world would look less sorry and bleak.

I felt a slight vibration; someone sitting on the metal bench. I opened my eyes. A gentleman about my age had seated himself at the other end, a newspaper in his hand. He was a handsome man, with a neatly trimmed brown mustache, dapper in his bowler and suit.

He nodded, and I nodded and smiled back. Our conver-sation started innocuously enough: comments about the weather, the recent Easter Parade. While we chatted, I found myself hiding my work-roughened hands. Vanity is a weakness, I suppose, but I saved my strength for more important things.

It had been a long time since I'd had a conversation with a man who wasn't an employer or the greengrocer (and the latter was in his sixties, so no matter how flattering his flirting, the answer was going to be no), and it wasn't something I'd thought about missing, but apparently I had. He was charming and intelligent, and although I kept my responses somewhat impersonal, in truth there wasn't much more a respectable woman would share with a strange man.

I relaxed, enjoying the day, the gentleman—Jonathan—and the shouts of Mary's laughter.

A short while later, Mary came running up to me, and I pulled her into my lap.

"What a fine young lady you are," Jonathan said. "What's your name. No, wait—let me guess." He screwed up his face in a silly expression, pretending to be thinking hard, and Mary giggled. Finally he said, "I think you look like a...Clara."

I felt as if someone had poured a glass of iced water over me. In the span between heartbeats, the entire situation had turned on its head. A pleasant gentleman sharing a bench with a young woman and enjoying a light conversation...or a man hired to find a woman who had stolen a child?

And while I thought Mary remembered nothing of her former life, would hearing her previous name dredge up some forgotten memory? Even at her young age, she wasn't shy and was quick to speak what came to mind, and there was no way I could stop her without seeming terribly suspicious.

Mary giggled. "No, I look like a Mary!"

"Ah, well, then your name must be Mary," Jonathan said. He smiled at me. "I have a niece called Clara."

Possibly he did, possibly he didn't. I convinced Mary we had to be getting home, politely said my good-byes. Her small hand firmly in mine, I walked away, resisting every impulse to break into a run.

This had been a sharp reminder that I couldn't let down my guard.

There was always the chance that Reginald had hired detectives to find us. I had defied him, and thus shamed him, and the worst thing for a man like him was to lose face.

I could trust no one with the truth, no matter how kind they seemed to be.

And even if I met a man with whom I could spend enough time to ascertain he wasn't someone hired by Reginald, I still could never start or build a relationship based on lies.

That left me very alone. At least I had Mary, sweet Mary, who had gradually accepted her new life and forgot her old one. Eventually all she knew was New York City; England was as unfamiliar to her as China.

I planned to tell her the truth when she turned twenty-one, an adult, old enough to make her own choices and to not be subject to any parental grasp. But would it be safe to return, even then? Being a grown woman didn't mean being protected from Reginald; I had no illusions that he could be inventive in finding ways to harm either of us.

In the meantime, I kept my focus on Mary and on my work.

My unique position of someone who had been cleaned for and now did cleaning meant I listened carefully to the other working girls. When I was growing up, we always treated our servants with kindness, but I heard story after story of employers who overworked their staff, underpaid them, or worse. The girls, like myself, who didn't live with a family but worked independently either in homes or offices, had little security. If they complained about long hours or a missed payment, well, they were easily and summarily replaced.

And most of them worked only until they found husbands, or had children. They pay wasn't enough to entice them to do more than they needed to.

I wasn't in that position—I wasn't going to find a benefactor. I wanted Mary to have the best opportunities I could give her, which meant I had to find a way to make more than what fed and clothed and housed us. I hadn't saved her only to deposit her into a life of drudgery.

So I went to the bank and applied for a loan to start my own business. The cleaning girls would work for me, and in return I would take steps to ensure proper payment, safe working environments, and other benefits.

By this time Mrs. Leary had found herself a new husband and he had taken a shine to Mary and me. He agreed to sign on the loan.

What I had learned at my father's knee paid off, and my business flourished. It still involved hard work and long hours, but I was grateful that those hours didn't involve so much time scrubbing floors. I was able to enroll Mary into a private school, where she too flourished, such a bright girl that she was. By the time she was twenty-one, she was working for me, and Williams' White Glove Cleaning Service had branches all over the city.

And on Mary's twenty-first birthday, I sat her down in the brownstone—now our house, as I'd purchased it from Mrs. Leary when she retired and turned it back into a single home—and told her the truth. I told her I wasn't her mother, I told her about her father, and I told her how her mother had begged me to save her, and so I had changed her name and mine and brought her to America.

She was silent through my speech, although she turned pale as milk, and her lips pressed in a thin line as if she were holding herself together. (A feeling I knew well.) When I finished, she asked,

"And what of my mother now? Is she well? And my brother?"

I told her I didn't know. I had planned to make some discreet enquiries leading up to her birthday, but then the War started, and there were more crucial correspondence to be made on all sides.

But there was this, too: I hadn't dared make any enquiries that might alert Reginald to our existence. And even though Mary was now twenty-one, an adult in all ways, she had been a child when I had taken her away. I could still be charged with kidnapping.

Not making those enquiries, though, in many ways, had been one of the hardest things for me.

I didn't even know if my beloved Mabel still lived. Whether Reginald had finally gone too far, or if now, with bombs raining down on London...

Mary stood, and without a word, collected her coat and hat and walked out.

Of all the things I feared, this cut deeper than I had imagined. I knew she might be angry that I had in essence kept her identity from her, but I had hoped she'd understand the reasons.

Like that first day on the ship, almost twenty years ago, I wept, and I prayed that Mary, my daughter in all ways except that I hadn't carried her in my womb, knew how much I loved her.

Mary did know, although in the days and weeks that followed, she struggled with her emotions. I had after all, turned her world upside-down for a second time, and this time she was keenly aware of it.

She was angry, of course, and I didn't fault her that. But I was still the only family she'd ever known, and she grew to accept, if not agree with, the decisions Mabel and I had made regarding her welfare.

I hadn't thought until now about how close she was in age to the age I'd been when I'd left Britain with her in my arms.

I was no longer a frightened 25-year-old fleeing with a tiny child. I had faced that challenge and survived, just as I had overcome every other challenge my decisions had placed before me: falling from British nobility to American cleaning woman, rising from charwoman to successful businesswoman.

I had never considered, though, the challenges facing Mary. I certainly didn't regret for an instant taking her to America; I believed, as Mabel had, that her life would have been peril had Reginald continued to have access to her.

But neither Mabel nor I, in formulating and carrying out the plan, had thought of how Mary would feel as an adult, learning that the only life she remembered was built on falsehoods and deceptions.

I had chosen to leave my family and everything I had ever known. Mary hadn't even had the chance to know her family—beyond me, of course, and she'd known me not as her aunt, but as her mother.

She should know her real mother...assuming her real mother still lived. If she did, Mary should have her in her life.

It was not my place nor my right to keep that from her now.

I would face whatever consequences that would come of it.

My hand trembled as I pressed the doorbell, and I clasped my fingers together as I listened to the chime sound deep inside the house.

Mabel had moved to this Georgian mansion on the outskirts of London before the War, and that was a fortuitous thing, given that our old London home had been destroyed during the Blitz.

It was smaller than I might have expected, but the time for a full complement of staff and hosting gala parties had long passed from this world. From the few letters we'd exchanged and the glorious, if hard-to-hear crackling phone calls during which we'd had to shout through the lines—but oh! to hear her voice again!—I'd learned that Reginald had died in the last months of the war.

Cancer had eaten him, a partner to the evil blackness he'd carried inside him.

There was no one left who might bring charges against me for my crime, but I hadn't known that when I'd searched for Mabel, and I hadn't cared. The only thing I cared about was Mary by my side right now, and that she would know her mother.

The woman who answered the door was closer to Mary's age, wearing a trim uniform: simple button-down black dress with a white lace collar, a starched white apron tied around her waist. She took our coats and hats, and I was aware of the disheveled state of our own dresses. We'd come straight from the airport, not wanting to waste an extra minute to freshen up.

But what an experience that had been, to return on a conveyance so much faster than the ship.

And yet, when the immigration agent had examined our passports, I'd felt an echo of my former fear. I had never completely stopped looking behind me, expecting a heavy hand on my shoulder, expecting my deceptions to be exposed.

On the plane, I told Mary the story of her telling the agent at Ellis Island that her name wasn't Mary, and she laughed.

"Well, I promise I shan't croak like a frog this time," she said.

The maid led us through to the back of the house, and I had time to admire the high ceilings, tall windows. The furniture was elegant but minimal, and no carpets adorned the floors.

At an open set of double doors at the back of the house, the maid stepped aside and indicated we should enter. I listened to her heels tap away on the hardwood. Beside me, Mary clutched her pocketbook so tightly, her knuckles whitened.

She made a motion similar to the maid's. "You go first," she said quietly. "She's your sister, and you haven't seen her in so very long."

One step in the door, and the scent of roses assaulted me. A particular strain, sweet and light—I'd known the name once, had learned all the classes and categories as befitting my station so long ago, but all that was forgotten now.

What the scent brought back was a gut memory of Mabel: this had been her favorite, and the smell was entwined with her inextricably in my mind.

It was a garden room, with a wall of windows looking out onto the back gardens. Walls painted white, décor updated with yellow accents—floral curtains, pulled back, and pillows—and bowls of the roses. It was beautiful outside today, bright and temperate, but I could see that even on typically dark British days, the room would feel cheerful.

From what I could see from the doorway, the gardens were beautiful, and there was a pool, too, glittering in the morning sun.

The house might have been less grand that those we'd had in the past, but there was still an opulence, and a graceful elegance to the furnishings and appointments that I attributed to Mabel. I'd forgotten her deft hand at deco-rating, the way she could flick a few stems and turn a vase of flowers into an artful arrangement, know which piece of silver to put here, which books to set there.

Mabel sat beyond the end of a sofa, her face turned toward the door. Twenty years on, still with a graceful neck and, although I couldn't truly see from here, but I knew, with eyes bright and kind. Her hair was different, her face had twenty more years of life on it, but I would have known her anywhere. Her face, pretty where mine was handsome, but still so much like the one I saw in the mirror.

The smile that bloomed on her face snatched the breath out of me.

She didn't stand to greet us, and a moment later, as I came around the sofa, I saw why.

I dropped to my knees next to the wheelchair and put my arms around her, breathing in the scent of roses, the scent of the sister I'd thought I'd never see again.

"I thought I would never see you again," she murmured into my hair, a catch in her voice. Her voice was lower, huskier.

"I know," I said. "I did, too."

But there was more to be done. I wiped my eyes, kissed her cheek, rose to my feet. Mary walked to me, and as if presenting a subject at court—only this was far, far more important—I said, "Mabel, this is your daughter. Mary, this is my sister—your mother."

———

We talked until our voices were hoarse. I let Mabel and Mary do the most of it, but sometimes Mabel and I would recount together a story from our childhood, or Mary and I would tell Mabel about something that had happened in our lives.

It felt like a dream, sitting in a pool of sunshine, breathing the scent of roses, seeing the family together. Only one somber thing dimmed the day: Mabel had chosen not to tell me over the phone that she could no longer walk, wanting our talks to be positive. It was, she said, simply a part of her now, not what defined her.

Reginald had been to blame. Fury rose up within me, hot and bitter, but Mabel said there had at least been something positive to come of it, in the end: Reginald's abuse had subsided after that. He never spoke of it, but she guessed that deep down, he knew he had gone too far. He had damaged his prize. His anger remained, his harsh treatment of everyone around him, but he became far less likely to lay a hand on her directly.

In the late afternoon, a young man of about twenty arrived: Mary's younger brother, Anthony. I saw Mabel in his features, less so Reginald, and more importantly, I could tell almost immediately that his demeanor, his gentleness, had come from Mabel as well. She had protected him from the worst of his father, tempered Reginald's influence.

Indeed, Anthony's studies to become a physician had been born from a desire to understand Mabel's injuries.

His mother had told him of our existence only after Reginald had died, so he was almost as new to the idea of a family as Mary was. But any awkwardness soon fled; he and his sister were so alike, it seemed almost unreal.

After supper, we sat outside by the pool—installed for Mabel's therapy, she'd explained—sipping sherry, watching the setting sun chase shadows across the gardens, listening to the low call of an owl.

Mary, sitting next to her mother, holding her hand, looked over at me. She mouthed the words, "Thank you."

I smiled at her, with all the love in my heart.

Save my baby, Mabel had said, and I had.

And now we had come home.

ABOUT THE AUTHORS

One of four pseudonymous writing Crowes, **Dory Crowe** resides in Nobtucket—a quintessential, if mythical, Cape Cod town. Crowe stories have also appeared in DAW Books, in Level Best Books' *Best New England Crime*, and in Fiction River anthologies, as well as in *Alfred Hitchcock's Mystery Magazine*.

Leah R. Cutter writes page-turning, wildly imaginative fiction set in exotic locations such as a magical New Orleans, the ancient Orient, rural Kentucky, Seattle, Minneapolis, and many others. She writes fantasy, science fiction, mystery, literary, and horror fiction. Her short fiction has been published in magazines such *Alfred Hitchcock's Mystery Magazine* and *Talebones*, anthologies such as Fiction River, and on the web. Her long fiction has been published both by New York publishers as well as small presses. Read more books by Leah Cutter at KnottedRoad-Press.com. and follow her blog at LeahCutter.com.

Dayle A. Dermatis is the author or coauthor of many novels (including snarky urban fantasy *Ghosted* and YA lesbian romance *Beautiful Beast*) and more than a hundred short stories in multiple genres, appearing in such venues as *Fiction River*, *Alfred Hitchcock's Mystery Magazine*, *Pulphouse Fiction Magazine*, *Heart's Kiss*, and DAW Books. Called the mastermind behind the Uncollected Anthology project, she also edits anthologies, and her own short fiction has been lauded in many year's best anthologies in erotica, mystery, and horror. She'd love to have you over for a virtual cup of tea or glass of wine at DayleDermatis.com, where you can also sign up for her newsletter and support her on Patreon.

C.H. Hung grew up among the musty book stacks of public libraries, where she found a lifelong love for good stories and lost 20/20 vision for good. Her stubbornly rational soul intersects with an irrational belief in magic, which means her stories are often as mixed up as she is, melding the plausible with myth and folklore. Her stories have appeared in *Analog SF&F*, *Ellery Queen Mystery Magazine*, *The Martian*, *DreamForge*, and *khōréō* magazines, as well as anthologies edited by Kevin J. Anderson and Kristine Kathryn Rusch, among others. Read more at CHhung.com.

Robert Jeschonek is an envelope-pushing, *USA Today* bestselling author whose fiction, comics, and nonfiction have been published around the world. His stories have appeared in *Clarkesworld*, *Pulphouse Fiction Magazine*, *Fiction River*, *Black Cat Mystery Magazine*, and many other publications. He has written official *Star Trek* and *Doctor Who* fiction and has scripted comics for DC, AHOY, and other publishers. Visit him online at www.bobscribe.com.

Michèle Laframboise feeds coffee grounds to her garden plants, runs long distances, and writes full-time in Mississauga, Ontario. Fascinated by sciences and nature since she could walk, she studied geography and engineering, but two recessions and her own social awkwardness kept the plush desk jobs away. Instead, she held a string of odd jobs to sustain her budding family: some quite dangerous, others quite tedious, all of them sources of inspiration. You can stop by at her website at Michele-Laframboise.com to say hello, or visit her publishing house EchoFictions.com to get a taste of her fiction!

Patrick Mammay lives in Arkansas. He's not sure how or why. He writes stories with dragons and stories without dragons.

C.J. Mattison's stories have appeared in anthologies from WMG Publishing, WordFire Press, and others. He writes in multiple genres, publishes novels in a space fantasy series, and dabbles in poetry. He lives in Dallas area with his wife and their rescue superhero dog Saber-Girl, calls his sourdough bread starter "Ursula" (K. Le Guin), and cooks crazy-good Cajun food for a Midwest Yankee.

Phillip McCollum hails from the sunny expanses of Southern California where he creates gaming experiences and writes speculative fiction.

Juliet Nordeen is a recovering engineer who lives on the gorgeous Kitsap Peninsula of Washington State. An avid reader and Dog Mom, she also loves to cook and so she has taken up recreational running to balance the scales, or at least to try to keep the scale in balance. You can find out more about her writing at www.julietnordeen.com.

Award-winning writer and editor Kristine Kathryn Rusch calls **Annie Reed** "a master short fiction writer." Annie is the author of well over three hundred short stories, some of which have been picked up for mystery best of the year volumes and short-listed for major mystery awards. But Annie doesn't write just mystery stories. She also writes science fiction, fantasy, and romance, as well as some stories that simply defy genre. Her stories appear regularly in *Pulphouse Fiction Magazine* and *Mystery, Crime and Mayhem*, and her short fiction has also been included in college entrance study guides in Japan. Annie's Unexpected series of short-story collections showcase the best of her work. She lives in Northern Nevada and can be found on the web at AnnieReed.wordpress.com.

Lisa Silverthorne has published eighteen novels and more than a hundred short stories, novelettes, and novellas in the fantasy, science fiction, romance, and mystery genres. She is the author of the A Game of Lost Souls series and the Experiencing True Purple series. Her work has appeared in numerous anthologies and magazines from DAW Books, Roc Books, *Pulphouse Fiction Magazine*, *Fiction River*, Wildside Press, and Prime Books. To discover more of her stories, visit LisaSilverthorne.com.

Stephannie Tallent is a 1989 West Point graduate. Since then she's served in the Army as a Military Intelligence officer, gotten a Zoology degree, gone to vet school, worked as a small animal veterinarian, and designed and published knitting patterns and books. Throughout all that she's always wanted to be a writer, and she's finally put all her type-A, soft-spoken, liberal, invisible middle-aged woman focus on that goal, writing everything from fantasy to science fiction to mysteries to romance. Check out her website StephannieTallent.com.

Rob Vagle has been writing short fiction for over thirty years with stories in *Realms of Fantasy*, *Strange New Worlds*, *Heliotrope*, *Fiction River*, *Pulphouse Fiction Magazine*, and more. He lives in Arizona after living more than a decade in the wet Pacific Northwest, and he was born and raised in Minnesota. Find more information on his books, and sign up for his newsletter, Dispatches From This Side of Wonder, at RobVagle.com.

ABOUT THE EDITOR

Dayle A. Dermatis is the author or coauthor of many novels (including snarky urban fantasy *Ghosted*) and more than a hundred short stories in multiple genres appearing in such venues as *Fiction River, Alfred Hitchcock's Mystery Magazine*, and DAW Books.

Called "a nail-biter" by *Publisher's Weekly*, her thriller story "The Scent of Amber and Vanilla" received an honorable mention in *The Year's Best Crime & Mystery 2016*.

Considered to be the mastermind behind the Uncollected Anthology project, she also edits anthologies, and her own short fiction has been lauded in year's best anthologies in erotica, mystery, and horror.

To find out where she's wandered off to (and to get free fiction!), check out DayleDermatis.com and sign up for her newsletter.

I value honest feedback, and would love to hear your opinion in a review, if you're so inclined, on your favorite book retailer's site.

For more information:
www.dayledermatis.com

ALSO BY DAYLE A. DERMATIS

EDITED BY

Fiction River: Doorways to Enchantment

NOVELS

The Nikki Ashbourne Novels

Ghosted

Shaded (forthcoming)

Spectered (forthcoming)

Standalone Novels

Beautiful Beast

Waking the Witch

What Beck'ning Ghost

COLLECTIONS

Devilish Deals and Perilous Pacts: A Spooky Collection of Deals With the Devil and Other Bad Choices

Five Funny Fantasies

Haunted (a Nikki Ashbourne collection, forthcoming)

Small Wonders: Ten Short-Short Speculative Fiction Stories

Umberto Scolari and the Five Mysteries: A Short Story Collection

Voices Carry and Other Stories of Women and Crime

Written on the Coast: Thirteen Stories of Magic and Mayhem Written in Lincoln City, OR

NONFICTION

Researching History for Fantasy Writers: How to Use Historical Detail to Make Your Fantasy Worlds Rich and Compelling

BE THE FIRST TO KNOW!

S ign up for Dayle A. Dermatis's newsletter for *free* fiction, plus the latest news, releases, and more.

Sign up at DayleDermatis.com.

For more in-depth conversations and special sneak peeks, you can also support her continued work by joining her community of patrons out Dayle's Patreon.

Patreon.com/Dayle.